Praise for

I0680760

Haven Security

Donna Gallagher has given us an exciting start to the Haven Security series with An Opportunity Seized. This is a wonderful blend of risk and romance that will leave readers anticipating the next story.
~ *Literary Nymphs Reviews*

The story is fast-paced, interesting, and I loved it. The sex is volcanic, the heroine's journey is epic, and I think you'll like An Opportunity Seized too.
~ *Manic Readers*

I almost immediately developed a little crush on Toni and Jason, and couldn't stop spending time with them and their adventures.An Opportunity Seized was a fun read. ~ *Cocktails and Books*

Totally Bound Publishing books by Donna Gallagher:

A Fruitful Intimacy

League of Love Volume One
Caitlin's Hero
Mandy's He-Man

League of Love Volume Two
Laura's Light
Pippa's Fantasy

League of Love Volume Three
Emily's Cowboy
Sarah's Soldier

League of Love
Cassie's Choice

Haven Security Volume One
An Opportunity Seized
An Opportunity for Redemption

HAVEN SECURITY
Volume One

An Opportunity Seized

An Opportunity for Redemption

DONNA GALLAGHER

Haven Security Volume One
ISBN # 978-1-78430-561-1
©Copyright Donna Gallagher 2015
Cover Art by Posh Gosh ©Copyright 2015
Interior text design by Claire Siemaszkiewicz
Totally Bound Publishing

Published in 2015 by Totally Bound Publishing, Newland House, The Point, Weaver Road, Lincoln, LN6 3QN, United Kingdom.

Totally Bound Publishing is a subsidiary of Totally Entwined Group Limited.

AN OPPORTUNITY SEIZED

Dedication

My darling Luke, I'm sorry I broke my promise but it
was just too good not to use,
love Mum

Chapter One

As soon as she spotted the little kiosk, all Toni could think of was tucking into a cold ice cream. The weather in London had been outrageously hot for the few days she'd been here. It was just her luck that a heatwave would hit town at the same time she did. She wasn't even going to feel guilty for the calories she was about to consume — well, maybe only a little. *Surely after all the walking I've done today I deserve a little treat,* she told herself as she waited to be served. It was such a pain having to worry about her weight — and she did have to keep an eye on her food intake. Toni had always thought it was so unfair that she took after her pudgy father and not her pencil thin mother in that regard. *Stupid genetics,* she thought, as she found a shady spot under the branches of a big plane tree in the grounds of St. James's Park to sit and enjoy her treat.

The park was opposite Buckingham Palace, and Toni watched the crowds of people streaming down the path. The changing of the guard had just finished and the sightseers were all headed off to the next attraction, just like she would be, after her quick rest break. London was a fascinating place and one Toni had been looking forward to visiting for some time. She was finding it hard to believe that she'd actually made it here and all by herself—still surprised that her parents had relented and let her go in the first place. The thought of her parents made Toni giggle—how horrified her mother would be if she could see Toni now, sitting crossed-legged on the grass, not to mention the frown that would crease her mother's perfect face at the sight of Toni eating such a fattening treat.

Toni knew her father would be horrified to think of his only daughter sightseeing like some common tourist. Her father had been invited inside the Palace, more than once, to attend some function or another, but those types of gathering were just not Toni's cup of tea. She much preferred to keep out of the spotlight, blend in with the crowd and experience life the same as the bulk of the population. Being a mining magnate's daughter was a difficult persona for Toni to uphold. She was plain, a little overweight and just didn't fit in with high society standards—much to her mother's disdain. She always managed to say something inappropriate or trip over her own feet at the worst possible moment, resulting in that look of disappointment and embarrassment her parents inevitably wore whenever she was around.

Just as she bit into the crisp cone Toni felt something hit her shoulder. At first she thought she'd been struck by a ball. That was until the wetness started seeping through her T-shirt. It felt like a warm sticky mass sat on her right shoulder and as she looked down, Toni gasped as she saw the green, gooey clumps that now covered her front.

Then the smell hit her.

"Eww!" she squealed as her stomach rolled. Nausea was threatening to bring her breakfast back up, and while she'd enjoyed the morning meal, revisiting it would not be pretty. What little of the ice cream she'd consumed also burned the back of her throat. The rest of the sweet treat was now melting and running down her right arm. *What am I going to do?*

The one small napkin she'd picked up at the kiosk was going to be of little or no use in trying to sop up the stinking, green lumpy mess, which had now made its way through her shirt to her skin. But if she didn't do something and fast, she could add her own vomit to her hopeless plight.

"Goose."

Toni heard the male voice, was shocked that anyone could be so mean as to call her that when she was in so much distress. She tilted her head up so she could at least see who it was that was making fun of her. Even in a strange town, Toni had managed to become the brunt of someone's cruel taunt.

The stranger was standing directly in front of her, looking down at her. He wore a baseball style cap and those horrible reflective sunglasses that Toni hated.

"I think its goose poo," the stranger added. "I've never really been a believer that a bird's droppings mean good luck, but if it does, I figure you should probably buy a lottery ticket."

Jason hadn't meant to make contact with her yet, if at all. His job was to follow and protect the target—Antoinette Grimaldi. It had been made perfectly clear to Jason that he needed to fulfill that charter without her knowledge while she holidayed in Europe. Her father, an extremely wealthy—no, scrap that, and make it ridiculously, filthy rich—businessman from Australia had used the firm Jason worked for on many occasions. So when his boss had given him this assignment, while not thrilled, Jason had agreed to take it for the good of the firm.

He'd expected his target to be a rich, spoiled brat that he would probably be spending many late nights at clubs or standing outside some playboy's apartment long into the early hours while she partied on to her heart's content. Jason had been wrong. When he'd seen the filth hit her and the mess it had left, he hadn't been able to stand by and do nothing. Just the look on her alluring face had torn at his heart.

Now she was looking up at him, her big brown eyes filling with tears.

"I think we need to do something about that mess real soon, luv, 'cause that smell ain't gonna get any better," he said, trying to keep his voice calm, project a soothing tone—the tears threatening to spill from her eyes making him panic slightly. Jason was not trained to deal with teary females.

"I thought you called me a goose."

It took a moment for Jason to realize that Antoinette had spoken to him and for what she'd said to sink in.

"I don't know what to do, how to get it off." Her whispered voice sounded so defeated. Every protective instinct in Jason rose to the occasion, bringing with it an overwhelming need for him to help her, whatever the cost. Without a moment's hesitation he unbuttoned the shirt he had on over his T-shirt and took it off, holding it out to her. "Take yours off and put this on."

"But I will have to lift it over my head and the poo will get in my hair and on my face, plus I can't take your shirt. I don't even know you," she replied sadly.

In the days Jason had been watching over Antoinette, he'd been shocked at the lack of care the girl had shown for her own safety. She'd never once looked over her shoulder to see if anyone was following her or given a second thought to wandering the streets of London alone, even at night, and now she was going to start worrying about the fact that she didn't know him. "Well, your accent would suggest that you're an Aussie, and so am I. My name is Jason and it would be my pleasure to assist a fellow countryman—or woman in this case—in her hour of need. I think your top is ruined so I could always cut it off you so you don't have to pull it over your head." Jason didn't bother telling her that there were goose droppings in her hair too.

"You have a knife?"

Way to go, idiot. Now she thinks you're a knife-wielding stranger. "I have a Swiss Amy knife on my key ring that has a small pair of scissors."

"Oh! I see..." she said, after a few seconds had ticked by.

Jason could almost hear the wheels grinding in her mind as Antoinette tried to work out whether to take his offer for help or not.

Finally, obviously having decided on her fate, she continued, "And yes, Jason, I am from Australia. I guess your plan is the only one I've got. I hope I don't get arrested for undressing in public, though."

The look on her face was priceless—she really was adorable and that was a word that Jason did not normally associate with women. Hot, fast or sexy were more the kind of words he liked to use when he thought of the opposite sex. Antoinette Grimaldi was sexy in her own way, he decided much to his own horror—the last thing he needed was to get emotionally involved with a client—especially one that was unaware of his employment. It was a major rule breaker in his line of work.

"I think we can pull this off without drawing any unwanted attention, luv. If you stand with your back to the tree trunk I can block the view from the front while we do the swap." Jason hoped that his idea would make her feel a little better about shedding her top in public. He wasn't a huge guy but he was big enough to block her small frame from passers-by.

"Well, if you're sure you don't mind lending me your shirt, I suppose it'll be okay." Jason could still hear the note of trepidation in her voice as she gingerly stood and started backing her way up to the tree. "Just try to make it quick and keep your eyes shut," she added.

"I think it's probably better if I keep my eyes open while I'm cutting off your clothes, honey. I wouldn't want to hurt you." If she didn't smell so bad and look so miserable, the whole episode would have been funny. Jason took the Swiss Army knife out of his pocket and flipped it open. Pulling the neckline of her shirt away from her body with his other hand, he quickly cut the fabric right down the middle, being careful not to let the sharp blade come into contact with her skin.

As the material split in two and fell away, Jason was left staring at a view of her breasts. She was clad in a simple white bra. Two perfectly rounded swells of creamy flesh peeked over the top of the cups and all the humor he had been feeling prior to that moment fled. In its place was a heart-hammering burst of hunger. The reaction was so unexpected that Jason had to stop and reel in his own imagination, which had taken off on an erotic journey that involved touching and tasting the luscious bounty in his sights, while he pressed Antoinette back up against the tree. He'd only have to move a step or so closer—just lower his head and capture between his lips one of the berry-colored nipples that were pressed against the virginal white fabric of her bra. The idea certainly had Jason's dick interested, as it swelled a little uncomfortably inside his jeans.

"Can I have the shirt now please...?"

Antoinette's plea shook Jason back to his senses. He grabbed the shirt that he'd slung over his shoulder while he'd had both hands full and held it out to her. A mixture of relief and disappointment fought for supremacy inside his head as she slipped into his shirt and fastened the buttons, removing the vision of her body that had rocked him.

"I don't know how to thank you enough for your help, Jason. Can I pay to replace your shirt?"

"Coffee, what do you say you buy me a cup of coffee?" Jason should have accepted Antoinette's offer or declined and moved on quickly, but before common sense had had a chance to influence him, he'd replied. He didn't really expect that the feeble attempt to stay in Antoinette's company a little longer would work, but it was worth a try. Following her around had left him feeling like she could use a friend. Jason was used to being in his own company— preferred it most days—but he could not comprehend why such a lovely young woman would be traveling on her own by choice. Surely there was a list a mile long of available suitors that would have given their eyeteeth to spend some time with the heiress to a fortune. She was way out of his league but it was only a coffee invitation after all. He tried to convince himself as he waited for her reply.

"Umm... I'm not sure that's a good idea..."

Antoinette's rejection affected Jason more than it should have. He felt the weight of disappointment in his gut.

"Why is that, luv?"

"I smell pretty bad. I'm not sure I should inflict this aroma on you or anyone else, for that matter."

Even though Antoinette had tried to laugh it off, Jason could tell that she was embarrassed. If he were honest with himself, he had to admit that the goose droppings stench was still very strong on her. But he didn't want to say goodbye yet and resume the impersonal act of following her around undetected. A job made more difficult now that she would recognize him.

"I can smell that your point is a valid one," Jason began, trying to add a jovial and friendly quality to his voice. "What say I accompany you back to your hotel and wait for you in the lobby while you get yourself cleaned up? Then we can have that coffee in comfort and without either of us having to shove a peg on our nose. I don't think I have one of those on my Swiss Army knife."

Jason waited, trying to portray an easy-going persona as Antoinette thought over his proposal. He'd pasted a friendly smile on his face to mask the desperation he was feeling. It was ridiculous. There had never been a time in Jason's life that he could remember when he'd wanted anything as much as he did the chance to have a lousy coffee and the opportunity to get to know this girl better.

"My hotel is quite a long way away," she finally replied. "I'm staying in Earls Court. I caught the bus here but I think I might need to catch a cab back. I can't travel on public transport smelling like this.

Maybe I can get your number and we can do coffee another time?"

There was no way Jason was letting her off the hook that easily. "Typical Aussie. We all stay in Earls Court. I'm at the Ibis. Where are you?" He knew she was also at the Ibis, had been surprised when given her itinerary that she'd booked such modest accommodation. The more he'd watched and trailed her, though, the more it had made sense. Antoinette Grimaldi did not advertise her wealthy upbringing.

"Seriously, the Ibis? That's where I'm staying. But you must have had other plans for the day. I don't want you to miss out on anything because of me. If we are both staying at the same hotel, I could meet you any time."

Jason couldn't miss the touch of pink that colored Antoinette's face as she made her offer. She was just so gorgeous. So shy and unassuming, nothing like the prima donna he'd been expecting when first lumped with this assignment.

"It would be my utmost pleasure to share a ride back to the hotel with you. To be honest, I'd really love the chance to chat with a compatriot, I've been missing the Aussie accent and feeling a bit homesick. You'd be doing me a favor. But there is one thing I need from you right now…"

The look of apprehension was plain as day on Antoinette's face, and Jason felt a little guilty as he watched her take a few steps away from him. Finally she looked up and faced him, those brown eyes of hers as big as saucers.

"And what would that be?" she asked him, her voice soft and sounding a little unsure.

Jason smiled broadly before he continued, "Your name, luv. You never told me what it was—I figure I deserve to know the name of the woman who takes the shirt off my back."

The sound of Antoinette's giggle was one of the most beautiful things Jason had ever heard. It wasn't loud and embarrassing or high-pitched — the type of noise that grates on your nerves — it was sexy, and her eyes took on a shine he hadn't noticed before. They sparkled back.

"Toni. My name is Toni, and I'm pleased to meet you, Jason."

Chapter Two

Toni didn't know whether to laugh or cry. Maybe Jason was right when he'd said being the recipient of a bird's dropping was actually lucky because she was not in the habit of receiving attention from men that were so drop-dead gorgeous. Yes, she'd had invitations from men before, but they were the ones who knew about her family's wealth. Toni had never been under the misconception that any interest directed her way from members of the opposite sex — or the same sex for that matter — were more about what she had to offer than how she looked or her personality. But Jason didn't know her and yet he seemed to be interested in her. Yes, she was feeling lucky — it was a terrible shame she smelled like a septic tank.

And what were the chances they were both staying in the same hotel? Yes, Aussies tended to stay in and around Earls Court — she didn't know why or when that had begun but it was fact. There were, of course, hundreds of hotels in this area, so it had to be a wonderful act of kismet, not just coincidence, that

Jason was staying at the Ibis as well. Toni was not going to knock back this display of luck that had been sent her way.

"Okay, we share the cab fare back. I go up and wash away this poo… I know it's in my hair and thank you for not mentioning it," she said and smiled, before continuing. "Then after I'm all shiny clean and smelling like a human again, I buy you lunch in the restaurant."

She was acting bold, forward even, but the excitement of what she was suggesting had Toni feeling empowered. She had just invited this sexy man—one she didn't know from Adam—out to lunch and she had done this while covered in goose poo! *Who knew I had it in me?* Full of nervous anticipation, she waited for Jason to reply.

"That sounds like a plan. I've been looking forward to riding in a famous London black cab and I can't think of a better excuse to mark that off my to-do list. Let's go," her sexy hero replied.

Relief washed over her as Jason agreed to her idea. She might have felt empowered by her boldness but she was still Toni, and opportunities like this didn't happen to her. So, when Jason held his hand out to her again, she didn't know what to do. This whole thing was starting to feel like some perfect dream come true. Handsome knight saves in-distress princess from disaster. *What the heck! I might as well make the most of it. My good luck must have a time limit. That's how it always goes in fairy tales.*

Toni placed her hand into Jason's, trying hard not to think about the fact that his height put his nose right above her smelly, goose poo perfumed hair, and headed off to locate a cab rank.

Jason's hand felt warm and solid around hers. Toni fell into step beside him. The idea that she would follow him straight into hell if he asked crossed her mind as they made their way from the park to the main road. Squirrels ran across the path in front of them, unperturbed by their presence, reminding Toni of some sappy children's movie with singing and dancing wildlife. She was being fanciful and she was enjoying every moment of it.

They found a cab on Buckingham Palace Road and Jason held the door for her as she climbed in. He sat opposite her in the back, facing her. As the driver wound his way through the congested roads of London, Toni couldn't help thinking that for someone who had said they wanted to take a ride in a black cab, Jason did not take much time looking at the scenery or enjoying the ambience. Instead he chatted to her non-stop, their conversation easy and comfortable. He had a way of making Toni feel safe and like she was the full focus of his attention. This experience was new to her—in one short taxi ride, Toni felt more alive and comfortable being herself than she could remember feeling in a long time.

"I can't believe we're here already," she said as the driver pulled the car up to the door of the hotel. "I don't think I looked out of the window once."

The sound of Jason's deep, throaty laugh had her insides melting. It distracted her long enough that she didn't have time to complain as he pushed the twenty pound note through the window to the driver saying, "Keep the change, mate."

"I thought the plan was that we were to go halves on the fare?" Toni finally managed to say after her insides had solidified again, as Jason helped her from the taxi and ushered her toward the front door.

"I guess I'm just a chauvinist at heart."

Toni laughed at the playful tone in Jason's voice. But the cheeky grin on his face as he waited for her to respond to his comment was enough to make her go weak in the knees.

"Well, Mr. Chauvinist, I've been warned and won't let you get the better of me again. I'm paying for lunch. Give me twenty minutes and I'll meet you on level one."

Toni didn't look back or wait for a reply as she scurried toward the lifts. "Twenty minutes? What was I thinking?" she muttered, as she stabbed at the lift call button more than once. "And what the hell will I wear?" As the elevator doors opened, she was mentally going through the articles of clothing still sitting unpacked in her suitcase, wishing that she had hung at least some of them on hangers when she'd checked in a few days before instead of just living out of her suitcase like she usually did. "Shower, wash hair, dry hair and iron something to wear all in the space of twenty minutes—this is going to be a hell of an achievement."

Jason watched her race away—he could see she was muttering to herself but he couldn't quite catch what she was saying. He'd decided to let her go up alone—he wasn't sure how she would react when she realized he had the room right next door.

Yes, there was such a thing as coincidence, but he figured that bit of news might push even that concept to its limits, so decided to take the stairs instead. It would be good for him to check out the stairwell one more time, and the exercise would do him good. Not to mention that being in such close proximity to

Antoinette in the taxi had taken its toll on his self-control. He needed time to pull himself together.

The whole journey had been spent in a silent battle with his own desire. Her full lips, perfect for kissing, such a temptation. He'd tried distracting his war of wills by chatting about the places he'd visited. Of course, it had been a little unfair considering that Jason knew Toni had also visited them. He had followed her to each and every location—seen the points of interests she'd paused at the longest. But when he thought about it, they were also the places he would have been interested in if, in fact, this trip had been a vacation.

You really should tell her the truth before this gets out of hand, said a voice of reason inside his head and he would, as soon as the right time presented itself. Maybe after sharing lunch, this infatuation—or whatever it was boiling his insides to molten lava—would be resolved and he could explain that he had been hired by her family to keep an eye on her, keep her safe. Of course that was not part of his job description—he was supposed to keep a low profile, not let the target know of his existence. That was a curly one. Jason wasn't sure how he would get around it, but he did understand that keeping it a secret, usually his forte, was not going to work in this instance.

He reached the top floor and checked that Antoinette was not in the corridor before hurrying to his door and using the swipe key to gain entry, breathing a sigh of relief when the green light appeared on the first go. He'd already had to get the swipe card replaced owing to a malfunction and now would not have been a good time for a repeat problem. He needed to get in and out of his room then back to the first floor to meet Antoinette, without her discovering his secret before he had the chance to explain.

Any control he'd regained over his rampant sexual desires with the stair climb and corridor dash quickly returned when Jason realized he could hear the water running in the shower next door and with that thought, his mind filled with erotic images of Antoinette — or more precisely, a naked Antoinette in the shower. He could almost feel the texture of her skin under his fingertips, could see the water cascading over her rounded tits and down her body like a heavenly waterfall, tempting him to explore its exotic path.

For God's sake, man, pull yourself together, he chastised his overstimulated mind, but it was of little use. He was rock-hard, his cock already leaking pre-cum thanks to his vivid imagination and the memory of those lush breasts confined by that modest bra he'd glimpsed as he'd cut the T-shirt from her body. Reminiscing over the sound of the ripping fabric was also not helping soothe his current state of arousal. There was only one thing he could do and as Jason stripped his clothes from his body and headed for his own shower, he had his hand firmly grasped around his erection, pumping vigorously.

"I need to take the edge off," he said loudly, as if the empty room would be of interest to his thoughts or actions. Leaning forward with one hand against the bathroom tiles for stability and still pumping his cock with the other as the cool water rained down on his back, Jason let go — gave his imagination free rule.

He pictured them both together under the running water. Imagined Antoinette's hands wrapped around his aching shaft, stroking him up and down until his balls were drawn tight and ready to explode. He gently pushed her to her knees and encouraged her to take him with her mouth.

The fantasy of her kneeling before him, lips parted, ready to take him into her mouth was enough stimulation to have him spurting cum onto the shower wall and spilling over the fingers he had gripped around his cock. Three more pumping strokes and he was spent.

Jason's legs gave way and he let himself sink to the shower floor for a moment while he regained composure. It had been a while since he'd had sex, maybe a month or two, but he didn't remember anything real or imagined that had resulted in him losing his load quite so quickly — or forcefully.

Finally sure that he would be able to use his legs again, Jason stood and turned off the stream of water. He grabbed a towel from the rack on the wall next to him and quickly dried himself off. Wrapping the smallish square of cloth around his hips, he gathered up the dirty clothes and tossed them out toward the chair in the next room singing out, "He shoots, he scores," as the clothes hit the target.

It was only a few steps to get to the drawers beside his bed to find clean underwear. Jason grabbed a collared shirt from the wardrobe and a pair of jeans that lay strewn over his bag, as he tried to make sense of what he was about to do.

He was an experienced soldier, one of the select few who had made it through the demands of commando training. He'd had more than enough tours of duty in extremely high risk areas under his belt before he'd resigned his commission and joined Haven Security. He was not new to this kind of assignment — it should have been a piece of cake—and yet he had broken protocol.

Spending time with Antoinette Grimaldi was going to cause him problems—exciting and enjoyable complications, he was sure—but he understood that a whole heap of trouble was headed his way if he wasn't very careful. The Grimaldi contract was an important one for the newly established Haven Security and he really should not have been doing anything that could risk it. But what was even more disturbing was that Jason had already decided that he couldn't care less. He needed to meet Antoinette and share a meal with her at the very least. There was something about this woman that intrigued him, enticed him—and that was a situation Jason had not encountered for a very long time.

Chapter Three

Deciding on the floral A-line dress, Toni gave herself one last look over in the mirror. Even though she felt that the flare over her hips made her look a little bigger than she really was in that area, she loved the bright pattern and the fabric was cool to wear. She'd only just managed to get everything done in the tiny amount of time she had given herself. Her hair was nearly dry and hopefully would not frizz, her makeup was minimal, as usual, and her one concession to vanity and excess — the beautiful strappy, red Manolo Blahnik sandals — were comfortable on her feet.

It's just lunch, no big deal. She had tried to convince herself more than once. But there was no hiding the feel of the thousand butterflies that had taken up lodgings in her stomach as she made her way back down the lift and headed for the restaurant.

Jason was standing by the entranceway and as Toni's eyes met his, the butterflies stopped. A sense of peace descended over her. There was no explaining why this happened. It just did. Toni was not one to ignore a sign from the universe and with a smile now firmly planted on her face, she walked confidently toward him. "I hope I didn't keep you waiting? I'm not sure what I was thinking giving myself only twenty minutes to shower and change."

"No, perfect timing. I just arrived myself," Jason replied. "And from where I'm standing, I'd say the timing was just right. You look gorgeous, Toni. Let's get a table. Shall we?"

Toni took up the offer Jason had extended her, placing her arm through the crook of his, allowing him to escort them in.

"I did have just enough time before you arrived to get the waiter to save this table for us. I hope that's okay," Jason said, as he pulled out a chair and indicated for her to sit down.

The table was tucked away at the back of the restaurant, quite intimate and very private. Toni was pleased with the choice. She hated to be the center of attention and sitting with someone as handsome as Jason, she figured plenty of eyes would have been on them.

"This is fine, thank you, but I warn you, I'm paying for this lunch. Don't you dare try and break our deal," Toni replied as she sat down.

"I promise I will be a good boy, at least on this occasion."

The waiter arrived before Toni could reply, but Jason's comment about being a good boy did not correspond with the devilish look on his face. It had given Toni goosebumps thinking about him acting like a bad boy. Toni tried to control her emotions by taking a sip of the water the waiter had just poured.

"Are you ready to order?" the waiter asked.

"Give us a few minutes, would you, mate? We haven't had a chance to look at the menu yet," Jason answered. "That is, unless you'd like to order a drink first, Toni. I'm going to have something soft at this time of the day, but if you want something alcoholic, go right ahead. With the morning you've just had, I certainly couldn't fault you for wanting something a little stronger, maybe, a nice green cocktail?" Jason gave a chuckle, and Toni's tummy did a flip-flop at the sexy sound.

"No, I went off that color just recently. I think I will just get a Diet Coke for now," she replied then could have kicked herself for ordering the diet variety in front of Jason.

"Goodo, then make that two Diet Cokes. We'll order when you bring back the drinks," Jason told the waiter.

Toni picked up the menu to give herself something to do other than stare at Jason. She couldn't decide what to order. She really wanted to try the roast of the day with Yorkshire pudding and gravy but her subconscious was pointing to the salad offerings.

"Hmmm, I'm not sure what to try..." she said.

"I'm going for the roast with all the extras," Jason replied quickly, putting the menu face down on the table. "Have you tried Yorkshire pudding yet?"

"Not in London, but I have had it in Australia. What I should be eating is a salad. Maybe a roast is a bit heavy for lunch. I should really be watching my weight." Toni felt the heat on her cheeks the moment the words had left her mouth. What had possessed her to make such a comment in front of Jason? *Seriously, the guy does not need to be reminded you're fat, stupid. Way to go.* She always managed to put her foot in it when she was out socially. It had been the bane of her life, her awkwardness. She couldn't even bear to look Jason's way. She was so embarrassed.

"Rubbish, luv. Take it from me...there is nothing worse than watching a woman push rabbit food around her plate when a bloke's getting stuck into some good grub. Have the roast if that's what takes your fancy. Maybe after lunch we can go and see some sights, walk off the food together, if it makes you feel better."

He was so charming and such an Aussie, the way he spoke. Toni couldn't help grinning at Jason's comment about rabbit food. She really was not a fan of salad — give her a good meat dish and potatoes any day. She also really liked the idea of playing tourist with him. Yes it was fun being away from under her family's influence, but it was a little lonely. So when the waiter returned, Toni did order the roast and was happy to see the smile and conspiring wink Jason gave her as she did.

"So what brings you to London, Jason? Are you holidaying or on business?"

It was crunch time. Jason had to make the decision to reveal his true reason for being in London or lie to Toni.

He'd been hoping this question would come up a little further into their lunch date or maybe even later — after he'd had the chance to figure out what it was about her that had him so tied up in knots. It was like his body recognized her, his mind already knew that she was meant for him, and this line of thinking currently rolling around his head had Jason stumped. He wasn't a romantic man, did not believe in love at first sight. That was just something women read about in romance books to make them happy. But here he was, a grown man, a man with quite an extensive sexual history, and he was having happy-ever-after thoughts like some ditzy teenage girl, for a woman he hardly knew and who was way out of his league.

"A bit of both really," he finally answered.

"Oh that sounds intriguing. What business are you in?"

"Security." He wasn't trying to sound mysterious but just couldn't think of the best way to come clean.

"So how did you get into that line of work?"

Toni's question gave him a bit of respite and Jason jumped on it immediately. If he could sidetrack her with stories from his past, maybe he could keep his secret for just a bit longer.

"I joined the Army straight out of school, spent ten years 'serving our country', as others like to put it. After a few stints in Afghanistan I decided it was time to bail. My mate Nathan had just started up Haven Security, and he offered me a job. It was a no-brainer really. Doing the sort of stuff I'd been trained for, thanks to the Australian Army. I've spent the last two years helping him build up his company."

Jason saw it—the minute he mentioned the name of the company, Toni reacted. She sat up a little straighter, her eyes opened wider and she started biting at her bottom lip. She had heard of the security firm her father had on retainer to look out for his company and family interests. *Of course she has, idiot. All the alarms installed in Toni's family home have 'Haven Security' written on them.*

He'd fucked up big time without even realizing it. She really had him operating off his game to have made that kind of rookie slip-up. Where was all that bloody training he'd just mentioned?

"Did you say Haven Security?"

Jason could hear the note of disbelief in her voice and wondered how long it would be until the penny dropped and she put two and two together. The fact that he'd just happened to be in the park at the same time as her, had come to her rescue, and the humdinger that they were both staying in the same hotel.

"Yes, Toni, I did."

Toni had started tapping her finger on the table, a nervous kind of habit someone might unconsciously do when they were upset. At least his training still had him noticing things like that. Studying human nature and how a person reacts when dealing with stress could be helpful in figuring out truth from lies — something Jason had been very adept at doing, which had helped him stay ahead of trouble more than once. Jason reached out and gently placed his hand over Toni's for two reasons — he hoped it would still her fingers and stop the tapping, and also prevent her from doing a runner on him.

"Please hear me out before you take aim at me... Before you jump to the wrong conclusion. You being here with me at this table is something I want for me. There is no ulterior motive in this lunch. I just want to get the chance to spend some time with a woman I'm finding hard to resist. The woman who has my stomach tied up in knots and my mind thinking things no respectable man should be thinking."

"My father hired you..." Tears had started to escape from Toni's eyes, and Jason wanted to punch himself in the head for being responsible for her sadness. Had she heard anything he'd just said?

"Please don't cry, luv. I never meant to hurt you. Yes, I was hired to protect you — but from a distance. I was never supposed to make contact with you unless there was a good reason — if you were in imminent danger. But I couldn't keep that charter. The more I followed you around, the more I wanted to get to know you, speak to you... My God, that sounds awful, like I'm some kind of stalker..."

Jason knew he was making a hash of things. The words weren't coming out like he wanted. He needed to explain that she meant more to him than some security detail—but that would sound even more desperate.

"I'm sorry I didn't tell you back at the park but I wanted you to get a chance to get to know me a bit better," Jason pleaded. "Maybe decide you liked what you saw. And then I was going to explain everything, probably starting off by admitting that I'm booked into the room adjacent to yours."

My father hired him.

She was such a fool.

Not only had she, just hours ago, been reflecting on the fact that her mother and father had finally let her do something on her own, trusted her to be able to look after herself—but the man that she had thought, ridiculously, had come to her rescue and shown a bit of interest in her, was in fact being paid to watch her—more than likely reporting back to her controlling father her every movement. And even more humiliating, she'd had no idea it was all happening until Jason had spelled it out.

Yes, she had recognized the name of the company he worked for. Of course she had. Toni had met Nathan Haven many times in her father's office at the family home. He'd even walked through the primary school where she taught... Just to make sure she was working in a safe environment—like teaching kindergarten kids was going to thrust her into the realms of danger.

But the way Jason is stroking my hand and the words coming from his mouth seem sincere. She was so confused, so upset. Her world had just been thrown off its axis and she didn't know what to do next.

"Roast beef and Yorkshire pudding?"

The waiter's question drew Toni back from her inner turmoil.

"Thank you," she managed to squeak out. She pulled her hand back from Jason's grasp and the waiter placed their plates in front of them.

"Is there anything else I can get you? Another drink, perhaps?" the waiter asked politely.

"Thanks, mate. I think we're all good for now," Jason replied while Toni was still trying to decide what she should do next.

Should I just get up and leave? Check out of the hotel and go somewhere else? Or should I stay and listen to what he has to say? How could someone as gorgeous as Jason really be interested in me? It's because of my name, the money. Toni felt sick to her stomach and the aroma of the food was making it worse. *So this is how I can lose weight — get a man to break my heart.* The last thought pulled her up short. Why did she feel like Jason had broken her heart? She'd only just met him. He didn't have that kind of power over her emotions — or shouldn't. This was about her family — the fact that Eva and Frank Grimaldi would not give her any space — not the man sitting in front of her, looking at her with such genuine concern. He was not to blame for just doing what he had been hired to do.

"Come back to me, luv. You're a million miles away... Say something. Please!"

Toni took a steadying breath then exhaled slowly, trying to calm down the maelstrom of emotion that was clouding her brain. "So, what you're saying is that you weren't supposed to make contact with me but you did? Why was that again? It's not like being covered in goose poo is all that dangerous to my well-being. Smelly…yes. Uncomfortable…yes. But certainly not putting my life at risk."

"I couldn't just stand back and do nothing—not when you needed my help. I'd been wanting to talk to you for days. There were a few close calls when I only just managed to stop myself in time. Like when you went to St. Paul's Cathedral, you spent so long reading about the history, I wanted to have a conversation with you. I love English history, have always been fascinated with the monarchy—not to mention the war and Britain's involvement. You went everywhere that I would've gone if I'd been on holiday. That fascinated me about you. It appeared we had a lot in common, and it didn't hurt that you happen to be the sexiest woman I've ever seen."

She'd been following along up until the part where Jason had said he thought she was sexy. Toni couldn't help it. She burst out laughing. "Me? Sexy? When was the last time you had your eyes checked, Mr. Security Man?" Toni managed to say when she had regained her composure.

"And that was before I saw you with your shirt off," Jason replied cheekily, causing Toni's face to burn with embarrassment at the memory. She didn't miss the accompanying wink either as Jason once again held out his hand to her and she placed her own in his.

There was no denying the spark between them and the way just the feel of her hand in Jason's made her heart race. She wanted to believe him because she was attracted to him like no other. "Well, you are definitely the hottest guy I've ever had give me his shirt."

"Good to know. Now, can we finish our lunch and do some sightseeing? I think I'd like to take a look at London from The Eye and I'd like to do that with my arm around you, not hiding behind a tree or a pole."

"Sounds like a plan to me. Bus, train or taxi? Your choice, Jason, but I warn you, if we catch a cab, you're not paying all the fare."

Chapter Four

"Look at the length of those queues. You sure you don't want to buy the fast track tickets? We could be standing around all day otherwise." Lunch had ended with Jason feeling like a weight had been removed from his shoulders. He still found it hard to believe Toni had forgiven him so quickly over his deception but he thanked heaven and earth that she had.

"What's wrong, Jason? Scared to stand in a line and chat? I enjoy being one of the crowd, experiencing the growing anticipation as the queue moves along, until finally it's my time to ride. Or are you worried I might find out a few secrets you're not ready to share?"

"I'm not worried. I was a soldier. Part of my training was how to withstand all forms of interrogation — even from sexy woman. But I'd much rather talk about you."

"Nice distraction technique but I'm not falling for it. Why don't you line up and I'll go grab the tickets."

There wasn't time for him to answer Toni before she trotted off toward the ticket sales window. He really shouldn't have let her head off into the swarm of people alone and so Jason remained on high alert until he caught sight of her curly hair bouncing up and down over her shoulders as she headed back toward him. It took her a few moments to spot him, but when she did, the smile she gave him made his heart beat a little faster.

"Here you are. I was worried I'd lost you. There really are a lot of tourists here today."

"Not much hope of that, luv. You're stuck with me and I wouldn't want it any other way. I must admit you've been a real surprise, though. When I was given this assignment, I thought I'd be following some spoiled rich heiress around the shops all day and shivering my nights away outside some playboy's apartment. I guess I shouldn't stereotype people before I know them."

Jason was glad Toni didn't take offense at his comments and, judging by her laughter, she found his fears amusing.

"I'm sorry I shattered your illusions but if it makes you feel any better, I think most of the people my parents would prefer me to hang out with would easily fit that description. I guess you got lucky then, Mr. Security Man. Although, now I think about it, maybe you deserve to follow me around the shops for a few hours. It would be my revenge on you for spying on me."

Taking Toni's hand in his, Jason brought it up to his lips and kissed her knuckles. "I'm not spying, luv. I'm protecting. Just think of me as Kevin and you can be Whitney."

"Does that mean I get to sing? I'm not very good. Even my students cover their ears when I try to lead them in the school song."

"I guess I could try to find a karaoke bar, but then I get to sweep you up in my arms and carry you off the stage."

Jason laughed when Toni poked her tongue out at him. He really enjoyed chatting with her. It was easy. They were making slow progress toward the boarding area for the pods that would take them high into the sky, but Jason didn't care how long it took them. He was enjoying himself. "What made you decide to become a teacher?"

"What made you decide to become a soldier?" she replied, quick as a flash.

"Isn't it every boy's dream to become a soldier and play with guns?"

"Really? Is that what all the little boys in my class want to be when they grow up? I was pretty sure some wanted to be firefighters or footy stars."

"Well, aren't you a feisty one?" He tapped his finger on her nose gently. "I play footy like you sing, so it wasn't an option for me. So, Miss Grimaldi, what about teaching does it for you?"

Toni went from giggling to serious in a heartbeat. "I love everything about my job — all those eager young minds soaking up information at such a rapid pace. Seeing the joy in their faces when they succeed at something new. I don't have to pretend to be someone I'm not. For a good chunk of the day, I am the center of their world and them, mine. Not that my parents can understand any of that. I think my choice of profession is a bit below their expectation. And worse, I teach at a local school, not some hoity-toity rich kid school. What made you leave the Army?"

"The senseless death. I did tours in Afghanistan and Iraq then joined the special commando unit and did some more time overseas. I saw too many buddies injured and worse. Got into a few close scrapes where I wasn't sure I'd make it and I think I just burnt out." Jason never spoke about his reasons for leaving the service but the words had just slipped from his lips before he had time to think. "Wow, so much for my anti-interrogation techniques." Talking about the past brought back memories Jason tried not to relive. He hated how emotional he felt thinking about the horrors of war he'd experienced, the things he had done under orders. It made him feel weak but when Toni wrapped her arms around his waist and hugged him, without a word, Jason could feel the pain in him ease a little.

"Look, we're up next, luv. Ready to see London from the sky?"

"See? That didn't take long at all. Don't forget you promised to do it with your arm around me."

Jason hadn't forgotten and he was doubly pleased that Toni hadn't either.

* * * *

Going around in the pod on The Eye had been more fun than Jason had imagined. The view of London was spectacular, but it was seeing and hearing Toni's reactions that had made it even more so.

After returning to their hotel — this time jumping on and off London's red double decker buses to get them there — they had shared a few drinks at the bar. Jason had decided that it was safe for him to relax a little, now that he knew Toni wouldn't be heading out again. As much as he had enjoyed every moment they had shared, Jason was finding it harder and harder, literally, to keep his hands off Toni. His cock had been semi-erect all day and he suspected that his balls would be a shade of blue if he didn't do something soon. But he didn't want to rush her.

The old Jason would have been thinking about bedding his date, getting the woman naked so he could pleasure her against the wall, on the floor or in a bed – it wouldn't have mattered just as long as they both orgasmed hard and were left sated and breathless. Then he'd take his leave.

Jason always made it clear that he wasn't the settling down type of guy before things got too out of hand. He'd seen first-hand what being 'in love' or married did to a couple – had lived his life caught in between his parents' constant battling. It had been the reason he'd joined the Army – deciding that if he were going to be in the middle of a war, he might as well be in one where he could be useful. But if a woman wanted some gratuitous sex then he was the guy for her – and he'd had plenty of action.

This thing with Toni – whatever it was – was different. Jason wanted more than just a quick romp in the sack. He wanted to hold her in his arms as they fell asleep, after a round or two of some mind-blowing sex, of course. Jason wanted Toni something bad, wanted to feel his cock push between the folds of her pussy. He wanted to hear Toni call his name as he licked and sucked her clit and drove her wild, until the resulting orgasm left her body quivering with satisfaction. Then he would enter her slowly, savoring every new sensation as his cock found space between those slick, wet walls of her cunt.

Even though he wanted this nearly more than he wanted his next breath, Jason had walked Toni to her door, and, after organizing a time for them to meet in the morning, he had kissed her lips gently then walked away. It had taken every ounce of his self-control to leave her there with her eyes burning a hole in his back as she'd watched him go.

As a result, Jason now sat in his room, calling himself every name under the sun for being such an idiot and not taking what he'd wanted—Toni naked and lying stretched out on his bed. All the while he ruthlessly pumped his hand up and down his cock to try to give his balls some relief.

He needed to clear his head so he could email the daily report of Toni's movements to Nathan. Well, as detailed as he could without giving away the fact that he'd blown his cover and was now lying in bed imagining all the ways he wanted to pleasure the daughter of the firm's biggest client. Yep, Nathan really did not need to read about any of that—his mate would go ballistic.

* * * *

Toni couldn't sleep. Looking at the clock again and finding out that only a few minutes had passed, she kicked the sheets off her legs with exasperation. Her body was on fire, the sheets too heavy against her skin. She'd flung off her nightie twenty minutes ago as the fabric had abraded her sensitive nipples—nipples that had remained hard and wanting—or, more precisely, wanting Jason ever since he had left her at her door. *This is ridiculous. I should just go bang on his door until he lets me in and gives me an orgasm so I can bloody sleep. What's the point of knowing he's next door if I can't take advantage of it?* It had been a bit of a shock at first when Jason had admitted to being in the room next to hers all along. Toni was convinced she had just invented a new form of torture.

She wanted to feel Jason's hands on her body so badly it hurt. As she unconsciously ground her pelvis against the mattress, imagining how it would feel to have his lips around her nipples with his hard body, heavy and warm, over hers, she'd been close to orgasm. It had taken Toni a few seconds to realize what she was doing. She'd been so busy imagining what it would feel like to have Jason touching her, she had lost control.

"Aaargh," Toni groaned again as she punched the pillow repeatedly with her clenched fist. *I'm going to look delightful in the morning, bags on bags, a bloody set of luggage under my eyes if I don't get some sleep.*

The bed linen felt like it was lined with barbed wire and ultimately won the war declared on her sexually frustrated and sensitized skin. She had suffered enough. Toni got up from the bed, then shook her head as she looked at the tangle of twisted sheets she'd left behind. She found her dressing gown and slipped her arms through the sleeve openings. The light and delicate fabric of her luxurious covering might as well have been a sheet of sandpaper rubbing against her body.

After tucking her room key into the pocket, she quietly opened her door, just enough to poke her head outside and check that the corridor was clear. Finding it empty and not hearing any sound of approaching footsteps, Toni pulled the door closed behind her until the sound of the lock clicked—a sound that in the still of the corridor seemed like the boom of a bass drum being struck.

She took the three steps that separated her room from Jason's and, summoning up all the bravado she could muster, Toni knocked on the door. It was really more like a brush of her fingertips against the two inch thick wood, but it was the best she could manage, given that she was already trying to quell the sound of her heart pumping so loudly that it was probably making enough noise to wake the entire hotel.

For one short moment Toni imagined a squad of firemen, fully suited up, with hoses and axes at the ready, racing down the hallway searching for the source of the loud thumping horn that sounded like an alarm but was in fact her heart beating. *If he doesn't open the door by the time I count to ten, I'm going back to my room and will just have to deal with the sexual tension I'm feeling myself... One... Two...*

Chapter Five

Jason had been able to hear Toni moving about her room. At first he'd suspected she was making a comfort trip to the bathroom but as he'd lain staring at the ceiling—something he'd been doing for the last hour or so as he'd tried, unsuccessfully, to make his mind and body relax so he could get some shut-eye—he'd heard the sound of her room door opening.

What the hell is she up to?

Was she making a run for it? Trying to escape from under his watch, have the holiday she thought she'd been having out from underneath her family's scrutiny, her father's control? Was his little sexy bird flying the coop while she thought he slept? Well, he had news for her. Maybe he would put her over his knee and paddle that ample and sexy butt of hers for the attempted break-out—or at least threaten to do it. He could hardly wait to see her reaction to his idea, his punishment.

Jason had sprung out of bed, dragged his jeans on and stormed over to the door, flinging it open so he could stop Toni before she had the chance to get down the hallway to the lifts.

What he hadn't been expecting was to see Toni standing in front of his door. And what was more unexpected was that she was standing there before him in her sleepwear, a filmy material that did nothing to hide the roundness of her breasts or the curve of her hips. It was mesmerizing, tantalizing. One second Jason had been imagining the pleasure of bending her over his lap and the next he was doing all he could not to fall at her feet and beg for mercy.

"Toni, what's wrong, luv?" he managed to croak out, trying to ignore the compulsion that was urging him to drag her into his arms and smother her lips with his own.

"I… I…couldn't sleep," she replied, her words coming out in a stuttering whisper that had Jason leaning in closer to make out what she was saying. It was a dangerous move on his part as the closer he came to her body, the more prominent the heady aroma of her scent teased his nose. His dick was now rock-hard and there was no way Jason could hide his reaction to having Toni so near.

"Why can't you sleep? Has something frightened you? Do you want me to have a look around, maybe check your room again?"

"I'd rather come into your room…if that's okay?"

Of all the things he'd thought she might say, that had not been one of them. *Come into my room?* How the hell would he be able to resist her when she was right there within his reach and wearing something so sexy?—nightwear that left little to the imagination, yet imagine was just what he was doing. The idea of him opening her robe, pushing it off her shoulders and sucking on her tits was in the forefront of his mind.

But he had to get it together. For God's sake he'd left her standing in his doorway, definitely not a secure position for her safety, and doubly so dressed like that.

"Sure, luv. Come in," Jason finally managed to say, his speech distorted as he struggled to control a tongue that did not seem to fit in the confines of his mouth anymore. "There's not much room in here. Just let me clear off the chair for you and you can sit and tell me what's keeping you awake."

As Toni stepped into his room, Jason closed the door behind her. He needed to clear his shit from the chair pronto. He'd never been the tidy type, much to the chagrin of his superiors in the force. Jason could not remember how many times he'd been written up and given extra duty for not having clean quarters. But the idea of Toni seeing his dirty jocks and socks was making his stomach roll. *Fuck, I'm totally screwed.* He made the dash for his undies. *How the hell can she make me feel like this when the toughest and meanest the Army had to offer couldn't?*

Toni took a quick glance around the room. It was smaller than hers and there seemed to be clutter on every available surface. Then her eyes caught sight of his bed — the sheets and pillows resembled her own, tangled and strewn about. She wanted to be in that bed and she wanted to be in it with Jason.

"Don't go to any trouble clearing off the chair, Jason, I think I'd be happy on the bed." Her cheeks were red, she just knew it, but she had come this far so there was no reason to not just go for it. She'd seen the bulge at the front of his jeans and was pretty sure that she was the reason for it. She reached out her hand and stroked her finger up and over his biceps. His skin was warm to her touch. She wanted more, wanted to lean forward into the broad of his back but she waited to see his reaction to her bold words.

It felt like forever before he turned to her. Toni heard the sounds of her own shallow breaths as she waited, but finally Jason spoke. "Are you sure this is what you want, luv? 'Cause, Toni…if I get you into my bed I'm not going to be able to control myself. I want you. I want to be buried deep inside you. I want to make you scream my name, as I make you come over and over until you beg for mercy and then maybe I might give you a moment's rest before I start all over again. Be sure, honey. Please be sure."

His voice was so deep, the sound of it made the hair on her arms stand up, just like when she heard a talented vocalist hit that perfect note.

She was so sure.

Had never been so certain of anything in her life.

With her pussy already wet and hot for him, she whispered, "I'm sure… Please, Jason, make love to me."

"Oh, honey, I plan to," was all Jason said before Toni felt his lips on hers.

His tongue probed for access inside her mouth and she capitulated, her lips shaping to his. The taste of him was amazing—better than any chocolate dessert Toni had ever consumed. Her tongue parried with his, as they discovered each other for the first time.

Jason tugged gently on her hair then he massaged her scalp, his strong fingers sending another wave of goosebumps racing over her skin. Toni had always thought the best thing about getting her hair done was the massage the hairdresser gave while spreading conditioner, but this was on a completely different level of pleasure. There was something incredibly erotic about the slight pain she felt from the pull of her hair followed by the soothing gentleness of Jason's caress. She was melting under his touch and they'd hardly done anything yet. Toni wasn't sure how she would cope when Jason moved his ministrations to her body, but she could not wait to find out.

It was delicious and even though Toni felt she could spend a lifetime kissing Jason just like this, she wanted more. Pulling her mouth away from his, she raised her hand to put a little space between them. "Can we get into bed now?" she purred.

Chapter Six

She was going to kill him. Her words, so simple and direct, had Jason's head spinning. Kissing Toni was like nothing he had ever experienced, and Jason had kissed many women. There was a definite zing, like an electric charge, as their lips met.

Taking her to his bed was the best idea ever spoken. "I'm trying not to rush this, luv, but if you insist, I'd hate to disappoint you, honey."

Jason was surprised by the gravelly tones of his voice. He was so used to being in complete control, yet Toni had him struggling to keep it together. Jason found himself dealing with a very uncharacteristic problem—he was nervous. He wasn't sure how long he would last before his dick or balls—or both—exploded. He needed to be inside her ASAP but first he wanted to hear Toni call out his name in ecstasy as he brought her undone.

"That robe is not hiding much but I think it needs to go," he said as he gently slid it from her body. "You're so beautiful, all curves and womanly softness. I can't wait to feel your skin against mine, honey." He couldn't resist the temptation of her full lush tits any longer and fell to his knees. One pink nipple now directly in line with his mouth, he licked the offering. The sound of her sighs spurred him on. Jason laved, nipped and sucked on the nub then repeated the same with the other breast. Fuck, he wanted to rub his cock between those two mounds of soft flesh and pump away until his cum covered them—just not yet. He needed to be buried inside her pussy this first time. But he would make the fantasy a reality sometime soon, he promised himself, as he concentrated on bringing Toni pleasure.

"I'm going to touch you now. My fingers are going to play with your pussy, tease your clit and make sure you are ready for me—hot and wet for my cock to slide into you."

"I'm ready for you now…" Her breathy reply.

"Oh, honey, that's good to hear because I'm ready for you. That's a fact."

Toni hadn't been kidding, Jason discovered. She was hot and slick, and he groaned at the pleasure of sliding his fingers between her soft cunt lips. "Oh, baby, you are so ready for me that you're killing me. You feel so fucking good. So wet, so hot…" He needed to taste that cream. Time was running out for him. He wasn't sure how long he could hold on to his load once his cock entered her wet cunt, but he'd be damned if he was going to miss this opportunity. He pushed her down onto the bed with his free hand, all the while delving and rolling the fingers of his other hand inside her pussy. She fell back onto the mattress, her legs opening a little wider as she lay back. Jason took the opportunity gladly and buried his head between them.

Her taste was heavenly, exotic. Jason had always enjoyed oral sex but this was something completely mind-blowing. Her taste was like nothing he'd experienced, nothing he could describe appropriately in words. He relaxed and enjoyed her erotic flavor.

It didn't take long, though, for Toni's body to start writhing and bucking in response to Jason's attention. Jason took hold of Toni's clit between his teeth and gently tugged. He tapped on her G-spot and within seconds he could feel her pussy walls tightening around his fingers, trying to claim the orgasm she had building inside her. He sucked a little harder, tapped a little more insistently, and was rewarded. The sound of her voice as she called his name, the rich tangy release that covered his tongue as he continued to ride her through her climax, was almost more than his poor, deprived cock could bear.

As Toni came down from her orgasm, Jason took the opportunity to grab a condom from his wallet. Scrambling out of his jeans—the movements not even close to smooth and controlled—he struggled to keep his balance while he fought with the denim to release its hold on his feet.

Finally rid of his clothes, Jason hurriedly donned the rubber then moved back into position between her legs. "I need to be in you now, honey, before I embarrass myself and come prematurely."

She had just had the best orgasm of her life—not that Toni had too many to compare it with—but this was so far and beyond anything she'd ever felt that she knew Jason had spoiled it for anyone in her future. There was nothing and no one that could compare to that, she decided, as she luxuriated in the warmth her release had created.

She was so wrapped up in her own pleasure that she nearly didn't notice Jason move from between her now lethargic legs. There was a moment of panic that crashed her back to reality when she thought he was leaving her. The pure relief she felt when she watched Jason roll the condom over his cock was short-lived as she spied the intimidating length and width. Her concern must have shown in her face as Jason soothed her, "It will be fine, luv, I'll take it slow and you tell me if I hurt you, okay?"

After the pleasure he had just given her, there was no way in hell Toni would have stopped him. She wiggled her way up farther onto the bed, opened her legs in invitation and tried to relax. Jason knelt over her body and aligned the head of his cock with her pussy lips. There was a slight burning sensation that bordered more toward pleasure than pain as his thickness stretched her until he was seated fully inside her.

"Yes!" The sensual satisfaction of him filling her set off a new wave of delicious tingles over her sensitive nerve endings.

"Am I hurting you? Do you want me to stop?" her knight in shining armor asked heroically.

She giggled at her own silliness before replying, "Stop and I may have to hurt you, Mr. Security Man."

"Thank fuck for that, luv, I'm not sure I could have if I tried." Jason was moving inside her as he spoke, his pumping rhythm managing to rub or touch every important or hungry nerve inside her.

Within moments Toni could feel another orgasm building. She drew her fingernails down the length of Jason's back as she flew higher and higher.

Jason thrust his hips against hers, rapidly. The sound of his cock entering and exiting her pussy, the slap of skin making contact with skin and the hiss of oxygen bursting from their lungs were the only noises Toni could make out as she soared.

"Come with me, Toni..." Jason whispered into her ear. He gently nipped her earlobe as his body tensed and he thrust one last time. Toni flew over the edge. She climaxed so hard she thought she would never come back from it. She heard a scream and delighted moaning in the distance as her body spiraled out of control—every nerve pulsating with pleasure and not realizing at first the sounds of ecstasy she'd heard were, in fact, from her own mouth. Of course they were hers. How could she not moan from the sheer force of pleasure Jason had heaped on her?

* * * *

Jason was still lying over her, his body covering her own—he was heavy but she didn't care. It was one of those perfect moments in time Toni knew she would never forget. She was tracing patterns over his back with her finger, spreading the moisture from the beads of sweat their lovemaking had produced into random shapes. It was when she realized that the shapes were in fact hearts that she stopped. She was getting ahead of herself. This was just sex, a night of pleasure that she had instigated. Hearts had no place in this. "Feels good... Touching my back... Relaxing," Jason muttered, his voice muffled because his mouth was against her shoulder. "I need to move... Too heavy," he continued, his lips brushing against her skin with every word.

It was an amazing sensation. It was turning her on. "You're not too heavy," she responded, and after a little giggle had escaped she added, "I'm enjoying having you flop all over me."

"Aargh! I'm not sure how to take that," Jason said as he lifted his weight from her, his bicep flexing as he moved. "I need to deal with the condom anyway. Stay put. I'll be back in a flash."

Toni didn't think she could move if her life depended on it. Every inch of her was languid, reveling in the memory of what had just taken place. She heard the sound of the toilet flushing and enjoyed the sight of a very naked Jason as he walked back from the bathroom.

Jason was glorious. His body was sculpted with muscle, not bulky like a weightlifter but every muscle still prominent and very enjoyable to look at. His stomach was flat, a channel formed from each hip that led to his groin. Toni wanted to run her tongue in the groove. She had seen pictures of the male physique with those tempting little valleys but Toni had always thought they were airbrushed on for effect. She certainly had never seen a man's body up close and in the flesh that resembled Jason's. His cock was relaxed but as she lay there staring at his body, she saw it flex and move slightly.

"Honey, if you don't stop looking at me like that, there will be a repeat performance of what we just did, very soon."

She heard the growling threat but the wicked grin that Jason was giving her and the twinkle in his eye left her feeling powerful. She was turning him on. Overweight and socially awkward Toni Grimaldi had this hot as sin man looking at her like he wanted to eat her up. For the first time in her life, Toni felt sexy. She also was very keen on the idea of Jason eating her up, again.

"Promises, promises," she replied. "Doesn't look like you've got it in you," she said as she brazenly reached out her hand and touched his cock. As her fingers made contact with his flesh, Jason hissed.

"Be careful, little lady. Don't rile the sleeping beast."

She burst out laughing. "Sleeping beast... That's funny. Didn't feel all that beastly to me. In fact it felt pretty damn good, if you ask me. What's the opposite of beast?" she asked as she traced her fingers up and down his cock.

"I don't know and if you keep touching me like that, I don't really care," Jason replied as he climbed back onto the bed.

She giggled again. For the life of her, Toni couldn't remember being the giggly type but it seemed that she was where Jason was concerned.

They lay in each other's arms for a while, caressing and stroking, each familiarizing themselves with the other's body. Toni was euphoric. She had never felt so bold, so confident about her own sexuality. So close to someone.

"You okay, luv?"

"More than okay, Jason," she replied, once again stroking her hand over Jason's chin, enjoying the prickle of beard stubble under her fingertips.

"I've never felt better than I do at this moment." The sigh escaping her lips was testament to the way she was feeling. "I'm glad you came to my rescue. Truth is, while I really was enjoying being on my own—or thinking I was—I was lonely. Today and tonight, sharing the sights, dinner and now this..." She waved her arm over the two of them. "It's just so much better sharing."

Toni was doing her best not to seem too desperate, keep things on the light side between her and Jason, but she was just so happy. She wanted to explain how much being with him meant to her. *But how far should she go?*

"I've had a pretty good day too, luv. You're good company. I'm used to doing things solo — comes with the job — but why are you over here alone? I thought someone in your position would have plenty of friends who would jump at the chance of a holiday. Yet here you are, halfway across the world alone. If you were my woman, there's no way I'd let you travel without me. It's not safe."

Just the thought of being Jason's 'woman', as he put it, sent a tingle up her spine. Oh how she wished she could find someone like him to share her life with, but it was the 'someone in your position' that brought her crashing back down from her fantasy world.

What had he meant by that? Did he think just because her family had money that she was popular, spent her days floating from one social event to another? It was so far from her reality it was laughable. He obviously didn't know her very well, hadn't done a thorough background check on her very boring life — a life she had created for herself, since she had refused so many invitations that they'd stopped coming.

In reality, Toni had very little to do with the rich, young socialites her family had hoped she would join ranks with. There was no way she wanted her picture splashed across the gossip pages, especially with her looks. She didn't fit in. She didn't want to live in that world and the 'normal' world never let her forget the other. She was a misfit.

"Will you stay the night with me?" Jason asked her "Let me hold you while we grab some shut-eye. We have a busy day of sightseeing tomorrow. I need my beauty sleep." Jason kissed her on the tip of her nose and she sighed.

Toni didn't want to go to sleep. She wanted to enjoy this feeling for as long as she could. Having his arms wrapped around her made her feel safe, content. Eventually, her new-found lucky break would end and Jason would come to his senses. Someone as gorgeous as Jason should be partnered with a tall, leggy blonde — some model or actress. Toni could almost imagine the woman that was meant to be with him. It was certainly not her. If it hadn't been for her father's money, she probably wouldn't have even registered on his radar, and soon this job would be over for him.

But for now, she was going to enjoy every second she had with her hero-turned-bodyguard. If he was hired to protect her for the length of her holiday, she had another glorious week to enjoy herself.

Chapter Seven

Jason had been watching Toni sleep for twenty minutes. He needed to take a piss, but was reluctant to disturb her by moving. She looked so beautiful lying next to him. Her breasts pushed up against his side, the softness and swell of her tempting cleavage not helping the morning wood he was sporting. Her curly hair was splayed out on the pillow, and Jason was playing with one of the springy locks as he took in her delicate features. Her eyelashes were long, her lips full and inviting, so kissable. She was small against his frame, her stomach and hips lush and curvy, just right for a man to cuddle into. His other arm was numb from having it wrapped around her body but he didn't care. He wanted to hold onto this moment for as long as he could. Jason wasn't sure what sort of reaction he was going to receive when Toni awoke. *Will she be embarrassed from the previous night's activities? Maybe regretful? Sorry that she's slept with the hired help, even if it isn't her that's paying my wage?*

He didn't think she was the type for a one-night stand but really, how could he know for sure? He'd only known her for a short time. He didn't really know Toni at all.

Why am I even thinking about this kinda shit? What does it matter how many blokes she's fucked or how often she does it? You're sounding like a lovestruck teenager, a fucking sensitive new age guy and you're no SNAG, there is nothing sensitive about you, bucko. Fuck 'em and leave 'em. That's the motto. Right? There's no real future for us. Shit, I've never wanted a future before. Why the hell would I want to worry about one now? 'Cause she's different, dickhead, the voice inside his head added helpfully.

But what did that matter? Different, bloody perfect or sexy as all get out didn't change the fact that she was the daughter of one of the richest, most powerful men in Australia. Like her father was going to let her hook up with an ex-soldier who came from nowhere and had very little to offer his only daughter.

"What's got you all scowly, Mr. Security Man? I bet you've got a case of numb arm from me lying on it all night."

The sound of Toni's voice snapped him back to the real world. She was looking up at him, her big brown eyes still holding a hint of sleepiness. He didn't know how long Toni had been awake or even how long he'd been lost in thought. What he did know was that Toni was moving her arm down his body, and that any moment now her hand would make contact with his dick and find it rock-hard. He really needed to take a piss before he could concentrate on anything else.

"Morning, luv. How'd you sleep?" Jason asked as he stalled her arm from its expedition with his own. "I need to take a leak. Don't go anywhere. I'll be right back."

Jason dragged his body away from hers, feeling the immediate loss of her warmth as he stood, already trying to decide what part of Toni's body he'd feast on after his trip to the bathroom. *Maybe I could spend some time sucking on her tits, get her to straddle my cock and take a ride at the same time. Yeah, I could definitely see the promise in that.* His fantasy was interrupted by the sound of her voice.

"...me too, and I am in desperate need of a shower and coffee. I just don't function well without caffeine, lots of it... I didn't think I'd fall asleep last night or this morning, whatever time it was. I planned to get up before you woke, go back to my own room and get ready for the day ahead."

Okay, so that pulled him up short—he hadn't caught all of what she'd said to him but from the bits he had registered, it sounded like Toni wasn't interested in them going for another round this morning, and while that idea disappointed Jason, it was Toni admitting she'd wanted to escape before he awoke that really knocked his ego around. After all, that was usually his forte... The irony was not lost on him. Putting a cheery smile on his face or hoping he was, Jason turned back toward her.

The sight of her stretching out on the bed gloriously naked nearly floored him. Her arms were stretched toward the ceiling, her back arched and raised off the bed, pushing her breasts up. Her nipples were hard and pointing up to the heavens. It was the hottest thing he'd ever seen. If he wasn't already sporting a hard-on—one that was now causing him a huge amount of discomfort—it would have given him another. *Fuck me, gotta get a grip... Stop drooling and say something, dickhead.*

"Okay, game plan is. I'll use the bathroom and then you can freshen up while I organize some coffee. White with one. Right?" he managed to stammer out as he spun away from the erotic view before him, then staggered into the bathroom before slamming the door shut behind him for good measure so he wouldn't be tempted to go back to the bed and take Toni again.

Waking to see the scowl on Jason's face had certainly shaken Toni's bravado. She hadn't meant to fall asleep and had been disorientated for a moment when her eyes had opened. When she'd seen his body next to hers, the memories had flooded back quickly. Remembering the night's activities, it was no wonder she was feeling a little stiff. It was a glorious feeling and Toni had been enjoying the reminiscing, until she'd noticed his scowl.

He didn't waste a second escaping from the bed either. She'd decided that as soon as Jason went into his bathroom she would jump up, grab her robe and go back to her room. She really didn't want to face any excuses or regrets from him until after she was clean and full of coffee. When she heard the sound of the door bang shut, it startled her into action. Toni swung her legs over the edge of the mattress and got out of bed. Trying to be as quiet as she could, she put on her robe and crept from the room, the click of the door as it latched closed behind her a somber sign that her fantasy night was over. Safely back in the sanctuary of her own room, Toni took time to evaluate the situation. She boiled the little kettle the hotel supplied and made a coffee as she tried to decide how she would play it.

It was obvious that Jason had been annoyed that she was still in his bed — his actions had confirmed that when he'd stopped her from touching him and fled. Of course he probably wouldn't say anything to her about it, given that he still had the job of shadowing her. *Maybe he'll ask someone else to take over?* The thought put her into a panic. *No, he'd need a good reason and it would take at least a day for someone to get here to replace him. Guess old Ma and Pa wouldn't want me traipsing around without their spies. If I can convince him I meant to go back to my room... That I'm not looking for a repeat performance... Maybe he'll hang around. I wonder if he really wants to do the whole sightseeing, touristy thing with me or retreat back to following me, hiding in the shadows?*

She was working herself into a frenzy trying to decide what to do. One-night stands or even relationships were not her field. She was flying blind and had no one to turn to for advice. Deciding that a shower was at least the first step needed, Toni quickly washed and dressed. Just as she was putting on her sandals, there was a knock at her door.

Hopping, one shoe on and the other dangling from her grasp, Toni opened the door.

"You didn't even look through the peephole," Jason growled at her. "Don't you have any kind of self-preservation instincts? You never think of your own safety. I know, I've seen it first-hand over the last few days. For God's sake, Toni, it's written on the back of your door not to open without checking first who it is. And that is advice for everyday folk, not just bloody heiresses." Jason pushed past her and stormed into her room.

He was so angry with her that Toni unconsciously took a step back, putting more space between them. She'd never been yelled at like that before and Jason was frightening her. All she'd done was open the door. Anyone would think, the way he was carrying on, that she'd walked into some gangster's house with a loaded weapon and demanded their drug money.

When he'd pointed out the heiress part, it was as if a barb had struck her heart. She didn't want him to see her that way—ridiculous really, given that he was hired to protect her and all. Not that it really mattered what he thought anymore. It was clear her luck of the previous day had run out.

"Don't yell at me," she finally managed to blurt out. "I can open the door or shut the door however I like. I can do and go anywhere I decide too—without your permission or advice. You do not get to lecture me. I get lectured enough by my parents. I do not need to hear it from the person that was hired to follow me and, might I add, without my knowledge or my approval. And not counting the attentions of the low flying goose with a significant bowel condition yesterday, I've managed to remain free from the clutches of evil and chaos all on my own accord."

The instant the words had spilled from her mouth, Toni wanted to capture them all and reel them back in, but it had been too late. She didn't know what had got into her. She never argued or caused a scene. Hated confrontation. But for some reason Jason had caused her to erupt.

The change in Jason was immediate. Her words had scored a direct hit. It was obvious by the way he straightened to his full height, the way his eyes became cold. Eyes that Toni had gazed into, taken comfort and joy from the warmth they had shown her, were now looking like icy glaciers. There was no emotion apparent on his face. It was even scarier than him shouting at her, the change in him. Toni could almost feel the wave of cold indifference hit her as he stared her down.

"I'm sorry, Jason... I didn't mean to—" she began to apologize.

"No, you're right. This is why I should not have made contact with you. It's crucial with the work I do not to get personally involved with a client. It can cloud your focus, your judgment. Be a distraction. I overstepped the boundaries. It's my responsibility to see to your safety. I had no right to speak to you that way. In fact, I have no right to converse with you at all. It won't happen again." Jason's reply was delivered without emotion, his voice flat and to the point.

Toni wanted to cry. This was not the way she had wanted today to go. She had been hoping that they could at least be friends, travel companions—that he could share in her excitement as they visited the many historical landmarks still on her itinerary.

Yes, she would have gladly fallen into his bed again but understood she had blown that opportunity. The idea that she had ruined any chance of their continued friendship was more than she could bear. Try as she might, Toni could not stop the flow of tears that were now rolling down her cheeks.

As he wrapped his arms around her shoulders, Jason guided her head to his chest, but still she could not stop blubbering.

"Shush, luv, don't cry. I'm sorry, so sorry. Please stop the tears," Jason pleaded as he rubbed the back of her neck. "I overreacted. I didn't mean to upset you or come on so strong. It's just when you've seen what I've seen, know what people can do, what sick sons of bitches roam this world... It makes you jumpy. I just don't want to see you get hurt... Not doing so great with that so far...huh?"

Between the sensation of Jason's fingers gently kneading her neck and the words he was whispering to her, Toni started to regain control. Her tears stopped, the joy of being held in this man's arms taking hold of her emotions. It felt so good to lean against him. Her nose buried into his chest, she could smell his scent, strong, masculine. Toni wasn't sure if it was Jason's cologne or just him, but she liked it. He was so strong yet, at that very moment, tender toward her.

"I don't regret for a minute that I let it get personal with you, luv. I really want to get the chance to know you, spend more time with you. The problem will be that it's a new experience for me. I've never felt this way before. I might become a little overbearing. Can you handle that, Toni? Will you forgive me? Give me another chance? Last night was amazing, waking up and seeing you lying next to me, holding you in my arms... I want that again." Jason paused for a moment.

Toni lifted her head from his chest, looked up. She saw the truth of his words reflected in the warmth of his eyes as he gazed down on her.

"Do you want that too, Toni? Can you see us spending time together? Or have I blown my chance? Am I relegated back to following you around in the background again?"

Toni's head was spinning. She was so confused. She'd thought she'd driven him away, yet here he was begging her to give them another chance. She'd been prepared to work to retain Jason's friendship. He was offering her more than that, talking about getting to know her and waking up with her in his arms. It was more than she could have wished for. But still a tiny voice in her head was telling her to slow down. *Will he feel the same way when it's time to go home or is this just a holiday fling for him? How will you cope when he says goodbye? You're already head over heels for him. What will your parents think if they find out?*

She didn't care. Ignoring the voices forecasting doom inside her head, she reached for him, pulling his head down toward her so her lips could reach his. Toni kissed Jason for all she was worth, hoping her actions were answer enough to his questions.

Jason cupped her face with his large hands and a shiver went up her spine.

"Judging by the heat of that kiss, you want to spend more time with me too, luv."

That was exactly what Toni wanted — more time with Jason in and out of his bed. She popped open the first button on his shirt.

"Let me show you just how much," she said, as she pressed her palms against Jason's chest, rubbing circles around his flattened, dark nipples with her finger.

"Mmm, I'm liking where this is headed," he replied.

Toni loved the firm contours of Jason's chest, the slight covering of hair that narrowed toward his hips leading a path to his cock. She wanted to get him naked, see his body in all its glory and worship it. He had other ideas, though.

Jason gripped the bottom of her T-shirt. "Let me help you with this, luv. You won't be needing any clothes on for what I have in mind for you today," he said, grinning wickedly.

Standing naked in front of Jason in the stark light of day was making Toni feel uncomfortable. Her hands involuntarily sought to cover her body from his view.

"Don't hide from me. You are beautiful. I want you, need you," Jason said, his voice gravelly as he pulled her hands away from her breasts. "Look at my cock if you need any proof. I'm as hard as a rock."

He tipped her chin up and his lips reclaimed hers. He licked and nipped at her mouth until finally his tongue swept inside. It was so glorious Toni forgot her anxieties the second their bodies met. Mouth to mouth, skin to skin, every nerve in her came alive and sang out for Jason's touch. He broke from their kiss and fell to his knees before her. "One day I will have you on your knees in front of me, just like this, as I feed my cock into the warmth of your mouth," Jason said just before his lips made contact with her skin. He licked a trail around her belly button before journeying even lower across her hip bones.

It was as if time stood still, Toni aware of his every touch, her pussy, her clit throbbing with need. Jason's words and actions both fueling her desire. Soon she was writhing and pushing her body against his.

"I need more…" she begged.

"Tell me what you need, Toni."

There was no time to feel self-conscious. If Jason didn't do something soon Toni feared she would lose her mind. "I need you to touch my clit. Make me come, Jason. Please." Toni moved her left leg a step to the side, widening her stance, eager to feel the touch of Jason's fingers enter her throbbing cunt.

He didn't make her wait long.

The moment he rubbed over her clit, Toni's pussy clenched and an orgasm swept over her hard and quick, like a tidal wave crashing over the earth. Her body shook from the force of her climax and her knees went weak. Jason did not relent. He continued to tease and rub her clit, not giving Toni a chance to recover. At first she tried to step away but Jason kept his hand firmly placed on her backside, keeping her locked into place and at his mercy.

"Come again for me, baby. I know you've got it in you."

"No I can't," she cried, her head thrashing from side to side. "It's too much."

Just when Toni thought she would die from Jason's unyielding, sensual torment, another orgasm began to build, the pleasure slowly growing inside her. Her toes curled as the yearning intensified. Once again she shattered, splintering into a million fragments of pure white light and paradise.

She was still recovering, basking in the pleasure she had just experienced as he lifted her onto the bed. Toni was vaguely aware of the sound of the condom packet being ripped open just before Jason positioned himself over her body, his cock nudging the lips of her channel. She wrapped her legs around his hips as he entered her in one quick thrust. Clinging to his shoulders, she reveled in the weight of his body on hers—a sensation that Toni had, only a few minutes before, feared she'd never experience again.

Jason's cock rocked in and out of her pussy slowly, a maddening pace, but rubbing against all the good spots as it did. To her surprise, Toni felt the fluttering of another orgasm begin to grow, the familiar clenching of her pussy walls as she strove to climb that peak to ecstasy. She buried her head against Jason's chest, her lips making contact with his nipple.

"God, you feel so fucking amazing, Toni. I could stay buried inside you all day and still not want to let you go, but I can't hold on any longer. Come with me..."

Jason's voice sounded strained but his words made Toni's heart sing. She moved her hips in unison with Jason's. She wanted him to feel the same pleasure that she was experiencing, enjoying. As her third orgasm in less than ten minutes hit and rocked her world, Jason's body tensed and he thrust inside her one last time before he stilled, shouting her name as he found his own completion.

Chapter Eight

"Lincoln is so beautiful, Jason. I had no idea it was such a historic town. The castle was built in 1068 by William the Conqueror."

Toni was so pleased they had decided to ditch her original itinerary. When she had made her travel plans, she'd decided on using bus tours to travel around the country. She'd felt a bit nervous at the thought of driving by herself. When Jason had brought up the option of hiring a car, not at all worried over the thought of taking on the unknown roads, she'd more than happily agreed. They'd set out on the M1 and headed north, stopping where and when they wanted.

"Neither did I, luv." Jason stood in front of Lincoln Cathedral, reading a plaque on the wall. "Come and take a look at this, Toni. It's a memorial to Sir Joseph Banks. He was born in the area."

Toni walked over and slipped her hand in his. "This is amazing. I never knew that. I'm going to take some photos. Grade three students learn all about Captain Cook and the *Endeavour*. How our Great Southern

Land was discovered and the coastline mapped. It will make it so much more interesting for the kids if I can say I've seen the memorial to the botanist that named so many of Australia's flora and fauna."

Jason laughed. "You think so, luv? Or are you just as excited to find something so linked to our Aussie history? I don't think it would have made much of a difference to my interest in schoolwork when I was eight. Botanists were nerds. I would have wanted to be the captain and carry a sword as I went exploring the unknown."

"Are you making fun of me, Jason Beck?"

"Maybe, sweetheart. But I do love seeing you get so excited by every castle, cathedral or Roman ruin we discover. Do you realize that you actually jump up and down and make these sexy little squealing kind of noises when you find some new piece of information that interests you?"

Toni tried to discount that Jason had just mentioned the word love in connection to her. *It's just a figure of speech. There is nothing more to it.* Toni was falling in love with Jason, she had tried not to but every minute they spent together, he wormed his way into her heart more deeply. She hadn't been able to get him to discuss their future. On more than one occasion over the last few days, she'd tried to talk to him about what would happen when they both returned home. Jason always changed the subject. He was gifted in the art of distraction and his aversion to speaking about anything to do with their future was frustrating Toni.

"I seem to recall discovering a few new things at night, Jason. Do I make the same kind of noises then? What did you call them…? Squeals?"

"No, they were more like sensual moans of pleasure, luv."

She grabbed his butt and gave it a squeeze. "What say you take me back to our hotel and see if you can get me to make those sounds again and we can decide what to name them?"

"Well, it is getting late and we have had a long day. Maybe that's just what we need, to go to bed early."

Jason was right about it being a long day. Each morning they had set off early, stopping frequently to roam hand in hand through historical points of interest, across meadows and moors, experiencing all they could in the short time frame they had. Toni had fallen asleep each night exhausted, not only from the day's adventures but also from the enthusiastic and insatiable sexual appetite Jason displayed as he explored and discovered her needs and desires. There was not an inch of her body that Jason had not stroked, laved and kissed.

As they were walking back, Jason's phone rang.

"Fuck, it's Nathan. I need to get this. He probably wants a report on what you've been doing. Let's just say I've not been all that forthcoming on the exact details of this trip."

As Jason answered the call to the head of Haven Security, Toni walked to a nearby bench. She sat down and tried to let the view of the picturesque river that ran through the town distract her. At times she forgot Jason had been hired to watch over her. The reminder made her heart heavy. With their time coming to an end, Toni was feeling the strain. *What if being with me is just a convenience for Jason? Now, not only is he getting paid for babysitting me, he's getting a willing sexual partner as well. It's a win-win situation for him.*

The sight of Jason walking toward her and the smile on his handsome face was enough to launch a thousand butterflies in her tummy and replace her dark thoughts.

"Sorry about that, luv. I know it must be hard for you—reminded all the time about how we met and why." Jason crouched down before her and placed his hands on either side of her face. "I'm happy I took this assignment. If I hadn't, I'd never have had the chance to get to know you, Toni Grimaldi." He touched his lips to hers briefly. "Let's go in and I'll make it up to you."

They hurried through the foyer, hand in hand, the sexual tension building as they waited for the lift to take them to their floor.

The moment they closed the hotel room door, Jason had his hands all over her. He tore the clothes from her body and Toni forgot all about the phone call. The only thing on her mind was Jason.

"I need you inside me, Jason—to feel your cock filling my pussy."

He groaned. "I need that too but I want to taste you first, hear my name on your lips as I make you come."

Toni lay on the bed. Spread her legs wide for him. Jason buried his face in her mound. He licked the length of her slit and Toni moaned in response to the pleasure. His tongue was pressed flat on her clit. Just the perfect amount of pressure. She thrashed her head from side to side. "Just there. That's perfect. Don't stop. Make me come, Jason."

Jason could smell the aroma of Toni's desire. He breathed the scent of her deep into his lungs, his longing for her overwhelming him. His cock was so hard with the promise of being buried deep in her wet cunt. He thrust two fingers into her pussy and finger-fucked her hard as he continued to tease her clit with his tongue. As her body arched, he changed the feathery-soft touch he'd been using to a prolonged pressure directly on her clit.

"Yes! I'm so close. More," Toni pleaded.

Jason had discovered what would push Toni over the edge so she would moan his name in ecstasy. He loved the little noises and sighs that spilled from her lips as she orgasmed — the way Toni's body shook as she was coming back down from her blissful high.

This time when he felt those telling little quakes, Jason climbed over her and buried his throbbing cock in her warm pussy, still pulsating from the strength of her orgasm.

"So tight. Your pussy is so tight... Feels so good wrapped around my cock."

Jason gave in to his need. He thrust into Toni. "Fuck, this isn't going to take long," he moaned into her ear. "Come with me, luv."

Her fingernails dug into his back. Her legs wrapped around his hips as Toni moved in sync with his frantic rhythm.

"I don't think I can," she whimpered.

He moved his hand between their joined bodies, found her clit and pressed down on the nub. Jason gave her what she needed to bring her to the brink with him.

He couldn't hold on any longer, the pressure from his clenched balls urging him on. Thrust after thrust, Jason spilled into Toni. Pleasure so powerful ripped through him he had to grit his teeth to stop from roaring. Jason feared the top of his head would be blown clear off. His brain overloaded by the surge of sensation seemed unable to deal with the intensity as every nerve ending came alive, sizzling with pure bliss.

Toni coming with him made it so much more potent. He had to fight the primal urge to beat his chest with his fists and claim her as his own.

But Toni wasn't his and never could be. He didn't belong in her world. Nathan had warned him not to get emotionally attached to her. Jason had originally laughed at the thought, foolishly believing he would be able to walk away from her at the end of their trip and put Toni Grimaldi out of his mind — that he could go back to his normal way of life, not caring what the future might bring, just living each day as it came. Toni had changed that for him. Jason had already started to mourn the future he had no right to imagine.

* * * *

They were back in London. This was their last full night together and Toni was determined to get Jason to open up. Tomorrow, late in the evening, they would board the plane for home and she might not see him again. As Toni dressed for what could be their final dinner, she tried to decide on the best way to approach the subject of where this thing they shared — whatever it might be — was headed.

It's time for us to talk, decide where this is all going — if it's going anywhere. I need to tell him how I feel, how much he means to me. Point out all the things we have in common. Convince him we could work… Yeah right, we love history and sex. What else in common do we have? I teach primary school, a nice safe and boring job, while he leads an exciting and dangerous life protecting people.

Toni had been going back and forth like this for hours, one minute feeling confident that maybe there was a future for them, then just as quickly talking herself out of it. It was doing her head in. If only Jason had given her the slightest hint of his true feelings. Yes, he had made love to her each night, passionately making her feel like she was the most important person in his world, but Toni was still not one hundred percent sure that it wasn't just her own wants and dreams projecting that sort of commitment.

That's why I need to make it clear to him. Spell it out. Take a chance for once. Otherwise I'll be living with regret, always wondering. So he makes it clear he's not interested in moving this forward when we return home...and his contract is over. At least I'll know where I stand. I will have tonight, I can make the most of this last time together. Content with the decisions she'd made, Toni applied a coat of ruby-red lipstick to her lips.

She was going all out tonight for Jason, trying to dress seductively — which was not an easy thing to achieve given that her one black dress now fitted quite snugly over her hips and stomach. A result she attributed to all the fish 'n' chips, Yorkshire pudding and pints of lager she had indulged in over the past few weeks.

I thought sex was a good way to lose weight. How come it's not working for me? Toni's cellphone began to ring as she was lamenting over the fact that life was not always fair, especially for the more cuddly-framed woman. She picked it up from the table and checked the screen to see who was calling.

Toni couldn't even remember having programmed Charles Baker's name into her phone. She wasn't a fan of the pompous, butt-kissing, permanent attachment to her father's side. *What the hell would he want?*

"Hello, this is Toni," she said as she connected to the call.

"Antoinette, I'm so glad I've caught you," Charles began immediately, ignoring the fact that Toni preferred not to use her given name. "I'm calling on behalf of your father, Antoinette. There has been an unfortunate incident at one of the family owned mines. It is causing the company a bit of bad publicity and your father believes that the Grimaldis need to show a united front to help deal with the issue. He wants you to return immediately. I've taken the liberty to book you on a flight leaving London Heathrow tonight and just this second emailed you the details. You need to get a car to take you to the airport in the next hour or so. Would you like me to organize that for you as well, Antoinette?"

What the…? Toni was still trying to understand what Charles was saying. "What sort of incident?" she finally asked.

"One of the mines had a cave-in or an explosion or something. We're not sure on all of the details. It's all quite a mess," Charles replied.

"Oh no, this is horrible. Is it very bad, Charles? Was anyone hurt? Is anyone trapped? Why haven't I heard about it over here?"

"It's been a dreadful incident. The papers are trying to put the blame on your father, saying that the mines were not following the workplace safety standards set in place by the unionist bureaucrats. Like Mr. Grimaldi would be aware of everything that goes on… He's a busy man."

"How many people are injured?" Toni shouted into the phone.

"The numbers aren't all in yet…"

"Charles, answer my damn question if you want any chance of me stepping foot on that plane…"

"Three dead, eleven injured and five still unaccounted for. Looks like the mine will be closed for months. There's already talk of a long drawn out investigation into all Cardona's operations and the possibility of the unions shutting down work on all Grimaldi interests."

Toni felt sick. "What exactly is being done to find the trapped miners, Charles?"

"How would I know those sorts of details? I can report an endless number of engineers, police, firemen and rescuers asking for all sorts of blueprints and paperwork. It's been quite time consuming, complying with their demands. You can see why I don't have time to argue with you about this, Antoinette. Be on that plane. Your father needs you."

Charles disconnected, much to Toni's frustration.

As Toni was checking the email with her new travel plans, the door to her hotel room burst open. The look on Jason's face as he stormed into her room foretold that he knew of the dramas going on back home.

"You need to get packed. We need to leave. I have to get you back home..." Jason began, his tone matching the 'take no prisoners' look in his stance and on his face. Toni wasn't sure what to be more surprised at, the fact that Jason had managed to unlock her door and enter her room or that he had already been notified her father demanded her return. *Then again, why wouldn't he know? He is, after all, in my father's employ.* The thought made her already sickened stomach roll again.

"So you've heard then?"

"Just got off the phone from Nate. He says the threats to your family are to be taken seriously and I am to get you back home. We need extra manpower to keep you both safe, Toni. Emotions are running high over the accident. It's times like this people take drastic measures…"

"Threats!" Toni gasped "Charles didn't say anything about threats…"

It was too much for her to take in all at once. People were hurt, dead and missing, and now her father's life was being threatened. Judging by the look on Jason's face, a threat he was taking very seriously. Toni began to shake. Her knees gave way and she had to grip the edge of the table just to support her own weight.

Jason was beside her in an instant, wrapping his arms around her body, helping Toni stay upright. The heat from his body dispelled the cold that had seeped through her as she tried to come to terms with all the horrible developments.

"Oh, honey," he whispered. "You didn't know about the threats? I'm so sorry for scaring you… You look so beautiful, by the way. That dress… If we didn't need to…"

She hadn't even thought about their last night together, the fact that it was now defunct. *I'm thinking about losing one night when so many families are dealing with so much pain and loss.* Her emotions now in check, Toni broke away from Jason's hold. She needed more details. "Tell me about the threat to my father, Jason. I need to know everything."

The way Jason was staring at her gave her the chills. Toni could sense that he was trying to decide what to say to her. His face was blank. Toni couldn't read any emotion from it or his eyes. It made Toni think back to one of their first conversations when Jason had joked about being trained to withstand interrogation.

"Please, Jason. I need the truth from you. I need to be able to trust that one person will tell me what's going on. This is all so horrible, so many people hurt.

There are still men trapped in the mine and I don't even know what's being done to rescue them. If my father is acting like a human being, for once, and putting the safety of the men and women who work for him before his own gain…"

Jason's tough, all action exterior thawed, his eyes softened as he gazed down on her. "Toni, honey, I won't lie to you, luv. This situation is bad. Nate's already heard rumors that the mine had safety issues and there's been some talk of bribes. Your family is going to be under the spotlight for months to come. If not worse… I'm with you all the way. I won't let anything happen to you. You have my promise. The death threat was not aimed at your father, luv. The danger is specifically toward you and your mother. But I've got you, Toni."

Jason had taken her hands in his own, as he'd spoken, moving his thumb over her skin in soothing motions as he'd explained the situation.

Her mind was running a million miles an hour. *Why would I be threatened? I've never had anything to do with the family business. Never have, never wanted to. How is Mum dealing with this?* "My mother…is she being protected? Where is the threat coming from? Who? Why us? We don't have anything to do with the running of the mine—or any of Dad's business dealings."

Toni knew she was rambling. It was just so unbelievable, unexpected. Her father was always going on about her safety, her security or lack thereof. Even the ridiculousness of Jason following her on this holiday, Toni had put down to her father being such a control freak. And what did Jason mean by rumors? Why was the mine not safe? Her family was rich. Her father made so much money every day it was ridiculous. Why hadn't he spent it on making sure people were safe? *He must not have known about the issues*? She quickly squashed and pushed that thought away, since she knew first-hand that her father made it his business to know everything about everything.

Toni had never liked being a Grimaldi, had never felt like she fitted the mold of an heiress. Now she thoroughly despised her heritage. Just the idea that her family might have had anything, even slightly, to do with this disaster or in not preventing it, made her sick to her stomach.

Jason was doing his best to keep his anxiety in check. He should have been all over this. His job was protection. It was what he was trained for. But the bottom line was, ever since the phone call with Nate, Jason had felt a heavy weight on his shoulders and—more unsettling—his heart. Just the notion that Toni could be under threat had his blood pressure soaring. Being able to wrap his arms around her as she bravely dealt with what was going on—probably better than he was—was the only thing keeping Jason from coming apart. He'd tried so very hard not to fall for her, to try to maintain some sort of emotional barrier between them. He had failed. That fact never more clear to Jason than when Nate had spoken of the letters sent to the Grimaldi home. The direct threats to Toni's well-being received on Grimaldi's private phone. His blood had turned to ice, imagining her hurt or worse. He could not let anything happen to her. Jason didn't think he could live with himself if even a hair on her precious head was harmed.

He'd already been struggling to come to terms with the inevitable—of living his life without Toni wrapped up in his arms, or having her in his bed again, before it had all gone to hell. But he'd understood that. That was his future—a future where Toni returned to her heiress lifestyle, and he returned to his one room apartment and back to his solitary life. That said, there was no way in hell Jason was going to let some nutcase get within a mile of her. Toni might not be his future but Jason was going to make damn sure she had a healthy one in her outlook—or die trying. "We need to get packed up and move. Just give me a few minutes to book another flight and we'll get going. Give me your passport, luv, I'll need it for the airline ticketing information."

"Charles booked my flight already," she said as she thrust her phone in Jason's face. "See? It's all in this email. Charles even had the hide to book me a first-class seat, despite all that's going on at home."

It sounded like the thought disgusted her, and while Jason couldn't fault the fact that Grimaldi's people got things done efficiently, it did leave him in an unacceptable predicament. How the hell was he going to pay the cost for a first-class seat? Yes, it could be recouped through expenses eventually, but he didn't have that sort of credit available to him up front. Jason didn't even know how much it would cost exactly but he figured over ten grand, easy—especially last minute. He'd already all but maxed out his credit card sharing the expenses with Toni over the last three weeks.

Toni must have picked up on his discomfort because she reached out her hand and stroked her fingers down his cheek. "What's wrong, Jason?" she asked, her voice full of concern. Jason could have punched himself in the face—a habit he was getting into around Toni. She was the one with all the drama ahead of her and yet here she was trying to comfort his arse. *Stop trying to be someone you're not, dickhead. Now is not the time to let your pride get in the way. Tell her you don't have the money to pay first class. She does. She's a fucking millionairess.*

It took all the strength he could muster to make the admission. Jason tried hard not to let the bitterness flow through in his voice with the embarrassment he felt having to ask the woman he had fucked every which way for the last few weeks to lend him money, but it had to be done. Her safety was more important than his male ego.

"I don't have the funds available to pay for a ticket like yours and there is no way I'm letting you get on that plane without me. Either you can buy me a seat close to yours or we wait until Nate can organize it from his end." Even though he felt like a fucking loser, Jason did not break eye contact with Toni as he made his humiliating confession.

"That's no problem. We can use my American Express card. It's empty. It's the one my father insists I carry 'for emergencies'," Toni replied as she raised her hands in the air and made quotation mark signs with her fingers. "I figure this rates as an emergency and after all, it is Grimaldi money and at the moment, you are working for a Grimaldi."

It was the first time Toni had not referred to Jason as working for her father, she had just said *'a Grimaldi'*. Was she now seeing him as her employee? He really didn't have time to dwell on the ramifications or meanings of her words. Toni had already pressed the numbers on her phone that would connect her to the airline. "I'll go get my passport," he muttered, trying as best he could to sound natural. While deep inside his soul, in places Jason hadn't known existed in him, he ached for the life he wished he could have shared with her.

Chapter Nine

Jason wished he could have enjoyed his first, and probably only, time traveling as a first-class passenger. The cabin was full of luxuries and the stewardesses more than attentive – in fact Jason had not missed the hints and flirtatious comments directed his way. What he hadn't taken into consideration, as he'd stood silently beside Toni as she'd paid for his ticket, was that their seats would be so far away from one another. He couldn't even see her at all now that she had reclined hers into the sleeping position.

Here he was cooped up in his own personal pod-like capsule, being afforded the best the airline had to give, and all Jason wanted was to be seated where he belonged, in the economy section of the plane – where the seats were so cramped that Toni would be snuggled in beside him, whether she wanted it that way or not. He couldn't even take advantage of the deluxe sleeping conditions. There was no way he was falling asleep and leaving Toni unprotected. Not that Jason could foresee anything happening to her in this secluded and secured section of the plane. There was no chance the cabin crew would be letting any of the riff-raff traveling in the back of the plane get anywhere near the privacy of first class.

"Is there anything I can do for you, sir…? Anything at all?" the stewardess once again enquired, her smile wide on her Botox-filled lips and her eyes twinkling with the unstated, but obvious, proposition of a sexual tryst with Jason.

Bet she wouldn't be so keen on me if she knew my bank balance. "No. I'm good. 'Thanks," Jason replied for the umpteenth time."

"Well, you let me know if you change your mind. We are here to meet your every need and make your travel more enjoyable for you any way we can," she offered before wandering away.

"Sheesh," Jason exclaimed loudly once the woman had moved out of earshot. She was laying it on thick with the suggestive comments and winks. He wondered if this was normal behavior or purposely aimed at him. He was so out of his league.

More disturbing was that a few weeks ago he would have happily joined the ranks of the mile-high club with the blonde, but now her forthright behavior was grating on his nerves. All he could think about was touching Toni. His hands itched to make contact with her. Fuck, his whole body did. *Should I go see if she's awake? Maybe we can just talk for a while? Take advantage of the bloody bar they have up here and have a drink together? Oh, man, you are really losing it.* Jason rubbed a hand over his face, trying to stop the relentless conversation going on in his head. It was not helping. *Relax, dude, watch a movie, get some shut-eye You'll need it for when we land. You'll need to be awake and alert if you plan to be of any use to her.* Jason wasn't even sure what plans Nate had put into place for Toni's security detail. *I'm probably persona non grata in Nate's eyes anyway. Wouldn't surprise me if my name's been purposely omitted from any future work that involves the Grimaldi family. Doesn't matter. I'm not trusting anyone else. Nate will just have to deal with it.*

Things had definitely become a little strained between Jason and his boss of late. Whether Nate had guessed that things had become intimate between him and Toni was not clear. Nate had never asked and Jason had never said. He'd just filed his report about what Toni was up to each day, where she was staying, without making any reference to their shared accommodations. When Jason finally did his expense account, there was probably going to be a heated discussion but he didn't care. What was the worst that could happen? Nate fire him? Unlikely. He would think twice before sending Jason on another bodyguard gig, though, Jason suspected, which was just fine by him. As long as it didn't interfere with him keeping Toni safe, Nate could do as he saw fit.

* * * *

"Jason, are you awake? Jason..."

Jason woke to the sound of his name being called, felt someone tapping on his shoulder. It took him a few seconds to come fully awake.

He'd been dreaming of Toni, of the night they'd spent together in Durham. Reliving the feel of her lips wrapped around his cock as she'd taken him into her mouth, sucking the length of him until the tip of his dick had touched the back of her throat. The sight of her on her knees in front of him, naked, his dick going in and out of her mouth had had him so fucking enthralled that he'd lost his mind. Up until that night, he'd been gentle with Toni, always committed to making it good for her, bringing her pleasure before he even contemplated reaching his own. But that night he'd lost control. He'd started bucking his hips against her face, pushing his cock farther and farther into the moist heaven that was her mouth. Holding her head in place with his hands as he'd fucked her mouth. It was the most intense moment of his life. Jason had never experienced pleasure like it. And it wasn't that Toni had used any special tricks—in fact it had been clear to Jason that she was not all that experienced giving head, the way she'd hesitated before she'd let her tongue explore the slit in his cock and the way she'd looked up at him. She'd actually asked him if she was doing it right. Fuck, if she'd done it any better, Jason might have died. As it was, he'd forgotten to warn her when he'd shot his load. It had gone down her throat, her eager lips and tongue licking every last drop of seed from his dick.

So at first he didn't register the sound of Toni calling his name. When it did become clear, Jason sat bolt upright.

"What's wrong...? Are you okay?" he asked as he pulled Toni down into his pod, so he could see past her, giving himself a clear line of vision to ascertain the possibility of any imminent threat. When Jason was satisfied all was as it should be, that there was no danger present in the empty aisle of the aircraft, his fight instinct subsided and another impulse took its place. His body began to react in response to Toni sitting in his lap.

"Umm, sorry to wake you, Jason, but I thought you'd want to know that Charles just called me. Who knew you could receive calls when you were flying?

The buzzing scared the crap out of me." Toni made a little noise that sounded like a stifled giggle.

Jason was surprised she hadn't known about the technology.

"Anyway, he said that Haven Security will have a car waiting at the airport ready to pick me up. I wasn't sure if you wanted me to mention you or not. Didn't know if you told them I knew about you, if that would get you into trouble, but they will be picking you up too, right?"

He was having a hard time concentrating on what Toni was saying, her shapely, soft arse cheeks sitting so snug in his lap a distraction. His engorged cock in particular delighted in the new seating arrangements. "Of course I am, luv. I told you I'm going to be by your side until we get this situation under control." *If I can get my body parts back under control so I can think clearly, it would help.* "As to your concern for me—I think Nate has picked up on our..." Jason was struggling to find the words to describe what he and Toni shared. *What will I call it? A relationship...? Is it? A close friendship, maybe?*

"I'm hoping the next word out of your mouth will be relationship, Jason. 'Cause that's how I see what we've just shared and I hope it will continue and even grow into something more when all this madness ends.

"I know this is probably not the right time for this sort of conversation, Jason. I've spent the last sixteen hours of the flight arguing with myself over whether I should, or should not have this conversation when so much is going wrong and so many are hurting, but I need to know. It's more unsettling than the knowledge someone out there wants to hurt me, not being sure whether I'm ever going to spend time with you again, kiss you again. Make love… It was always more than just sex to me, much more than that."

Toni's bluntness took Jason by surprise—they were words he'd wanted to say, had been thinking. She was braver than him.

He could see how much his answer meant to her, there were tears rolling down her cheeks and falling from her chin. "I'm sorry. I promised myself I wouldn't cry, no matter what your answer. I think I'm just tired. I just need to know if this is over between us now."

He needed to answer her, but he didn't know what to say. *If I tell her the truth—that there's nothing I want more than to see where this is headed—will that just cause more heartache later? She deserves so much more than I can offer her but am I selling her short? If she wants to give us a try, why shouldn't we? I'm not ready to let this go, let her go.*

"I want the same thing you do, luv. More than you'll ever know. But I think us having a relationship, or trying to, might end up being a little more complicated than we imagine. Even though it's what we think we want right now." It was a total cop-out and Jason knew it. *Why the hell can't I just say 'I love you, Toni' and be done with it?* Jason was stunned by his own admission, albeit a silent one. He waited for a feeling of panic to set in or that prickle he got between his shoulders when something was not right.

Nothing happened.

He felt calm. Well most of him did anyway—his dick was still rock-hard, enjoying the feel of Toni's butt cheeks against it. *I love her. Well, whaddya know? I've fallen for her and it's not freaking me out at all. Who knew I had it in me?*

They spent the remaining few hours of travel sharing Jason's pod. The stewardess that had been all over Jason, giving him the 'come on' for most of the flight, could not hide her disappointment when she was forced to wake them from their cozy slumber as the plane began its descent.

Chapter Ten

Jason was holding her hand as they made their way through immigration but as they headed to the carousel to retrieve the bags, he suddenly let go, taking a few steps away from her.

"Nate, how the hell did you get in here?" Jason growled.

Toni noticed the large bearded man standing in front of them and Jason's actions became very clear to her.

"I have my ways, Beck," the bearded man Toni recognized as Nathan Haven growled back, before turning his attention to her.

"Miss Grimaldi, nice to see you again. I hope the flight was bearable. I have a car waiting to take you to your father's office. He would like a word with you before we take you home. I just want you to know that we will make sure you are taken care of and that Haven Security and the police are working on catching the ones responsible for all this."

"Thank you, Nathan. My flight was fine. I think having Jason with me helped. It's all just so awful what's been going on, all those people injured. I've been so worried for the families involved." Toni could feel the tension in the air between the two men. She just hoped her words helped the situation and didn't make it worse for Jason. "Do you have any news on what's been happening at the mine site? Do you know if they've found everyone yet?"

"Let me fill you in once we're on the road, Miss Grimaldi."

"Toni. Please call me Toni, Nathan. I'm not too fond of my last name at the moment." Toni turned her focus toward Jason and held her hand out to him. "Let's get our bags then."

Please take my hand, Jason. C'mon, don't let them come between us so soon. I need you.

Just when Toni was about to give up, her hand dangling now for an awkwardly long amount of time, she felt the familiar warmth of Jason's touch. His hand wrapped around her own.

Thank you, God, universe, Mother Earth.

"C'mon, luv, let's go." His voice was gruff, maybe held a bit of embarrassment in its tone, Toni wasn't sure. She was just so grateful that for the moment at least, she still had Jason in her life—that he was prepared to show her affection in front of his boss, even if it was just by holding her hand.

"Nate, stop with the deadly glare, already. It's not going to work, you know. I'm not scared of you like some rookie might be. I'm not stepping away from this, just in case that thought might have crossed your mind. Toni is my responsibility. Mine. Got it?" Jason said, as he gently tugged on her hand. Turning their backs to Nathan, they headed toward the baggage claim area.

Toni's heart beat a little faster as she waited for Nathan Haven to respond to Jason's rather aggressive statement. She liked the sound of his 'mine' in reference to her.

"You and I are going to have a conversation very soon, Beck, but for now, I think we all just need to focus on the matters at hand."

Toni stood by a trolley, Nathan at her back while Jason collected their luggage—she let out a little sigh at the sight of Jason's bicep flexing as he easily swung the bags from the moving carousel like they weighed nothing, reminding Toni of the times he'd swept her up into his arms just as effortlessly, making her forget for a few moments that she was overweight. "So sexy, mmm."

"He's not the settling down type, Toni. Never seen him with the same woman twice."

The deep whispered voice came from behind her. Toni hadn't realized she'd voiced her thoughts until she'd heard Nathan's warning. She wasn't even sure it warranted her reply, but she couldn't help herself. She turned to face him, angered at not only his disloyalty to Jason but the fact that he believed he had a right to comment on their relationship. "Jason and I have spoken of his past and mine—not that this is any of your business, Mr Haven. I have no need of or interest in your input on how I choose to live my life."

Once again Toni was shocked by her behavior—shocked but pleased that she was finally finding her voice and standing up for herself and what she wanted. Being with Jason had certainly drawn her out of her mousy disposition, and Toni found she liked this new side to her personality, a lot.

"That is where you are very much mistaken, Miss Grimaldi. At the moment your life is my business and you will listen to what I have to say. Your safety depends on it."

Nathan's tone was so grave it caused a shiver to run along Toni's spine.

Wow, these guys really take their jobs seriously. I can't see how these threats can be all that dramatic to warrant this kind of attention. I bet that's all this is about, someone trying to get a bit of attention. Dad's probably concocted the story to get some sympathy from the press. Toni's last thought turned her stomach. *Oh God, he wouldn't have...*

"All set, luv. Let's roll— Toni, are you all right? You've gone pale."

So upset at her current line of thought, Toni threw herself in Jason's direction. She needed to have his arms around her, needed him to distract her, chase away the horrible images she'd formed of what her father might be capable of. Jason caught her, tucked her safely against his body but it didn't feel like the same kind of embrace as the times he'd held her over the past few weeks. This was more like Jason was shielding her from an imminent attack. "Whoa there, Toni, what is it? What's happened? What the fuck is going on, Haven?" he roared.

"I dunno, Jase. One minute she's giving me a mouthful, the next she's looking like she's seen a ghost or something," Nathan answered. "Let's just get out of here. Maybe it's jet lag or shock setting in. With everything that's been going on, you couldn't blame the poor kid for losing it."

Kid? Toni couldn't believe her ears. *What the hell? I'm twenty-six years old, for heaven's sake. Why does everyone always treat me like I'm some helpless teenager? 'Cause for the past twenty-six years, that's how you've let them.*

As Toni let Jason lead her out through customs, his body somehow blocking her view of the terminal and the goings-on around them, she made up her mind to change her life. It was time to stand up to the people that continually tried to control her—her father and mother top of that list. First she needed to find out what was being done to help the families that were suffering because of the mine collapse. Even if it meant calling in on each family personally, to check on their well-being or pass on her condolences, Toni was going to make it her priority.

Toni was still making notes in her head, a mental checklist of what needed to be done, as she sat in the car traveling toward the city and her father's office. It was comforting to have Jason sitting beside her, his hips and thighs so close to hers that they touched. Holding Jason's hand was giving Toni strength to feed her new outlook on life and to bring those ideas to fruition when she heard her name.

"Toni? Are you listening? I think it's important you have all the facts and I can also fill you in on the latest developments with the search and rescue teams."

His mention of the search and rescue teams garnered her full attention.

"So let me start from the beginning... The mine collapse two weeks ago—"

"Two weeks ago?" Toni parroted Nathan's last words in disbelief. "How did I not hear about this before now, if it happened two weeks ago? The first I heard was when Charles rang me last night, in London, however many hours ago that was..."

"That's a good question, Toni. Maybe you were too busy enjoying other things to worry about what was happening in the world."

Toni did not miss Nathan's verbal slap.

"Fuck off, Nate. I doubt the English newspapers were running it as their top story and Toni was on holiday. Catching up on the news isn't usually top billing on your itinerary when there is so much to see and do. Maybe someone should have taken the time to let her know," Jason snapped back in her defense.

"Anyway," Nathan continued, ignoring Jason's outburst, "there is still no clear evidence as to the cause of the explosion that caused the cave-in. Preliminary reports are suggesting a gas build-up in one of the tunnels could be to blame. The total number of injured is eleven men. Five are still in a serious condition with crush type injuries."

"How many are dead, Nathan?" Toni asked, tears already threatening to fall just from hearing the number of injured, dreading Nathan's answer but needing to know all the same.

"Six, counting the three poor souls still missing. Search and rescue teams don't hold out much hope of finding anyone else alive."

"Oh my God!" Toni sobbed.

"What about the threats? What's happening there, Nate?" Jason asked, as she battled to control her emotions, images of those poor men lying crushed and alone under a wall of rock filling her head.

"It's been a cluster fuck from the get go. I didn't get wind of anything until Mrs. Grimaldi's car was purposely run off the road…"

"Is Mum okay? What happened? When did this happen?"

"Your mother is fine, Toni. She was a bit shaken up and as much as I hate to say this, it has made my task of protecting you all a lot easier. She and your father are finally taking the threats seriously. And I can guarantee no one will get that close to her or you again. Fuck, it wouldn't have happened in the first place if I'd actually been informed of the notes and calls your father was receiving. It wasn't until after the accident that Grimaldi—I mean your father—brought me up to date. Since then, we've managed to intercept a suspicious parcel addressed to your little girlfriend, Jason. Nasty piece of work it was too. Had to hand it over to the local boys after I defused it. Stupid cops got all up in my face for touching the evidence. Had no clue the fuckin thing might have gone off at any second. Didn't have time to wait for the bomb squad to roll on in."

"Got anyone in the frame for it?" Jason asked.

Jason's grip on her hand tightened. It was almost painful. She wasn't about to make him let go any time soon, though, after hearing that a bomb had been sent to her.

"Well, my gut feeling is that this has nothing to do with what's going on at the mine. The wording of the threats, the earlier ones, don't even mention the cave-in. It's like the un-sub has just used that accident as a convenient excuse. Maybe head any investigation in that direction."

"Un-sub?" Toni cut in, not understanding what Nathan Haven had meant.

"Unknown subject," Jason answered.

Nathan continued speaking, completely ignoring Toni's question.

"This is personal. Someone wants Grimaldi to suffer. Unfortunately, I can't find any firm reason why or what Grimaldi might have done to warrant this kind of hatred, revenge. To build a fucking bomb and send it to his daughter? That's just fucked up." Nathan looked directly at Toni, his lips drawn together in a firm line.

The way he was staring at her—his eyes the color of a winter's night and just as cold—made Toni uncomfortable. It was like he was reading her mind and what he found there was not to his liking.

Then just as abruptly, Nathan looked away from her. "No one is talking, telling me the truth so I can find the bastard or bastards that are doing this."

"I will," Toni said. "If it helps keep us all safe. I just don't know much about the business...yet."

Chapter Eleven

Traffic was heavy as usual at this time of day in the city so Jason had time to make the most of the close contact he and Toni shared in the car. It was probably the last time for a while that they could be themselves. In a few minutes, Toni would be thrust back into the life of excess and luxury. Jason was worried that between the stress of what was happening in her life and the influence of her family, he would get shoved aside.

He was so proud of her, though, the way she was dealing with it all. Jason had nearly lost his mind when Nate had calmly informed them of the device he'd intercepted. The sudden urge he'd felt to punch Nathan in the face for telling Toni about it so callously, was hard to resist. The bastard was an insensitive arsehole. Didn't he even think how that sort of information might affect her? It wasn't a normal occurrence to be sent a bomb with your name on it. *Stupid fuckwit.*

Glad he knows what he's doing, though. Better to have Nate on my side than the other. Wouldn't mind running a check on her father, though. Got to be something in his past... Something he has done that's putting my woman in danger. Jason paused as he reflected on his choice of words. *My woman? Yeah, I like the sound of that.* Jason swiveled his head so he could catch a glimpse of Toni's face as she rested against his shoulder. There were dark circles under her eyes, her lips were turned down and there was a frown, owing to her lack of sleep or maybe just sadness.

Jason lowered his head until he could brush his lips over her temple. "It'll be okay, luv. I'm not gonna let anyone hurt you. Nate's the best man I know for this kinda thing. We're lucky to have him on board. It's going to be all right."

Jason didn't respond to Nathan's snort.

The car finally pulled to a stop outside the high-rise building that housed Grimaldi Holdings. He and Nate had already decided that the underground car park was not where they wanted to be, given that the unsub had experience with explosives. Better to make a quick dash from the curb, both men shielding Toni.

All hell broke loose, though, the second the entourage entered the Grimaldi building. Security was everywhere, unfortunately not all of it Haven men. Police were crawling all over. They were just about to enter the lift when Jason felt a hand on his shoulder.

"I need you to step away from the elevator door, sir, and identify yourself," someone demanded from behind him.

"Not a chance, bud. I'm taking Toni up to speak to her father and no one is about to stop me," Jason replied with enough of a threat in his voice to make it clear he was dead serious.

"I said stop... I'm a police officer and have given you a clear directive. If you don't comply immediately, I will arrest you."

Jason heard Nathan chuckle. If he wasn't so pissed off with this skinny kid—the one who couldn't keep from prancing from foot to foot, showing just how nervous he was about the confrontation—Jason might have laughed too. But the reality of the situation Jason did not find amusing in the least. *This cop wouldn't have a clue how to stop a real threat to Toni's safety.* Jason just growled in the kid's direction and directed Toni through the now opening lift door, checking first that the car was empty.

"He's with me, Constable. I'm Nathan Haven, head of Mr. Grimaldi's personal security." As the lift doors closed, Jason glimpsed Nate holding out his identification.

"I hate coming here," Toni's voice was a whisper beside him.

"We stay until you tell me it's time to go. Okay, luv?" Jason used his index finger under Toni's chin to tilt her head up, so he could look into her face. "I do what you want. Remember that. Your father doesn't have a say anymore. It's me and you." Jason brushed his lips quickly over Toni's, heard her little sigh as their mouths connected and felt a sense of relief. It was the same sexy sound he had come to enjoy over the past weeks.

"Most people, including myself, find it difficult to go against my father's wishes, Jason, so I will understand if you can't hold up to that promise. Just don't disappear without letting me know, okay?"

She still doesn't get it. There's no one on earth that could keep me from her side. Nate, Grimaldi... No one. I'm with her for as long as she wants. Toni not wanting Jason around would be the only reason he'd go and it was a reason he hoped he didn't have to face at all. He'd be happy to add the word forever when it came to Toni but Jason still feared that would never happen. Eventually Toni would see him for who he was—an uneducated ex-soldier with nothing to offer her and she would move on to some man more acquainted with her way of life.

The lift doors opened and Jason had his first glance at what it was like to be a Grimaldi, to live in that kind of world. The view from the floor-to-ceiling glass windows looked out over the city and harbor. It was spectacular. Turning his head to the side just a little so he could see more of the panoramic view, Jason let out a whistle.

"Okay, so the view is quite breathtaking. I'll admit it." Toni shrugged her shoulders. "Just not enough of a payoff for the rest of the visit. Just wait, you'll see what I mean, Jason."

"Miss Grimaldi, finally! Your father has been waiting for you all morning."

A squirrelly looking man hurried toward Toni, and Jason automatically took a step in front of her, blocking the squirrel's path. He felt Toni's hand on his back as she stepped up beside him.

"Please, Charles, give me a break. You and my father knew exactly what time my plane touched down and how long it would take me to get here from the airport. Go be useful. Organize some coffee for Jason and me. Oh and, Charles, we'll have it in Dad's office."

Jason watched on in amusement as Mr. Squirrel's eyes grew round and a big blue vein popped up on the squirrel's head. Jason thought the guy was going to blow a fuse. Toni had given him a bit of an earful.

Jason had never really heard her stick up for herself like that. She never queried waiter mistakes or got annoyed if people pushed in front of her in a queue. She was normally so calm—perhaps a little timid. But this Toni was staring Mr. Squirrel down. Jason couldn't help chuckle when the squirrel lowered his head and scurried away, muttering something inaudible.

"Way to go, luv. Don't take shit from anyone. I've got your back."

Toni turned to face him. "I wish you had me on my back."

Jason nearly swallowed his tongue. His dick, in complete agreement with Toni, started to twitch, show its interest.

"Antoinette... Antoinette. I thought I heard your voice. Thank God you have returned, my darling daughter, where I can see for myself that you are safe."

Frank Grimaldi in the flesh, as the average height but quite rounded figure rushed up to Toni and threw his arms around her.

"I'm so glad to see you, Antoinette. Thank you for coming here first from the airport and not home. I'm sure you are weary from the long flight but I needed to see you were safe with my own eyes," Grimaldi gushed, and Jason swore he saw a tear in the old guy's eye. This was not the greeting he had been expecting from Toni's father, considering the way she had spoken of the man.

Grimaldi finally stopped hugging Toni and turned his attention toward Jason.

Jason readied himself, sure that he was about to hear Grimaldi dismiss his services, now Toni was safely back in her father's arms.

"Jason Beck, I presume," Grimaldi said. "I've heard good reports about you from Mr. Haven. He says you are his best man. I'm hoping the last few weeks keeping my daughter safe have not tired you and that I can count on your continued services to keep my Antoinette out of harm's way?"

Jason was stunned! He nearly didn't see the hand Grimaldi held out to him. *The man wants to shake my hand – wonder if he'd feel the same way if he knew what other things I've done to his daughter.* Jason accepted Grimaldi's outstretched offering.

"Nice to meet you, sir," Jason said as they shook hands. *At least he's got a firm grip.* "You have my personal guarantee. Toni is my top priority. No one is hurting her on my watch."

This is not the way my dad behaves. What the hell is going on? Toni couldn't believe the way her father had hugged her. She couldn't actually remember the last time he'd even touched her, let alone nearly crushed her ribs with the force of his embrace.

And now he was shaking Jason's hands like they were friends. Frank Grimaldi hardly ever shook hands with anyone. Toni could remember a time, at some dinner party somewhere, when her father had left the Prime Minister hanging. Yet here he was pumping fists with her Jason. Of course her father was unaware of her relationship with the man he'd just begged to keep his daughter safe.

"Good to hear, Jason... That certainly is good to hear. Antoinette, come let your mother see you. She has been as worried as I."

Toni was beginning to think she'd been transported to some kind of twilight zone. Her mother was in the office? She never came here. "Mother is here?" she blurted out.

Still finding it hard to imagine, she took off in the direction of her father's inner sanctum to see for herself. She burst through the door and there indeed, Toni found her mother, Eva, sitting in one of the big leather chairs that were scattered about the room. Owner and CEO of Grimaldi Holdings, Frank Grimaldi's office was a huge area that took up more than half the entire floor. "Hello, Mother." Toni noticed it took her mother a considerable amount of effort to get to her feet as she rose slowly from the chair. "Mum, what's wrong? They told me you didn't get hurt in the accident."

"Of course they did, dear. I didn't want you to worry when you were so far away. It's nothing really, bruised ribs and spleen from the seatbelt more than anything," Toni's mother explained as she patted Toni on the arm. "I will be fine, even better now I know you are home safely."

This was getting really eerie—her parents were acting just like Toni had dreamed on many occasions they might. But this time it was no dream. *Jason must be thinking I'm a liar, whinging and moaning about how horrible my parents are to me. Seriously, have I gone mad or something? Am I dreaming this whole thing—Jason, the holiday, all this drama? Only one way to find out…* Toni pinched her own arm with her thumb and index finger. "Ouch!"

Jason pulled her hand away from her arm. "What are you doing, luv?" he asked, his voice full of concern.

"Just checking I'm awake. Nothing to worry about, Jason, just had a bit of a twilight zone moment."

"Why don't we all sit down," her father said. "I heard you ask Charles to bring you some coffee. He should be here soon. There are some things we need to discuss, unfortunately."

Toni, her mother and father sat. Jason remained standing beside the office doorway. Toni was just about to call him over, include him in the discussion that was about to take place, when her father beat her to it.

"Mr. Beck, please join us, have some coffee. You need to be part of this discussion as well."

Toni wasn't sure who was more shocked by the offer, her or Jason.

Now they were all seated, Toni's father began to fill her in on what was happening at Grimaldi Holdings and the Cardona Mine, and, more important to Toni, what was being planned to help care for the families involved in the disaster at the mine site.

Chapter Twelve

Up to this point in his life, Jason had thought he had a concept of how the other half lived. He'd been wrong. Now having experienced life in the first-class section of a plane, standing on the floor that housed Grimaldi's office in the building the man owned, and now seeing the mansion the family lived in—all in the space of one day—made his head spin. It was pure opulence. He could not even imagine the amount of money that would be needed to achieve such excess. It made the divide that he was sure existed between him and Toni even harder to ignore.

"So this is where you spend your nights," he muttered as he took in the size of her bedroom, a floor space that would encompass his own home twice.

"Yep. Pretty hideous, isn't it? I had nothing to do with the gaudy décor. That was all Mum," Toni replied. "I just never could be bothered arguing with her about it. It does have a nice big bed, though," she added with a smile that made Jason's insides quiver. "Wanna try it out?"

"Don't tease me, luv. Just the mention of you and bed has me thinking dirty, wicked thoughts. But this is your father's house—what if someone walks in? How do you think he will feel about me and you—?"

"Stop right there, Jason," Toni cut in, her hands pushed against his chest. "I don't care what my father thinks. It has been one hell of a day, and I need to feel your arms around me. I want the touch of your body next to mine, reminding me that some things in my life are the same as they were yesterday. Please don't push me away. I can see it in your face that you are uncomfortable with what my family has. I don't care about any of it. I never have. Don't you see that?"

Jason could not deny Toni or himself any longer. He swept her up in his arms. "I'm trying, baby. I really am. I think my fragile male ego is finding it all hard to deal with," he said, trying to make light of his concerns as he carried her to the bed. "One thing I do know is I want to touch you, have wanted to get you naked and sprawled out on a bed since the moment I saw you all dressed up for me back in London. It seems like a lifetime ago."

He'd hardly lowered Toni to her bed before she was up on her knees, her fingers moving frantically as she tried to undo his belt buckle. He covered her hands with his own. "Let's make a deal. I'll ditch my clothes if you take care of yours. Last one naked is at the other's mercy." The words were barely out of his mouth before Toni was scrambling to get out of her top.

Jason couldn't decide if he wanted to win this bet or not. Usually he took the dominant role in any sexual encounter—it was just in his nature to stay in control—but everything about Toni had Jason tied up on knots. She made him feel things he'd never experienced before, emotions so unexplainable they churned up his guts, made his heart feel like it was about to explode inside his chest. That was even before his dick entered into the equation.

Jason levered off his boots one by one then stripped out of his clothes, before leaving the discarded items in a heap on the floor. He crawled toward her on the bed. "You are so fucking hot, Toni. I lose my mind whenever I even think of you naked, but nothing compares to seeing you that way. I just gotta get me a taste of that sweet honey of yours. Spread those legs, sugar, and let me feast on that warm, sweet cunt." Jason hoped the crudeness of his words didn't offend Toni. *If we're going to try to build on this, there's no point hiding who I am or how hot seeing her naked gets me.*

As he buried his head between her thighs and swiped his tongue along her wet opening Jason realized he'd had no reason for concern. Toni was just as hot for him as he was for her. He could taste how his words had affected her. The rich, exotic tang of her arousal filled his mouth as he drank it in. Looking up over the curve of her stomach, he could see she was enjoying him tongue-fucking her cunt by the pleasure that shone in her heavy-lidded eyes.

"I'm so close... Pl...ea...se," she cried out, her voice a breathless stammer.

Jason plunged two fingers into her pussy, curling them so he could tease behind her clit as he pressed his tongue flat onto the sensitive nub. He built her up over and over again before stopping at the last moment, not giving her the chance to fall. His mouth was dripping with her arousal as he continued the sensual assault on her body. His cock and balls ached with the need to be inside her but Jason was determined to keep Toni on the edge for as long as he could so that when she did explode, it would be the best orgasm of her life — one he hoped would ruin her for any other man, his efforts and his love for her never to be outdone.

He was trying to send her insane. Toni didn't know whether to cry or demand that Jason give her the relief she craved, but it felt so good. Each time he built her up, teased her with the promise of an orgasm before denying her at the final hurdle, Toni thought she would scream, convinced that the torment would be too much for her to bear. Until his wicked tongue and magical fingers would again begin to move and she would be teetering up on the edge of that sweet abyss once more.

"No more, Jason, please. I can't take any more."

Jason must have heard the desperation in her voice. This time as Toni began her ascent he did not stop. Waves of pleasure rocketed through her pussy, her nipples contracted, tiny stars formed before her eyes. The sensations went on for so long Toni thought she would never recover. It was delicious.

"Worth the wait, I hope, luv?"

Toni heard the teasing note in Jason's question. She didn't care that she'd had to beg him, more than once for the orgasm that had just rocked her world. It had been worth it.

"Mmmm," she mewled. "I guess so."

"Just admit it, honey. That's the best orgasm you've ever had."

He sounded cocky, but Toni couldn't fault him. It was the best orgasm of her life. And considering that Jason had also delivered Toni her second, third and fourth best orgasms he did have a lot to crow about.

"I admit it... You are a sex God and I'm the luckiest woman around," she replied, trying to keep a straight face. Toni couldn't, however, stop the giggle that escaped her lips when Jason nodded in agreement.

"How's that ego doing?" she finally asked when her fit of the giggles ceased.

"Ego is just fine, but my cock...now that's another story. Up on your hands and knees, woman. This is going to be hard and fast."

Jason lifted her into position. It was like she weighed no more than a feather the way he manhandled her and Toni loved it. The sensation as he entered her from behind, primitive, dominant—she was under his control. Jason crouched over her as he drove his cock into her. It was all she could do to keep her hips in the air. Toni dropped her head down to the bed and enjoyed the carnal ride. Jason strummed her clit with just the right amount of pressure to bring her to the edge again. "You're coming with me, luv," he whispered in her ear, his voice strained, breathless.

She didn't think it was possible, not after the force and potency of her last orgasm, but before she knew it Toni's body was soaring again.

"C'mere, luv," Jason said, as he positioned Toni snuggly into the curve of his side, his arm around her waist and his hand splayed out over her tummy. "We need to get some shut-eye."

That's how they remained until the next morning.

Chapter Thirteen

He was fucking Toni on a beach, the white sand warm against his back as he plunged his cock in and out of her pussy. Toni was sitting on top of him, her bountiful tits bobbing up and down in sync with the rhythm of their thrusts. The bleating noise in the background was annoying him, though, distracting Jason from the pleasure he was experiencing. Getting louder.

"Answer your phone, Jason," a voice said from beside him as he felt an elbow poke his ribs.

The dream faded away, much to his disappointment, as Jason realized Toni was the owner of the voice, and she was lying beside him, her leg flung over his own. More disconcerting, though, was that Jason realized he was still in Toni's bed.

Having found his pants and recovered his phone from the pocket, Jason answered the call. The irritating bleating noise ceased. Toni made a sighing noise and snuggled into her pillow—it was a beautiful sight and one Jason thought he could get used to seeing each morning for as long as he lived.

"Beck," he finally managed to squawk.

"Well, hello there, sleepyhead, I hope I haven't interrupted your beauty sleep." The sound of Nathan Haven's voice attracted Jason's full attention immediately. *Shit.* He'd forgotten all about reporting in last night. *What the hell time is it now anyway?* He looked around Toni's room for a clock or some way of determining how long he and Toni had been sleeping. Jason could see through the gap in the curtain that it was daylight outside.

"Nathan," he replied trying to sound normal.

"I guess you've caught up on sleep now. Not feeling any effects of jet lag, buddy?" Nathan enquired, his voice sounding way too friendly for Jason's liking. Nathan Haven was usually blunt and to the point when he called. Even though he and Jason had a history and were close friends, their telephone conversations were rarely chatty. Neither man worried about the usual pleasantries when dealing with the other, so Jason knew something was up.

"I got some sleep," he replied non-committally.

"Yes, so I heard. Frank Grimaldi's exact words were and I quote, 'My daughter and your best man must be very worn out—neither stirred when I went to call them for dinner. In fact they seemed very comfortable in each other's arms and I haven't seen so much of my daughter since the day she was born.'" Nathan paused, obviously giving Jason time to absorb the full meaning of his words. "I actually wrote it down exactly as he told me, so I didn't forget anything he said. What the fuck are you doing, Jason? Not only are you banging the man's daughter under his own roof but it's not like you to miss the sound of someone sneaking into a room. What if it had been the fucking un-sub?"

Nathan had been roaring so loud by the time he'd finished his rant that Jason had moved the phone away from his ear but he hadn't missed a word.

What the hell was he going to do now? How would he face Frank Grimaldi? Jason was still old-fashioned enough in his beliefs that he understood it was disrespectful to fuck a man's daughter under his own roof — unless you intended to put a ring on the finger of the man's daughter. *I could offer to do that — tell Grimaldi I want to marry Toni. Yeah, he's gonna love that option. That's if I even get the chance before he gets me thrown off his property. Maybe if Toni and I speak to him together, explain how we feel about each other?* That line of thought was quickly quashed when Jason realized Toni had never even told him she loved him. It wasn't like she was going to agree to marry him just so he didn't feel guilty about her father knowing they'd slept together.

"You still there, Beck?"

Once again the sound of Nathan Haven's voice recaptured the attention of Jason's wandering mind.

"Yeah, I'm still here," Jason replied a little more sheepishly.

"Well, why don't you and the little missus get your butts out of bed and join us *all* in the breakfast room. Can't believe this place has a room set up just for breakfast. Oh and, Jason, don't forget to put some clothes on first."

Jason did not miss Nathan's emphasis on the word 'all'. It looked like he was about to face the firing squad. "Right. We'll be down in five," he told his boss before adding, "I'm not surprised, Nate, the house is big enough to eat a meal in a different room every day for a week, maybe more."

After Jason had disconnected the call, he woke Toni.

"Honey, time to wake up, luv. We need to get down to the breakfast room. Everyone is waiting for us."

Toni opened her eyes slowly. Jason could see she was digesting what he had just said and by the way she hurled herself up from the bed, he guessed that she understood.

"Who is waiting for us, Jason? And who was that on the phone?"

Jason didn't hesitate to answer Toni's quick-fired inquisition. Usually he bristled up when a woman got demanding or too inquisitive. Toni was different.

"Nathan called to let me know our presence was required and also to point out that I'm losing my touch. Apparently I missed your father's visit to your room last night. Not much of a bodyguard if I don't hear someone enter the room — or leave it again."

It was really worrying Jason that he'd not heard Frank enter. He usually slept so lightly that the slightest noise stirred him, but last night he'd been dead to the world. Nathan was right — if it had been the maniac who'd sent Toni the explosive parcel he might have done her some real harm before Jason had had the chance to stop him. The knowledge did not sit well with him. *Maybe I need to step aside, let someone else take over. I couldn't bear the thought of Toni getting hurt, let alone on my watch.*

The sound of Toni laughing interrupted Jason's thoughts — he hadn't been expecting that reaction from her. Maybe she didn't understand what he had said, that her father had caught them in bed together?

Toni could not stop laughing — the look on Jason's face was priceless. Her big, strong protector — the man who had made love to her for hours last night, his touch inciting responses in her that no man would

115

ever be able to reproduce — was terrified to face her dad. He really didn't get it. She did not care what her father thought. Her parents could go jump if they had any negative opinion about her choices. This was the new and improved Toni. She wasn't going to let her parents get in the way of what she wanted anymore. And Toni wanted Jason. Her biggest fear was not her mother or father. It was learning Jason's true feelings for her.

"Don't look so worried, Jason." Toni thought it was time to put Jason out of his misery, and time to let him know how deeply she wanted them to be together. There was also the important fact that she had fallen in love with him to disclose. *Better to know now before I start a fight with my folks over him. I need to know for sure that there is something worth fighting for here.*

"I don't care what my family think about us, good or bad. I love you, Jason. Everything else is irrelevant — the money, this house, the company. I don't need any of it to be happy. I have my job teaching and I hope I have you as well. That is all I need." There, she'd said it. She'd stood up for what she wanted and strangely, Toni didn't feel nervous. She felt calm and strong as she waited for Jason to reply. The fact that she'd been stark naked as she'd made her declaration had not even registered.

Jason was staring back at her. Toni could tell by the way he was fidgeting about that her words had made him uncomfortable — her Jason was not the fidgety type.

"Toni, I don't know what to say to you... How can you love me? You hardly know me."

That was where Jason was wrong, Toni did know enough about him, knew what kind of man he was. "I don't know all there is to know about you, Jason, but

I'm guessing it takes a lifetime together before you can say you really know someone. But I know a lot. I know you are thirty years old, you served for ten years in the Army, did three stints in Afghanistan where you saw and did things that give you nightmares. I know your usual *modus operandi* is to leave a woman's bed after sex because you didn't believe in love, as a result of spending your childhood listening to your parents quarrel and rip each other apart. How am I doing so far?" Toni asked before continuing, not really needing to hear Jason's reply just yet.

"You never wanted a woman to get past the emotional wall you put up, that is, until you met me – we've spent the last three weeks curled up in each other's arms and you haven't broken a sweat about it. There's been sweat, but for very different reasons altogether. I also know you are the type of man that could not let a woman suffer the trauma of getting shit on by a goose without coming to her rescue. You open doors for me, you talk to me, we laugh together, love exploring historic sites together and we have explosive, phenomenally satisfying sex – and you snore." Toni paused to take a breath, gather up her resolve. She only hoped that she'd finally broken through that wall she'd just mentioned and that what she was about to say wouldn't come back and kick her in the teeth – or heart.

"But if I'm wrong and I've just imagined all that about you, wrong in thinking that you do have strong feelings for me no matter how scared that makes you, then tell me now, Jason. I can take it. I sure as hell don't want to make a fool out of myself any longer, in front of you or my parents."

"You remembered everything I ever told you?"

Toni couldn't help it. She rolled her eyes. *After everything I just said, that is the best he can come up with?* She nodded as indication of a yes to Jason's question.

"I think I'm in love with you too."

He'd said it so quietly Toni wasn't sure she'd heard right, thinking maybe her imagination was playing games with her. She needed to know for sure. "What did you just say?"

"I said I'm in love with you too, Toni. And you're right. I've never felt this way before. No woman has ever made me feel this crazy—this out of control. I hate being away from you for even a minute. Just looking at you turns me on. I've been walking around with a semi ever since I first laid eyes on you. More than that, I've never felt so comfortable talking about myself with anyone. You know more about me than Nate and I've known him for over ten years. I've fantasized about being with you when we're both old and gray but I can't give you any of this..." Jason lifted his arm and waved it about, obviously indicating through his action that he was talking about her room, her life.

"I hear you when you say you don't need any of it, but what if you change your mind? What if your father disowns you? Are you really ready to live your life struggling to make ends meet on a teacher's wage and my meager salary?" Jason added.

"You need to listen more carefully, Mr. Security Man. I've already told you this more than once. But I will repeat it again, this time *real* slow so you can keep up. I. Don't. Care. About. Any. of this. I. Love. You." Toni mimicked Jason's action by waving her arms around just as he had done. "And for the record, my teacher's salary isn't all that bad."

He smiled. Toni smiled back.

"You really are hot when you get all testy, luv. Come give me a hug. I love you, baby."

She didn't hesitate—happily wrapping her arms around Jason's waist, Toni buried her head into his chest. It was becoming her favorite way of standing. Her heart felt like it would burst. It was beating so hard and fast she feared her chest would rip clear open. It was better than any dream. This gorgeous, sexy hunk of a man—one she could never have imagined showing any kind of interest in her—had just declared he loved her. Nothing could spoil this moment for her.

* * * *

Hand in hand they walked into the breakfast room. Toni had laughed about the way her mother called it that, saying it was just her mother's way of showing off in front of company and that they also ate other meals there.

Nate was the first to notice them. "Well, glad to see you finally deigned to join us, Beck. Hope we didn't pull you away from anything important."

Yep, Nathan was really pissed off—he always used 'Beck' when he had the shits with him.

Ignoring his sarcasm, Jason responded, "Sorry we took so long. Toni and I had a few things to discuss first. I think the traveling finally caught up with us last night. We crashed and burned, but we are both feeling wide awake now."

"Why are you waiting for us anyway?" Toni chimed in. Her hand still firmly grasped in his. She began to pull Jason toward the table, and he could see the look of amusement on Frank Grimaldi's face as they neared their destination. Toni's mother was not looking quite as happy. He pulled out a chair for Toni to sit on and took his own place in the seat next to her.

"Well, while you two were...sleeping..." Nathan began to speak again, and Jason was sure that no one in the room missed the way he'd hesitated over the word 'sleeping'. "You will be relieved to hear that the police have arrested a suspect they believe to be responsible for all the threats. Seems this guy took exception to a recent hostile takeover of his family company by the Grimaldi group. From what I've been told, he reached out to a few lowlifes on the best way to build a bomb. Seems the idiot also told anyone who cared to listen how he was paying Frank Grimaldi back for stealing his birthright. Luckily for the cops, one of the guys he spoke to was a police informant."

"It was hardly a hostile takeover," Frank Grimaldi added in quickly. "The company in question was so far in the red that I did the family a favor taking it off their hands. I took over all the debt as well."

"Well, it seems the son didn't see it that way and decided to do something about it. He even used his own car to try to run Mrs. Grimaldi off the road. Said car is already at the police impound. Forensics is having a ball writing up all the evidence." Nathan gave a little chuckle before continuing. "The good news is I don't have to figure out how much sedation I'd be needing to bring you down, Jason, after I told you I'd decided to take you off this detail. Guess I don't need to point it out now that you screwed up, mate. I've never known you to sleep through a door being opened, let alone someone walking into a room while you slept. I think you've lost your edge."

Jason didn't know how to reply. Nathan was right— no one had ever managed to get past him like that before. Probably also spot on in his decision to take

Jason out of the game but it would have taken enough sedative to fell an elephant before he'd have ever let it happen.

"So that means this is all over then?" Toni asked him.

"The security detail, honey. That's all. I'm not going anywhere." The words had slipped from his mouth so instinctively, so easily, that Jason had forgotten Toni's parents were sitting right there next to them. Well, within hearing distance, anyway. It wasn't until Frank Grimaldi made a throat clearing type noise that Jason even thought of what they might think about the situation.

"Guess I'm not needed here anymore," Nathan chimed in. "Good luck, buddy. Check in when you can... Or if you need some protection." He was laughing as he left the room.

Jason made a mental note to kick Nathan's arse first chance he got.

"Antoinette, I must apologize for entering your room last night. I did knock. I was worried when I didn't hear a reply from either of you. Jason— I can call you Jason, can't I?"

Jason nodded his consent, surprised that Toni's father wasn't kicking his butt by now as the man continued, "I was a bit shocked at first. I haven't seen that much of my little girl since the day of her birth."

Then much to Jason's disbelief, Frank Grimaldi started to laugh. It was a deep bellow of a sound and yet it made Jason's cheeks heat with embarrassment. He was thirty years old and what Frank was *not* mentioning was making Jason blush like a schoolgirl. If the roles had been reversed and Jason had walked in on his own daughter naked and lying in the arms of a man he hardly knew, Jason would have torn his head from his shoulders. The image of a young girl, with Toni's beautiful curls but with eyes that reminded Jason of his own, filled his mind. He looked over at his gorgeous woman. *She'd make such a great mother.*

"Oh my God, Dad, did you really have to tell me that...? I feel a bit sick." Toni started to laugh as well.

Jason just looked on in amazement.

"Well, I have to admit, I'm a bit jealous I missed out on all the fun," Eva Grimaldi added. Her voice was prim and reserved, not sounding the least bit like she ever had fun, as far as Jason was concerned. "Wouldn't have objected to catching a glimpse of Jason naked. I have wondered what all those muscles might look like."

"Mother!" Toni squealed

Frank Grimaldi guffawed even louder.

Jason squirmed.

Chapter Fourteen

"I can't believe I found a few pieces of furniture that you liked. But I do have to say on my own behalf, they are quite exquisite." Toni's mother was beaming with happiness as she sat across the table from Toni in the upmarket restaurant. "Thank you for meeting me for lunch and accepting mine and your father's house-warming gift."

"Mum, I'm not sure a few pieces is really how I would describe furnishing nearly our whole apartment, but I thank you for your generosity. I just hope Jason agrees because I really love them. That bedroom suite is perfect for us and the leather of the lounge feels so luxurious. But they are a bit extravagant."

"Hush now. You're my only child. Nothing is too extravagant when it comes to you. Why, I spent nearly as much on Judith Renway's fiftieth birthday present and I can hardly tolerate the woman."

Toni giggled. "That's a terrible thing to say, Mum. Mrs. Renway can't help her pompous ways."

"So, Toni, how are things with you and that sexy man? It fills my heart to see you happy. It's all your father and I ever wanted for you—to enjoy life and find someone to love."

Every part of Toni's life was just so perfect. She and Jason had moved in together. They had rented a new apartment in both their names. The rent was a bit steep but they were determined to get by on the wages they brought in. She'd taken an extra leave of absence from her teaching position so she could help set up the Grimaldi Foundation, a charitable organization that helped families cope both mentally and financially with workplace accidents. Toni was finding her new role so fulfilling—she loved being able to help, using the family resources and notoriety to convince others to pitch in as well. It was as if she was seeing her parents for the first time. Toni had insisted that her father pay her the appropriate wage for the work she was doing, promising they would re-evaluate the situation when the Foundation was fully operational.

"I get that now, Mum. I don't know why it took me so long to realize it. I thought I was a disappointment to you and Dad—that I couldn't be what I believed you wanted me to be, and I blamed you both for having too high an expectation of me. When really, it was my own insecurities feeding those beliefs. It's all seems so silly now."

"You were never a disappointment, Antoinette. We love you but were concerned about you. I admit that. You were always fighting with us, rebelling against any of our suggestions. But then again, my mother would probably have said the same thing about me. God rest her soul."

It turned out that Toni's mother and father were quite fun people to be around. The family business had kept her father busy but Toni had never bothered to notice the strain it put on him. Yes, the couple acted more formal when they were in public but that was more because the press were always looking to share some juicy gossip about them. Once her parents had explained that to her, Toni had understood their public persona so much more. She and her mother had even started putting pressure on her father to wind back his interests — to start enjoying the benefits made from all his long hours and stress.

"I love you too, Mum. Let's hope Jason still loves me when he sees all the gifts."

"Of course he will. I can tell by the way he looks at you — those dark, brooding eyes of his, the way they are always so focused on you, as if you're the only person in the room. That hint of a smile he wears when you are around, it says it all. He is madly in love with you. Ah youth..." Her mother let out a wistful sigh that made Toni laugh again.

"Who knew you were such a romantic, Mum?"

"Did Jason mention your father offered him a job? One he refused. I told Frank he didn't have a hope of getting Jason into the firm... Just yet, anyway."

"Yes, he did. Actually Jason admitted he thought about the offer for a moment or two. Luckily his rational side took back over. I would have been devastated if he'd taken it. Jason loves what he does. It would've been about the money, the reason he'd even contemplate the idea for more than a second. It worries him that he can't support me in the same way you and Dad have. Like I'd even care, Mum. Seriously, I've spent most of my life rebelling, as you put it, against our money. I just want to be with Jason. Materialistic things just aren't important."

Jason was still working for Haven Security but he had taken on more of the training and contractual side of the business. Toni had never really asked too many questions about what Jason was doing now but she did get the impression there was more to Haven Security than she had originally believed. There were certainly a lot more tough, hard and fit looking men employed there than were needed to fit alarms and keep rich young women safe. She was relieved that Jason didn't have to spend many nights away from their bed but did sometimes wonder if he missed being out on a job — doing the kind of stuff he used to do, whatever that might have been — before she'd come along.

Many times as they'd lain in bed recovering from their latest sexual tryst, a tangle of sweaty, languid body parts, Toni had questioned Jason on her fears but he always smiled and told her that he didn't want to be out somewhere in the dark anymore, when he could be with her instead.

"It's a man thing, honey. You just have to find ways of convincing him he makes you happy. And with a body like that, I'm sure that won't be a hardship for you."

"Mother!" Toni exclaimed. "You really need to stop looking at my boyfriend in that way. It's a bit creepy. I'll tell Mrs. Renway what you said."

"My goodness, girl, resorting to blackmail. Good for you." Toni's mother laughed and patted her on the hand. "Finish up your coffee, dear, so I can settle up the bill. I need to get home and cook your father some dinner. He promised to come home from the office early tonight."

Toni wanted to get away early too. Each night she raced home from her office at Grimaldi Tower and cooked dinner for Jason. Sometimes they even ate it before the urge to tear at each other's clothes and bodies got too hard to resist. They had christened each square inch of their new home — in some places more than once. She looked forward to christening all their new furniture as well. Jason had an insatiable sexual appetite and Toni enjoyed every aspect of his hunger, particularly when Jason was feeling all alpha male and dominant. Jason taking control of her sexual needs was always very rewarding.

"That must have been some thought. Your cheeks have just turned a lovely shade of crimson, but it's not really working with your pink blouse, darling. Bit of a clash of color."

"Jealous, Mother?" Toni replied and winked. But she could feel the heat in her face.

"Absolutely, my dear daughter. Absolutely." Her mother grinned at her.

"We have had a few bumps lately, though, Mum. Jason really doesn't want me to go to the Cardona Mine site."

It was the only thing they had disagreed on. Toni needed to see for herself that the families were managing. She understood that the wives and children left behind would never recover from losing their husband, father, or son completely. She just wanted them to know that she was there if they needed anything — that Grimaldi Foundation was there for them.

"Your father was not all that happy with the idea either. I could never see any problem with it, myself," her mother said before taking a sip of water. "Frank has wanted you to get involved with the business for so long. I told him to stop being such a fool now that you'd shown some interest. That you were a big girl and could make your own choices."

"So was that before or after he and Jason colluded to protect me?"

She and Jason had finally come to an agreement—one Toni's dad approved of whole-heartedly. Jason would accompany her around the site, keep her out of harm's way. Toni found it amusing that her boyfriend and father were under the impression she might fall into a hole if they didn't watch her every step. But it was still sweet that they cared about her. Toni was beginning to understand her parents' side of things. She'd been dreaming of babies lately, gorgeous little bundles that resembled smaller versions of Jason.

Toni knew that if she was ever lucky enough to share a child with Jason, she would protect it with her life. She often giggled about how crazy it would make Jason. He was such a control freak, always expecting the worst but with a foolproof plan to avert any such event if it happened. Toni loved him so much.

"That's what you have to deal with when you fall in love with a dominant male," Toni's mother replied sagely.

* * * *

"Did you organize with the bank to forward our rent?"

"Yes."

"Is your father sending a car here or are we meeting it at the office?"

"That's a good one, like you and Dad haven't gone over this a thousand times. What's up? Jason, we've been over this, heaps of times. I know you know the car is coming here. Like I know for some reason one of your guys is driving us. I think just this once you might be going a bit overboard. No one is out to get me. Everyone is looking forward to meeting me, glad the Grimaldi family care about them." She wrapped her arms around his waist, her gaze fixed on his face.

"I don't know what it is, luv. I just get this feeling between my shoulder blades when something feels off." He was being a jerk, Jason knew it, but he just couldn't shake the feeling that something was about to happen. His hunches had never let him down before and that scared the shit out of him. He couldn't work out what the threat was or where it was coming from. He'd been over Toni's itinerary with a fine toothcomb, even seeking out help from Nate, hoping a fresh set of eyes might turn up something he'd missed. There was nothing either of them could find that should cause any concern.

"We will be fine, Jason. In a week we will be back here fucking like rabbits and you will have forgotten what it was you were so worried about." Usually when Toni talked dirty to him, it really turned him on. This time Jason was far too distracted.

He loved her. There was no denying it. There had been times when his need for Toni had overpowered him and he had taken her forcefully, without gentle caress or tender words, pounding his cock into her pussy until they'd both exploded. Jason had been amazed that Toni had enjoyed these times just as much as he did, when he'd worshiped her body for hours. They were perfect for each other in every way. He'd even started questioning his own sixth sense, or whatever that sensation was that he got when he sensed danger. Maybe he was confusing his own possessive streak for Toni with the one that made him feel she was under some sort of threat.

He was not proud that he wanted to keep Toni safely tucked away, out of the reach of all the scum that roamed the earth, but he was trying to deal with it—push those impulses away. Up until now he'd managed to do that. But it was time to man up and let his woman do what she thought was right.

"Let's just get this over and done with." Jason removed Toni's hands from around his waist and picked up his phone.

Jason's phone beeped, indicating that Chris had arrived. It was time to get a grip on his concerns and take Toni to do what she so desperately wanted to do—make people feel better, care for others. Show the world that being a Grimaldi was more than just making money.

"C'mon, luv, time to get this show on the road. Chris is downstairs."

Jason helped Toni into the car. "You remember Chris, Toni? You met at my office."

"Hey, Chris, glad to see you again. I'm sorry you have to play nursemaid to me for a week. I hope it's not too boring." Toni's reply held a fair hint of sarcasm, and Jason couldn't blame her, considering his behavior.

"Hi, Toni. Not a problem, honey. Let's make a deal—you promise to stay out of trouble and I will just pretend we are all on a nice little holiday in the countryside, okay? We better get on the road, though. It's a five hour drive."

"My father did offer the use of the company jet but I thought the drive would be nice—that Jason and I could spend the time chatting. I'm starting to think that might have been the wrong decision."

He deserved it again. He'd been such a bastard it was no wonder Toni wasn't looking forward to being in his company.

"I get to pick the music, though, luv. I don't think Chris would appreciate listening to your choices. There are only so many sad love songs a bloke can handle."

"It's better than that old head banging music you listen to."

* * * *

They'd been traveling for a few hours. Jason was relieved that Toni seemed to have forgiven him as they chatted and reminisced about their holiday. He was starting to relax a little.

"Chris, would you mind pulling over at the next rest stop? I need to go to the toilet."

Jason hadn't planned for that. Stopping. He'd not considered all of Toni's needs. He'd been so busy worrying.

"Is that a problem, Jason? Is there a high probability that I might be snatched from the ladies' toilet while you're not looking?"

"Pull over the first chance you get, Chris."

"Righto, J-man."

The toilet break was not the only time Toni asked for the car to be pulled over, though. Toni wanted to see the countryside up close—see what impact her family's mining interests had had on the area. Wanted to walk the land her family leased. Jason had not been happy about her unscheduled stops but he kept his concerns to himself. He was pleased that Chris remained alert and watchful, making sure the area was clear. Jason had known Chris for years. They had been in some tight spots together, and knowing Chris was taking his uneasiness seriously made Jason feel better and worse at the same time. Chris didn't question Jason's ability to sense danger, having witnessed the benefits of Jason's insight first-hand over in Afghanistan when Jason had somehow just known there was an IED ahead. One their truck would have rolled right over the top of.

Finally they made it to their destination.

* * * *

"Seriously, guys, you're starting to make me jumpy," Toni complained as Jason and Chris scouted the area before they finally let her into the accommodation she'd booked for their stay during her visit.

Every time she had asked Chris to stop the car, the men had gone into full macho mode. *Anyone would think I was about to go skipping through the desert scattered with land mines in some Middle Eastern country, the way they carry on.* It was starting to get to her. Jason was more overbearing and controlling than ever and without the promise of an orgasm at the end of it.

"Stop acting like I'm about to get murdered or something. No one is out to get me. We're in the middle of nowhere and the only people around here are employees of Grimaldi Holdings or people who benefit from them. Can't we just relax and try to enjoy these few days away from the hustle and bustle of the city?"

Jason and Chris just glared at her.

"Fine. Suit yourselves, but I'm not going to let you get in the way of what I'm here for. If you don't stop with the frowns and the 'I'm a big bad arse, don't come near me' vibes, I'm going to leave you here in the motel room."

"The hell you are," Jason bellowed at her.

"Well, smile, Jason, and pretend you're happy to be here." Toni skipped toward her brooding man and touched her lips to his. "I booked Chris a room a few doors down, just in case we get a bit loud later on."

Jason's lips twitched into a half grin of sorts. *Finally something that makes him smile.*

"Let's leave our bags and go meet Tom. He told me he'd be on site at the office around this time." Toni was looking forward to meeting Cardona Mine's general manager so she could see first-hand what was being done. Unfortunately even after drilling more than eight exploratory boreholes, there had been no evidence that any of the missing miners were still alive. After so many weeks, not many held hope of finding more survivors. The death toll was horrible but Toni thought that not recovering the missing bodies made it even worse for the three families involved. Not being able to lay your loved ones to rest, unacceptable. The only problem was without evidence, it was hard to send a crew into the mine. Their safety had to be considered. The last thing anyone needed was for any rescue team to be injured — or worse.

"Don't you want to freshen up a bit first, luv? It was a long drive. Maybe Chris needs some time."

Nice try, Jason, but that's not gonna work. "Well..." Toni began, making her voice sound all cheery and innocent. "If Chris is too tired from the looong drive, maybe I can just drive myself. I do have a driving license, you know." *There. Suck on that one, Mr. Security Man.* Jason's jaw clenched. *Wow, if looks could kill, I think I'd be a goner.*

"I'm good to go whenever you are, Miss Grimaldi," Chris declared.

Toni guessed he had noticed Jason's reaction as well. "Please call me Toni, Chris. And good, let's get going then."

The three of them piled back into the car—Chris up front, Toni and Jason in the back. Jason was holding her hand again, making Toni smile. He might not be happy but at least he still showed her that he cared, no matter how annoyed he was with her.

Toni quickly realized that her early statement about the area being deserted was wrong. Even after all this time, television crews and reporters were still camped outside the gates to the mine. There were a team of security guards who checked their identities before the gates opened. Reporters swarmed the car, cameras pushed up against the windows.

"Fuck." Chris' expletive was loud as he tried to maneuver their vehicle safely through the melee.

"No one here, Toni? Seriously, did you really think the place would be deserted? Have you not watched the news, read the papers? This is still a big story. Now can you see why I'm concerned? Do you think you will be able to cope under the scrutiny of the press? They are going to be desperate for a new headline, having been out here for so long with no new development to report on."

Jason's tone was calm, but the seriousness of the situation was clear to see—Toni didn't need Jason to yell at her for her to realize she was way out of her depth. But if she could talk to some of the press, explain her plans for the Grimaldi Foundation—what she hoped to achieve—maybe it would help. People would see her father was doing the right thing for his people and maybe Toni would attract other big donations in the process. Her head was swimming with ideas of how she could pull this off to benefit everyone.

"We can check out the guests before they enter the lunch thing, J-man—make sure they are all employees. Maybe even enlist the help of some of these security guys, although they all look a bit green to me," Chris said over his shoulder as he pulled the car into an empty spot out the front of a one-story building structure. The head office of Cardona Mine didn't look much more than an upscaled shed.

"I'll make it happen, Chris. I reckon five or six men covering the lunch should do it. I'll make all the arrangements when I meet this Tom character. It will be first on my list of what needs to be done. Frank assured me this guy would comply with all my requests," Jason replied, the man talking as if Toni wasn't in the car or able to make any decisions of her own.

Typical that my father would be in the mix as well. When are the men in my life going to treat me like an adult? Not some precious pet they need to keep safe? Jason was no better than Frank.

"Enough. I'm sick of all this. I'm going in to meet Tom—and, Jason, I don't want you to come with me. Stay here in the car with Chris. You are both acting like bodyguards, so if you're both on the job then that makes you my employees. And I'm ordering you to sit or fall back or whatever the right terminology is..." Toni flung her car door open, breaking one of her nails in the process. She was so angry, so frustrated. She stomped her way over the red dirt then up the metal steps, only pausing long enough to twist the doorknob to open the office door. She pulled it shut after her, just as Jason was bounding up the steps behind her.

A tall man in a crumpled gray suit jumped up from behind a desk. "Miss Grimaldi, it's a pleasure to welcome you to Cardona Mine. I'm just so sorry it has to be under these awful circumstances."

"Tom?" Toni replied, as she held out her hand in greeting to the man.

"That would be me, "Tom said, as he took hold of her hand and gave it a quick, firm shake. "Can I get you something to drink, Miss Grimaldi? Coffee? Tea or water, perhaps? The dust has a way of coating everything around here, even your throat."

Toni had heard the sound of the door opening behind her and she could feel the heat of Jason's body at her back but she refused to acknowledge him just yet. Instead, she decided to take up Tom's offer.

"Coffee would be lovely. Thank you, Tom, and please call me Toni."

"I'm Jason Beck. I'm sure Frank Grimaldi informed you I would be accompanying Toni on her...visit?" Jason said, as he reached past her and shook hands with Tom.

"Yes he did. Glad to meet you. I'm more than happy to offer any assistance you might need while you are here," Tom answered.

Again Toni got the feeling she was superfluous in the equation as the men bonded and took control.

"Coffee?" she blurted out feeling bitchy and sounding the same.

"Yes, yes, of course, Miss Gr—Toni. Let me make a phone call and get some sent over from the canteen." Tom looked a little flustered as he stepped back behind his desk and picked up his phone.

He can probably feel the tension in the air.

She felt Jason's breath on her neck. "I'm sorry you are angry with me, luv, but this is what I do. I protect people, keep them out of harm's way or stop them from getting into it in the first place. Don't you ever storm off from the car again without me or Chris at your side. Do you understand me? I'm am not opposed to throwing you over my shoulder, strapping you back into your car seat and driving you straight back home. God, sometimes I think I should just keep you tied to our bed for your own safety and my peace of mind."

The words Jason had whispered into her ear made Toni want to scream, but her body's reaction to the warm puffs of air from his mouth as he spoke made her even angrier—with herself. She was so turned on, her panties were wet. She checked that Tom was still busy with his phone call then slowly turned her body around to face Jason, making sure her now hard and pointy nipples brushed against his chest as she did. She should have been thinking about slapping him for ordering her about that way. Instead, Toni's thoughts had turned to sex.

As her eyes met his, Toni saw the moment Jason realized she was turned on. At first his gaze was hard then Jason's nostrils flared a little and his features softened. A little grin formed on his lips.

"Don't look at me like that, luv—you know what it does to me."

"I'm not proud of myself about it, I can assure you, Jason. That little outburst of yours, all that ordering me around should make me want to punch you in the nose," Toni replied in a huff. "I just can't help it sometimes—your dominant side just gets to me."

"Well, I'm glad I have that effect on you, honey, but I do need you to take what I said seriously. I'm really not feeling right about any of this." Jason took her in his arms, hugging Toni to his chest. "It's not just me anymore either. Chris feels it too. I can't let anything happen to you, sweetheart. I can't live without you and can't stand the thought of you being hurt."

The sound of Tom clearing his throat reminded Toni that they were not alone.

"Is everything okay?"

"Yes, Tom, at least it will be, I'm sure," Toni replied, never lifting her head from the warmth of Jason's chest.

Chapter Fifteen

"There's a hell of a crowd here, J-man, but everyone has produced identification and if their name wasn't on the list, they didn't get in. I made sure to give the media contingent my best 'don't fuck with me' face, just to keep 'em honest."

"Thanks, mate." Jason knew the look Chris was talking about, had seen him use it to intimidate even the toughest of men—and it usually worked. Chris was a scary son of a bitch when he set his mind to it.

"Fuck, I wish she didn't insist on this lunch thing. Bloody hard to keep a decent watch over the room when bodies are shifting about all over the joint." Jason rubbed his temples, trying to reduce the tension that had his body coiled as tight as a spring. He hated that he didn't have total control of the situation. Toni was floating around the room, introducing herself and chatting with all the guests. Jason just wanted to shout out for everyone to take a seat and stop moving around. He couldn't see all the hands, needed to know that they were all empty—that no one held some sort of weapon.

Jason had hoped after his and Toni's little altercation at the office the day before — which had resulted in the best makeup sex of his life — he'd be feeling more relaxed.

He'd certainly not wasted any time yesterday getting her back to the motel room, naked and flat on her back. He'd been so shocked when Toni had turned to him, sure she'd been about to give him a spray for what he'd said. Seeing her face and realizing that she was turned on had just about blown his mind. Seriously, the woman had him tied up in fucking knots most days. His dick had gone ramrod straight at the sight of her chewing on her own lip and that had been before he'd noticed her nipples poking against her top, just begging for his attention.

He'd paid homage to those rose-colored peaks the first chance he'd gotten. Teased, nipped and sucked on them until Toni had been a writhing mass beneath him. Then he'd kissed a trail down between her ribs, her abdomen, swirled his tongue in and around her navel before continuing his journey. His resting place? The haven between Toni's thighs. Holding her pussy lips apart with his thumbs, Jason had plunged his tongue deep into her cunt. Savored the taste of her arousal that had filled his mouth.

He'd drunk deeply from her creamy wet cunt until she'd screamed his name in ecstasy and even then, he hadn't stopped. He'd been a man possessed, intoxicated by her sweet perfume and her exotic taste. He'd been coiled up so tight with worry that he hadn't been able to control his own emotions. It hadn't been until he'd felt Toni's hand brush against his forehead, in an attempt to push him away, that her pleas of "Stop" had registered. He'd lifted his head and seen her tears.

Terrified that he'd hurt her, scared her, he had torn himself away, backed himself up against the wall, horrified at his actions. But Toni had once again thrown his equilibrium off kilter. She had climbed off the bed, walked right up to where he'd stood and knelt down before him. She'd wrapped her fingers around his cock and she'd looked up at him, her eyes still glistening from the tears she'd shed, and apologized to him. "I'm so sorry, Jason, for making you so stressed — for not understanding that you really are worried about me, for not remembering what you've been through, what you've seen. I didn't think about it from your side. I was just thinking of myself, how it affected me. I'm so sorry I'm making you crazy. I promise I will listen to everything you say from now on."

Then Toni had sucked his cock into her mouth, while he'd stood there like a frickin' statue, trying to figure out what the hell had just happened. Toni had made him forget his own thoughts soon enough. Her wicked little tongue and mouth performing magic on his throbbing cock. She'd sucked and licked every inch of his dick and balls, taking him so far into her mouth he'd felt her throat tighten around his head as she'd swallowed.

They'd made love again a short time later, more slowly, taking time to caress and love each other. Then he'd fallen asleep, feeling more relaxed than he had in days — Toni tucked up safe and sound in his arms.

But that feeling was long gone now, and Jason knew this was not the time or place to be reliving such erotic memories. Toni was about to start her speech.

Jason's gaze was immediately drawn to her, as she smiled at the crowd before she picked up the microphone.

"Hello and welcome. For those of you that have not met me, I'm Toni Grimaldi. My family and I are deeply saddened over the horrible tragedy that has occurred on this site. We want you to know that we are standing here with you, beside you. We grieve for those that have been lost and hope the injured will heal quickly. We will do everything we can to help."

Some of the attendees started out aggressively, taking out their frustrations over the accident and the current mine closure on Toni. It made Jason bristle hearing them accuse her—the Grimaldis—of not doing enough.

"She's doing fine, mate. Calm down. You look like you're gonna start throwing punches. Toni has the room wrapped around her little finger."

Chris was right. Jason had realized his fists were clenched by his side. He had to get a grip. Toni was holding her own. He was so proud of her—the way she was answering all the accusations and questions thoughtfully and with a calm self-assuredness that was quickly winning the hearts of all that were present. Jason could see it in their posture. Most of the guests were sitting back in their chairs, nodding in agreement as Toni spoke of the efforts being done by her family's company.

"I'm okay. She's bloody awesome, the way she's handling herself. I don't understand how Toni ever felt she didn't fit into the role of socialite or mining magnate's daughter. She's a natural. Once this is done, we've only got to worry about the visits to the families of the deceased. I guess Toni sitting with a few widows, sharing a cup of tea and sympathy, could hardly be classed as dangerous. "

"I hate to mention it, J-man, but I think your radar might be on the blink. I think there would be a mass revolt if anyone threatened a hair on her pretty little head."

"You might be right, Chris, but if you ever make me think you are paying that much attention to my girl again, we may have a problem. I'm the only one that gets to notice how pretty she is. Got it?"

"Calm down, lover boy. It's just a figure of speech. She's not my type anyway. Toni's a settlin' down kind of woman and that scares the shit outta me, J-man. I'm still surprised she managed to get her hooks in you. The J-man I knew wouldn't have gone near her. She's got you so wound up that if she pulled the trigger, you'd be spinning around like a friggin' tornado."

Chris was still chuckling at his own humor when Toni joined them.

"What's so funny?" she asked, as she placed her hand in Jason's. She looked so happy. Jason couldn't blame her either. The lunch had been such a huge success and Toni deserved to feel pleased with the outcome, with her efforts. Jason couldn't wait to reward her.

"Chris thinks he's got a future in comedy but I have my doubts. You, however, luv, are bloody awesome. You had them all hanging off your every word. You should be really pleased with what you've done here and what you will achieve in the future with the Foundation. There's plenty of Grimaldi in your genes, babe. You just hadn't found the right outlet for it."

Jason watched in horror as Toni's eyes filled with tears. *What the fuck did I say this time? Sheesh, women — never understood 'em.*

Without warning she flung her arms around him, her strength quite astonishing as she squeezed Jason's ribs so hard he thought she might actually crack one.

"I love you, Jason Beck. Meeting you has given me so much more than you'll ever know. I'm a different person now. I got brave. You gave me the strength to find the courage to reach out for what I wanted. I wish I was just as good for you. Instead, I just give you more to worry about."

"Oh for God's sake, you two, get a room. All this lovey-dovey stuff is making me feel all skittish and girly," Chris said, the sound of his laughter fading as he walked away.

* * * *

She paused in front of the green door a moment to gather her thoughts. The lunch she'd organized had gone without a hiccup. She'd been so nervous, bordering on terrified at the thought of facing the media whilst delivering her speech. Scared that she would trip over or spill food down the front of her neat two-piece suit, in front of everyone. But none of her predicted disasters had happened and Jason's fears had been unfounded as well. It had all gone smoothly. But these visits to the widows were taking their toll on her. Today, Toni was meeting Mrs. Carlton. Her husband had been a miner for almost forty years and now he was gone. What could she say that would make any difference? *I can let the woman know I'm thinking of her.*

After taking a deep breath then releasing it slowly, Toni knocked on the door. The sound of muffled footsteps approached before the door swung open.

"Well, hello, dear, you must be Miss Grimaldi... Or are you one of those New Age girls that likes to use the Ms. title? Never understood it myself."

Mrs. Carlton was a small, dainty woman. Her silver-gray hair was neatly pinned in a bun on the top of her head. She wore an apron that was so bright that sunflowers seemed to jump from the fabric, and Toni had to fight the urge to pull out her sunglasses.

"Hello, Mrs. Carlton. Yes, I'm Toni Grimaldi, Toni. I'm glad you had time to see me."

"Time, that's all I have left, dear. Come in, Toni. Is that short for something? Antonia, Antoinette…" Mrs. Carlton was still talking as she led Toni into the house. "I've been doing some baking. My Harry used to say if he came home and found the kitchen full of cakes and scones, he knew something was up."

There was a wonderful aroma filling the house and after spotting the assortment of baked goodies on the kitchen counter Toni understood why. Lamingtons, scones, muffins and cookies filled every available space. "They look delicious and smell even better, Mrs. Carlton."

"Call me Bea, dear, short for Beatrice. Would you like to try something? There is quite a lot here…"

Bea paused. Toni waited for her to continue but she appeared to be lost in thought. Toni wasn't sure if she should say something or just keep silent.

"I think I may have gone a little overboard this time," Bea finally said but her voice held such sadness in it that Toni wanted to wrap her arms around her.

"I'm sure there are families who would be happy to take them off your hands, Bea. I could help you deliver them if you like? That is, after I try one of your lamingtons. Is that fresh cream inside?"

"Of course it is, and homemade jam as well. I might make us a pot of tea. So, Toni, why have you come visiting? Not that I'm complaining. It's nice to have a lovely young woman to chat with."

"I wanted to make sure you were doing okay and let you know my family are thinking of you, that we are so sorry for your loss and to offer any support you might need, now and in the future." Her words sounded so inadequate considering the circumstances, and Toni was embarrassed by them.

"That's very kind of you, dear, and your family. Pass on my thanks." Bea poured tea into a cup then handed it to Toni. "I'll get you a lamington."

Toni took a moment to look around the kitchen. Despite all the cooking Bea had obviously done, the room was spotless. Benches were neat and tidy, the kitchen sink sparkled. Sunshine beamed through the large window, bouncing off the lemon colored curtains bringing an extra brightness to the room. A total contrast to the dark and gloomy reason for her visit.

"Here you are. Enjoy." Bea placed the cake on the table in front of Toni. "I'm not sure there is anything anyone can do for me. It is going to take some time to get my head around the idea that Harry will not be coming home. But, unfortunately, that is the way of life. People you love are taken from you too soon. I'm very lucky to have had my husband for so long. We've been married for forty-five years next March. Harry and I met in primary school. I guess people call us childhood sweethearts, and we were. I loved him and he loved me. We had our share of hard times but always worked through them together. Do you have a special someone, Toni?"

Toni had eaten half of the lamington and it tasted wonderful. The cream in the filling had been mixed with something, possibly a liqueur of some sort, and the jam was tangy and sweet but it was all curdling in Toni's stomach. It was all so sad. She and Jason had only known each other for a moment compared to the life Harry and Bea had shared. "Yes I do, his name is Jason. It's all very new for us, though. We only met a short time ago."

"My advice to you is if you love him, don't hesitate. Grab hold of happiness with both hands and don't let go. Live life like there is no tomorrow. I wouldn't trade a minute of my life with Harry. We spoke of the dangers involved with his job, I understood that this day might come, but what could I do? Mining was in Harry's blood. His father was a miner and his grandfather. It was rumored that Harry's great-grandfather was a rebel during the Eureka Stockade. It's a tough job and Harry's working days were coming to an end. He would have been forced to retire soon. He was getting on, you know." Bea winked.

"Was it hard, worrying about him when he went off to work?"

"I didn't worry, Toni. Harry knew what he was doing. He didn't take risks and he wasn't foolhardy. You can't waste time worrying about things out of your control. It doesn't help anyone. People are taken from this life every day, expected or not. Doesn't change a thing if you make yourself sick with anxiety over the what-ifs. Don't get me wrong. I'm still half numb trying to come to terms with my loss. Harry was my life. I'm not sure I ever will, completely. Of course I'd hoped and said a few prayers that this kind of accident would not happen to my husband. But it has, and now I have to learn to live with that loss and sorrow the best I can."

This tiny woman was so strong. Tears rolled down Toni's cheeks as Bea spoke of times she and Harry had shared. It was almost unbearable to Toni that this couple, who had loved each other for so long, were now parted. It was difficult not to feel responsible. If he hadn't worked for her family... Maybe.

"As to my future, I will have to think about that. God didn't favor us with children but I do have a sister in Perth. I don't really want to leave. This is my home, has been since Harry started working here. Long before your family took over the lease, my girl, so get that look off your face. I know your family took all the safety issues seriously. Harry would not have let the miners go in if he didn't think it was all above board. He wasn't the union representative but he certainly was well-known and respected. The men listened to him."

How did she guess what I was thinking? "You stay here for as long as you want. That is something I can help you with. I don't want to embarrass you and talk financial matters but if you ever need anything — I mean it, Bea, anything at all — you call me."

"That's very thoughtful of you, dear. I think all those matters are being taken care of and Harry did think ahead. He was like that. Looking out for me, making sure I would be okay..."

Toni's tears flowed even harder. "I don't know how you can be so strong, so forgiving. I don't know how I would cope if I lost someone I loved. How can you bear it?" This really wasn't what Toni had planned when she'd come up with her idea to visit the widows. She'd wanted to help them and here she was bawling her eyes out and asking for answers to the questions she should be finding the solutions for.

"You have to. What other choice is there? Harry wouldn't want me to just give up. He loved life and would expect me to go on. He loved his job. I don't know what it was about those tunnels but Harry lived for it. It seems almost appropriate…" Bea paused. She focused on something outside the window.

Toni tried to see what had captured Bea's attention.

"I will always love Harry and think of him as I do the everyday things. Maybe he will enjoy watching me, from where he is now. You need to live your life without regret, Toni. Enjoy it. Embrace the good times and the bad times. Go make some memories with your man. My life is so much the better for having my Harry. I've been lucky. I have friends here—some that have suffered a loss as well. They will help me get through the lonely times. We have our quilting group and our reading group. I can bake." Bea handed Toni a napkin. "Dry your tears. Don't fret over me. But I thank you for coming and visiting. It was very thoughtful of you. I do appreciate it and I'm sure Harry does too. He always said that Grimaldi was a great company to work for. See? You proved him right again, dear."

Toni didn't want to leave but she had been with Bea for over an hour. She was surprised Jason hadn't already come barging in. He'd been trying so very hard to control his concerns for her safety, to not let her see the worry he was still feeling. Toni didn't want to push her luck or give Jason more reason to be concerned. It was time to go. "Bea, the pleasure has been all mine. You are amazing and I will never forget our visit. Please promise me you will call if I can help in any way—you or your friends."

"I will, dear."

Toni rose from the chair. Hugged Bea. "Good. Don't forget."

Walking away was hard and as Toni heard the front door of Bea's house close behind her, a fresh batch of tears welled. She made her way toward the car. Jason was standing leaning up against it, making her even more upset. They had only known each other for such a short time, their love so new when compared to the woman she'd just left who had been married for more years than Toni had been alive. Toni could not imagine how broken she would be if Jason was not a part of her life.

"Oh, luv, stop crying. I'm here. Come on. Let me hold you." Jason helped her into the car. Cradling her in his arms, he whispered sweet nothings in her ear until she cried herself to sleep. She woke briefly as Jason carried her in his arms from the car.

"Thank you, Jason. I'm sorry I'm so emotional but that woman was just so…"

"Shh, luv. I think you need to get some rest. We can talk about it all when you wake up. I'm going to tuck you into bed for a few hours. No arguments, okay?"

"Just don't leave me."

"Never, luv. Never."

* * * *

Toni lay snuggled up against Jason's side as the sun peeked through the curtains heralding a new day. Jason had placed his arm over her body at some stage during the night and Toni was grateful for the connection.

She'd learnt so much over the last few days. Tom had taken her on a tour of the whole site, explained all aspects of mining the best he could in the short time he had. Toni had listened intently as he'd explained the differences between open-cut mining and subsurface mining—the ever present dangers involved even with all the safety guidelines put into action and adhered to. He'd showed her all the reports about the cave-in. The thorough investigation had concluded that a small underground earthquake a few weeks before the accident, which had hardly registered on the Richter scale was the most likely cause. That the earth shifting around the beams and poles, which had been erected to shore up the working areas as per safety standards, had become compromised by the quake, causing the rockfall.

"Morning, luv," Jason said, his voice gravelly from sleep and so sexy it made Toni's heart flutter. "What time is your first visit?"

"I've got one at ten and then another at two. I'm not sure what I can say to these women. We haven't found their husbands yet. I just hate that with all our money we can't do this for them, give them a chance to bury their loved ones properly."

Jason pulled himself up to a sitting position, his chest bare as he propped himself up against the headboard. Even the sight of Jason shirtless couldn't shake Toni from her gloom.

"I know it's hard, luv, but the truth is…mining's a dangerous business. Like being in the Army, you know the risks but you still do it anyway."

What Jason was saying was true. Exactly what Bea Carlton had said, Toni knew that, but it didn't make it any easier for her to accept. She was truly grateful she hadn't met Jason while he'd still been serving — she didn't think she could have coped with the constant fear that he might get hurt.

"Why don't we go and get some breakfast," Toni suggested, trying to distract herself from her maudlin thoughts.

"That is an option but the dining room isn't open for a while yet and I have another idea."

"And what would that be?" Toni asked, knowing full well what Jason had in mind as he started nipping at her shoulder. "Are you hungry for something else?"

"I'm always hungry for you," he growled in reply.

Sighing at his touch, Toni forgot about everything. Jason licked up the curve of her neck. He was being so gentle with her, nibbling at her lips until she opened to him. The kiss started off soft and sweet but Toni wanted more. She plunged her tongue into his mouth, desperate to show Jason just how much she needed him. Their kiss grew harder and deeper as their desire for each other grew.

Jason broke from the kiss first. Covering her breasts with his hand he teased her nipple until it puckered into a hard bud. "Feels so good, luv, your breast in my hand, your nipple hard, responding to my touch."

Toni moaned in agreement. She stroked his back as Jason drew her nipple into his mouth and sucked gently on it, before moving to her other breast and repeating the tantalizing action.

"Mmm. You, Toni, taste better than any breakfast could."

Chapter Sixteen

At ten o'clock, Chris pulled the car up in front of a small weatherboard house. Toni immediately noticed the overgrown lawns and drawn blinds on the modest dwelling. Heather Cain was the name of the woman Toni was about to meet. Tom had given her a brief outline of Heather's situation. Her husband was one of the men they had not been able to locate. Joshua Cain had only been new to the mining business, he and Heather having moved here from the city to try to get some money behind them for their young family. Joshua, a sparky by trade, had only been down the mineshaft laying cable for lighting. Something so innocent, just installing light for the miners, and yet enough to put him in the line of danger. It was heartbreaking.

"Do you want me to come with you this time, luv? Give you some moral support?" Jason asked her as she stepped from the car.

"No, I'm okay. I can do this. I want to do this," Toni replied, as she closed the door on her smiling lover and turned toward the house. Her heart was heavy, though, as she knocked on the door and waited for Mrs. Cain to open it.

As the door swung wide Toni couldn't hide her shock at the state of the woman standing a few feet away in the shadows of the dimly lit entry. Heather Cain was very pregnant but she didn't look well. Her hair, limp and unbrushed, fell to her shoulders, her dress crumpled and stained, stretched over her swollen belly. Her eyes were dull, lifeless. This woman was struggling. Toni made a mental note to speak to Tom about it as soon as her visit was over.

"Heather Cain, I'm Toni Grimaldi. I was wondering if I could come in and have a chat with you. I thought Tom Church had organized this time with you, but if you're not up to it at the moment, I'd be happy to come back—at your convenience, of course."

Heather's hand shot out and grabbed her on the arm, her grip on Toni painfully tight. The woman moved so fast it took Toni by surprise "No, I've been expecting you, Miss Grimaldi—looking forward to it, in fact. Finally, getting my hands on the people responsible for keeping my Josh from coming home."

Heather was strong, despite her fragile appearance, and she pushed Toni farther into the house. As Toni's eyes adjusted to the dimly lit room, she could see that the area was very tidy despite Heather's own appearance, and that a single chair, one normally found at a dining table, was smack bang in the middle of the room. "You sit right there and don't move while I get Tom Church on the phone. He keeps telling me they are doing their best to find Josh, but I want you to order him to send my husband home right now." The already high-pitched sound of Heather's voice becoming even more shrill made the hairs on Toni's arms stand up. "I want my Josh to come back. He's been away for weeks and the baby is due soon. I don't want him to miss her birth."

This is not good. Just do what she says, try to keep her calm… She's bloody hysterical already. How can I calm her down? Thoughts were ricocheting through Toni's head as she tried to make sense of what was going on. Heather was obviously emotionally unstable and the fact that she now held a gun in her hands and was waving it about did not help the situation at all. Toni was in real danger. The whole situation had developed so quickly, so unexpectedly, that she hadn't even had time to let fear set in until now. Seeing the gun made it very real. *What should I say? How can I help her?*

Toni looked on helplessly as Heather dialed her phone with one hand, pointing the gun at Toni with the other. The line must have connected to someone, judging by the look on Heather's face but Toni had seen Tom's schedule for the day — he was in a meeting with the head of the rescue squad at eleven, so she knew it couldn't be him.

Heather started to speak into the phone, "I need to speak to Tom Church right now," she said.

Then there was a pause.

"Well, you tell him to ring Heather Cain as soon as he gets back. There is someone here that needs to speak to him, urgently," Heather shouted into the phone before slamming the handset back into its cradle. The noise was so loud it made Toni jump.

Heather's eyes clearly showed that the woman had passed the point of rational thinking. Now distraught to the point of madness and out of her mind with grief, she had not accepted the reality that her husband was dead. Toni didn't know what to do. *Do I tell her that her husband is not coming home, that he is dead, buried under a ton of rock? That Tom is busy meeting with the people trying to retrieve her husband's body right now? Probably not going to work in my favor. Maybe I can try to get her to think about something else?*

Toni thought anything was worth a try. *If I can just keep her calm until Tom rings back and then I can try to say something to alert him to the situation.*

"Your baby is a girl?"

Heather remained silent, but Toni noticed Heather's grip on the gun change — she moved the barrel of the rifle so it rested against her baby bump, and what was more of a relief. Heather's finger was now away from the trigger.

"Do you have any names picked out yet? Is this your first child?" Toni already knew the answer to her second question — she remembered reading that the couple had a little boy aged two. Toni hadn't spotted him yet, wondered where he could be. A niggling, worrisome thought entered her head. *Is the boy okay? Has Heather harmed him in her distressed state?*

After a few tense and silent moments, Heather finally opened her mouth to speak. Toni managed to breathe again.

"Sally, after my mother, that's what we were thinking."

Toni tensed at Heather's 'we', hoping it didn't bring Joshua back into the equation and was relieved when she kept talking. "Dylan is named after Joshua's dad. He's in his room sleeping. I put him down for his nap before you got here. I didn't want any distractions. When will you let Josh come home?"

Shit, back there again. I need to keep the conversation away from Joshua. She racked her brain for some other way to connect with the woman. "I don't think it is good for the baby to get yourself worked up like this,

Heather. You should be resting. Why don't you sit down too?"

"I am tired and my back aches all the time now..." Heather replied. The woman glanced toward the couch and back to her.

It's working.

"I promise I won't move from this chair, but I'm worried about you, Heather, please sit down," Toni said trying to keep her tone soothing even though she was terrified of what Heather might be capable of. She'd also finally managed to get her thoughts under control and had remembered that Jason was sitting in the car, waiting for her to return.

If Toni didn't get out of the house soon, somehow, there was a real possibility of Jason storming in and taking matters into his own hands. Toni didn't want to see Heather get hurt, didn't want to put Jason in the position of hurting the pregnant woman because of her. It was such a mess but Toni was determined to talk Heather down. So she kept up a string of idle chat with topics that she hoped would not provoke her captor.

The longer Toni engaged Heather in conversation, the clearer it became that Heather really didn't want to harm her. The distressed, pregnant young woman was just overwhelmed, had convinced herself that Joshua was being kept at work and not allowed to come home for some reason. Heather had obviously had a mental breakdown of some sort, and who could blame her? Toni couldn't.

It was horrible the events that had pushed Heather over the edge—her husband's grim death only the beginning of the struggles that lay ahead for her. Trying to manage a toddler and a newborn on her own would be hard for Heather. Toni hoped she had family or that Joshua's would be around to help. The Grimaldi Foundation and Toni herself would be making sure they did all they could, and not just in the short term — Toni had already made the decision that the Cain children would have all the financial support they needed. Heather was certainly going to need some professional care too. Toni was convinced of that.

Now if she could just get Heather to put down the gun and let her help, life would be a lot less stressful.

* * * *

The tingle in Jason's back had progressed steadily in the last few minutes to that of a knife stabbing him. There had to be a concrete reason for his ill ease.

"How long has she been in there?" he asked Chris for the second time since he'd watch Toni walk up the path to the house. Even though he'd been watching her every move, Toni had disappeared inside so fast Jason hadn't even got a glimpse of the poor widow. These visits were taking their toll on Toni, and Jason was looking forward to them coming to an end. *Only one more to go. Only one more and it will all be over.*

Jason could see Chris' eyes reflected in the car's rear-view mirror. Chris had been watching him intently for a while now. "It's been ten minutes, J-man. What's got you so antsy today? Toni normally sits with them for over an hour. What's up?"

Jason heard the apprehension in Chris' questions and wondered whether it was for him, his state of mind, or if Chris was sensing something too.

"I wish I knew, mate, but I don't feel good about any of this. The state of the house, the drawn curtains, the fact I didn't see this Heather Cain woman before Toni disappeared inside. I'm probably just letting my imagination run away with me, but I just dunno." Jason rubbed his hand over his chin and neck trying to soothe the tension in his jaw line.

He heard the rustle as Chris shifted himself around to look him in the eye. Jason had seen that look on Chris' face before, recognized it for what it was. "You feel it too?" Knowing that Chris was concerned didn't make Jason feel better. Any sliver of hope that perhaps he was overreacting ripped away with the knowledge that Chris was sensing something too. They both couldn't be wrong on this. Toni was in trouble.

"Yeah I do. This whole thing smells bad. I think you should go check on her. Or do you want me to, so Toni doesn't rip your balls off, if we've both got it wrong?" Chris offered.

Tempting as it was to get Chris to do his dirty work, Jason needed to see Toni was okay with his own two eyes and needed it to happen in the next few seconds before he lost his mind completely.

"Thanks for the offer and your concern for my well-being, but I think I can handle this one," Jason replied but the comedic element he was trying for to lighten the mood didn't work.

He opened the car door and got out, before shutting it silently behind him. With a soft tread, Jason made his way toward the front door of the house. He took a moment to stop and listen through the door. *Maybe if I can hear her voice, hear them chatting like woman do, I won't have to announce my presence and I can slink back to the car and forget it ever happened. Chris will keep quiet about the whole paranoid episode...*

He couldn't hear a thing, not a sound. The stabbing feeling between his shoulder blades got worse. Surely he'd be able to make out some kind of sound—the house wasn't that well built? At least some noise from the kid. Jason had read all Tom's reports and the Cain family had a two-year-old boy. Jason didn't know much about kids but what he did know was that they were usually loud.

Noiselessly Jason inched his way toward the front windows. The curtains were drawn but he hoped that he'd be able to set his sight on Toni or her host through a gap somewhere.

He was in luck. There was an opening on one side of the window. It looked like someone had pulled the curtain closed too firmly. As he took a quick peep through the opening, Jason's heart nearly stopped. Toni was sitting in the middle of the room on a wooden, straight-backed chair. Her head was turned away from him. Jason couldn't see her face but he could see what was holding her attention. There was a woman sitting in a chair to her left holding a gun, positioned awkwardly across her lap.

The fact that he had been right all along was not really any comfort to Jason at that moment, as he tried to digest all the information at hand. The soldier in him overrode the desperate and panicking man to take control of the situation. He had to get out of sight but taking his eyes off Toni at that moment was the hardest thing Jason had ever had to do. Forcing himself to crouch back down below the windowsill took an enormous amount of self-discipline. Jason did his best to breathe normally, his heart racing, as he tried to figure out a way to get Toni out of there.

There has to be another way in. Strategies and plans to accomplish the objective started to form in Jason's mind — where possible entry points in a house of this design would be found. *If Chris can get in there from somewhere out back, distract the woman with the gun, it will give me time to come through the front and surely between the two of us, we can disarm her. No, Chris needs to disarm her first. Maybe I should distract her, give him an opportunity to get that gun. She won't be expecting an attack from behind.*

Keeping his body low to the ground and out of sight, Jason crept back to the car to fill Chris in on the situation. The distance may have only been a few yards but it felt like he'd traveled miles before he reached his destination. Chris was already out of the vehicle waiting for him.

"What do you need me to do?" Chris asked, his voice lowered, but it was clear he'd figured out that all was not right.

"We need to get her out of there. Toni is sitting in the front room just a few feet from that window—" Jason pointed out the location to Chris. "There's a woman sitting to her left, holding a rifle on her. You need to find a way into that house from the back and be ready to move when I go in the front door. That gun has to be taken out of the equation first, and quickly. I'm thinking if I cause a distraction, you can get your hands on it."

Jason was regretting his decision to leave his gun back at Haven Security headquarters. Australia's gun laws were strict, carrying a weapon very unusual for the common Aussie. He'd had to go through some strict licensing requirements to even own a firearm. So there weren't that many occasions Jason thought it necessary to be armed, let alone feel the need to draw his weapon.

He more often than not carried a stun gun—not completely legal either but a better alternative to putting a bullet in someone. Jason had always believed, after seeing so much death with his time in the Army, that it was better to try to defuse a situation without the use of deadly force. But that all had changed now his woman was being threatened. If he'd had his Glock 22 strapped to his ankle, he'd have been tempted to put a bullet in Heather Cain then spend the next fifteen to twenty years behind bars. And he would have done that time happily, knowing Toni was out of reach of that damn rifle and the woman who wielded it.

Jason and Chris synchronized watches, Chris believing a five minute time frame was all he needed to be in place and ready to roll. The seconds ticked by slowly as Jason waited.

Chapter Seventeen

"Heather, I really think you should take the opportunity to lie down and rest while your little boy is sleeping. Maybe I could look after him for a bit if he wakes up? I'd enjoy spending some time with Dylan. Have I mentioned I'm a kindergarten teacher? So you can trust me with him. I love children. Precious little gifts, aren't they?"

It was a long shot thinking that Heather might leave Toni and lie down, but anything was worth a try. Toni knew time was running out. Jason would be coming to look for her soon—she wasn't sure how long she'd been sitting in this uncomfortable chair but it felt like forever. Her shoulders and back were stiff from the tension Toni was trying hard not to show.

Heather made no reply.

"It's great that your little one is such a good sleeper. I've heard some of my students' mothers complaining their toddlers stopped taking naps quite early on." Toni kept prattling on, smiling and trying to connect with Heather on a more personal note. She was sure she had seen this tactic used in movies, hoped it was the right thing to do. "I can't remember if I was a napper or not..."

"Dylan slept through the night from the moment we brought him home from hospital. He is such a good boy. Never gives me any trouble..." Heather's eyes glazed over, as if she was remembering back to the time she spoke of.

Toni heard a noise. It was coming from the front door. A small rattling sound, as if someone was trying to open the lock. Toni knew who it was trying to gain entry to the house so she kept her gaze fixed on Heather and the gun. It was clear that Heather had heard the noise too. The poor woman's face lit up, a smile formed. *She thinks it's Josh coming home.* The confusion and anger that had previously turned her features into those of a mad woman were gone, replaced by hope. It was heartbreaking for Toni to observe this change in Heather, knowing it would not last long. Joshua was not at the door.

Heather struggled to get up from her seat, her pregnant tummy hindering her actions. Then, out of the corner of her eye, Toni noticed movement on the other side of the house. She hadn't heard any sound from the toddler. *Oh my God, please don't let that be Dylan awake.* Toni was in a panic over what could happen. *Does he sleep in a cot or a bed? Is he about to come wandering into the middle of this just as Jason storms in?*

Jason picked the lock with ease. He slid inside the open door, quickly surveying the layout of the house, getting his bearings. He only had a few seconds to get in between Toni and the gun. He went straight for the living room, the room his woman was in, fully focused on his objective of spotting Heather Cain before she saw him and getting that gun away from her.

Heather was on her feet and a big smile lit up her face—not the reaction he'd been expecting. And she was heavily pregnant. Then her smile faded. It was about this time that Jason got his first good look at the rifle, as she pointed it in his direction. It was an old Winchester double barrel, possibly dating back to the fifties and not in the best condition—which led to a whole new world of problems for Jason to take under consideration.

If the gun wasn't well cared for—cleaned and oiled regularly—it could be damaged. If the gun was fired—and Jason hoped that wasn't going to happen—the round could jam or hang fire, release a few seconds later and explode anywhere. Maybe rushing the gun carrier was not going to work. Jason just couldn't stand idly by and do nothing, though. He'd much rather be the one to take a bullet if that scenario played out. He moved, positioning himself in front of Toni, blocking her from Heather Cain's line of sight.

"Heather, relax, it's just my driver. He was probably wondering what was taking me so long. You must have left the door unlocked. Maybe he didn't want to wake Dylan by knocking. Jason knows how cranky two-year-olds can get if they're woken abruptly."

Jason could hear Toni's voice behind him. She was obviously trying to keep the situation from deteriorating, doing her best to keep everyone calm and tell him there was a kid asleep somewhere in the house. She knew Jason didn't have a clue about cranky kids. *Clever girl…* His eyes never left Heather's position. *But you'd better stay put behind me…*

Chris was inching his way slowly toward Heather. Jason could see him over the woman's shoulder. Any moment now, Chris would make his play. Jason had to be ready to react, throw his body over Toni's. But he had to give his buddy a heads up on the condition of the gun.

"No need to be alarmed, ma'am, I just need to pass a message on to Miss Grimaldi," Jason said presenting his hands, palm up, to Heather in a non-threatening manner. "You should be careful holding onto that gun, ma'am. It looks pretty old and there's so much rust, it can damage a gun. Make it more dangerous," he said, not needing to fake the concern in his voice at all.

The more Jason studied the ancient weapon pointed at him, the more certain he was that if Heather fired it, she would be the one injured. If Chris didn't comprehend his warning and grabbed the gun at the wrong time, then he and Heather would both bear the brunt of his predicted misfire.

"Have you ever had it cleaned, ma'am?"

It looked like Heather was going to say something. Her mouth opened, but before any words came out, Jason heard a long, high-pitched wail. It sounded like a child. Heather's head swung in the direction of the noise. Chris took advantage of the distraction and pounced. He snatched the gun right out of her hands. It was so quick, all over in a split second. As Jason moved toward the now unarmed woman to contain her, Toni's hand touched his back.

"Let her go to her son, Jason. I think now you all are here, she can't do anything else. Thank you for getting the gun away from her, Chris. Maybe you can follow Heather and make sure she and Dylan are okay."

Now I've heard it all. Toni was worried about how Heather was feeling. The woman was going to be the death of him. Nodding to Chris in approval, he waited until they were both out of sight then spun around to face Toni. Seeing her safe, out of danger, was enough to make his knees go weak. He dragged her into his arms, hugging her to his chest. Not sure if it was to comfort her — or him.

Chapter Eighteen

With a blanket around her shoulders, Toni sat in the car. The local paramedic had said that her body was more than likely going into shock. Judging by the way her bones shook and her limbs trembled, he was right but she refused to leave without Jason by her side. It had been awful watching Heather being carted away by the police. Even though the doctor had sedated her, Heather had been weeping uncontrollably. Toni hoped the medication kicked in soon so the poor woman could feel some peace, even if it was artificially induced by drugs. Little Dylan had looked so sad and confused, crying out for his mother the whole time.

Toni had tried to explain to the police officers that Heather had not really intended to harm her – an idea she clung to just as much for the sake of her own sanity as in trying to help Heather's cause. She'd ignored the dirty looks Jason had sent her way, as she'd tried to make excuses for the woman's behavior.

He had been right all along, that stupid sixth sense probably the reason they had survived the ordeal without injury. She was never going to hear the end of it. So far, though, Jason had done nothing but praise her ability in handling the difficult and delicate situation. He'd told her how proud he was. Even Chris had commented on her ability to handle such a stressful confrontation. He'd given her a brief and awkward hug before Jason had manhandled him away.

There was so much in her life that Toni could feel grateful about—the weeks since her return from London had been the biggest learning curve of her life. Her meeting with the people involved at the Cardona Mine site had impacted on her life. And not just because of her traumatic experience with Heather Cain or her emotional visit with Beatrice Carlton. Toni had come to the conclusion that Grimaldi Holdings was more than just a way to make her family money.

It was much bigger than that. Her father, their company, was responsible for so many employees, giving them the means to live and raise their own families by making sure jobs were safe, wages fair and forthcoming. She really hadn't understood anything her father did. No wonder he worked so hard. Toni could only imagine the pressure he was under. Yes, they lived well—better than most. Maybe it was okay for her mother to spend too much on gifts every now and again as long as Toni ensured there was plenty of Grimaldi money to support the employees that might need a hand.

And there was Jason.

Her lover, friend and protector.

Ready to put his body on the line for her.

Toni never wanted to put him in that position again. She'd nearly had a heart attack when Jason had stood between her and Heather's gun. And Toni knew it had been more than Jason just doing his job, which also scared the shit out of her, because it had been for his love of her. She'd figured that bit out when Jason had nearly fallen to his knees as he'd hugged her after Chris had disarmed Heather—his body vibrating against hers from the strain of it all, the words he'd whispered into her ear about love and not being able to stand the thought of not being with her every day of his life. Saying that he wanted her with him, by his side forever… Words Toni believed with all her heart. Toni had held the same beliefs as she stood trembling behind the safety of Jason's broad back. Willing Heather to not shoot, praying for the sad, disturbed woman to spare Toni the same agony she was going through from losing her husband.

It was all over now. Soon Jason would drive her back to their motel then Toni was going to show her man how grateful she was to be loved by someone like him—that was if she could ever stop her body from shaking. *Maybe a nice warm shower, together, would help? If the heat doesn't help, I know Jason will be sure to distract me.* The idea brought a smile to Toni's lips.

"If I didn't know you better, I'd think that smile was due to a wicked thought," Jason said as he knelt down beside the open car door, their faces now level.

My God, I love that man. "Well, sexy, I was just thinking about having a shower to warm myself up. So maybe you're wrong."

"A shower sounds like a plan. The cops are finished with us. What say we go back to the room and I can assist you with that shower? I've also got a few of my own ideas on how to help heat you up, luv."

"I like the sound of that a lot, Jason."

Epilogue

They'd gone back to their motel room and Jason had come through on his promise to warm Toni up. He'd squeezed his body into the cramped shower stall with her and helped her forget the horrors of the afternoon the best way he could. He'd lavished love on her body with his hands and in her mind with his words. Toni had never felt so cherished in her life.

Snuggled up in the bed together, Toni remembered her conversation with Bea – what the wise woman had suggested to her. To grab happiness with both hands and live each day as if there was no tomorrow. Toni made a decision. She felt so right wrapped in the safety of Jason's arms, his body next to hers. She was courageous. Jason had taught her that about herself. She needed to reach out and take what she wanted.

"I want to ask you a question, Jason." She started a little hesitantly, trying to find just the right words for such a momentous occasion. "You don't have to answer me straight away but I want you to give it some thought. I've been thinking about some of the things Mrs. Carlton and I talked about, and I think she's right. I need to grab hold of the important things in my life. You are my life, Jason. I love you so much. Seeing you standing in front of me, thinking I could lose you before we made enough memories to see me through, scared me. I want you to marry me. I want to have a family with you. Will you marry me, Jason Beck? Be my husband?"

Jason stopped caressing her, his hand stilled. Toni held her breath, hoping that she hadn't pushed him too hard, too fast. She knew he didn't really believe in marriage or long-term relationships. Jason's parents' unhappy union had soured him in that respect. But she hoped her love for him might have changed that view. His love for her might have shown Jason that their life would be different from that of his mother and father.

"Like I said…just think about it," she said, trying to hide her disappointment that he hadn't answered her straight away.

Jason changed their positions so fast Toni gasped when she found herself lying on top of him.

Their eyes locked. Their lips met.

Jason's kiss was full of passion before he pulled back.

"Yes," was all Jason said before crushing his lips to hers once more and Toni was swept away on a current of passion that she knew would see them together, forever.

AN
OPPORTUNITY
FOR
REDEMPTION

Dedication

To the wonderful Sydney ARRA ladies — Helen, Lyn, Laine and Barb — your encouragement, friendship and faith in me keeps getting me over the line. Thanks also to my editor Sarah, Emmy for the beautiful artwork she creates and Holly for answering all those emails.

Chapter One

Dear Nathanial,

I'm sure you are probably shocked to be receiving this email from me after all this time. I'm reaching out to you out of desperation and fear, Nathan. My son is dying. His only hope is a transfusion of bone marrow from a suitable donor. I have exhausted every avenue in my search for that compatible match but have failed. It's why I reach out to you now, with the hope that you might do me this huge favor and have your bone marrow tested. Not for me, Nathan. I don't deserve any acts of kindness from you – but for the sake of my son.

The testing procedure is a simple one, requiring only a small sample of your blood to be taken and sent off for analysis, to determine if the HLA – Human Leukocyte Antigen – is a match.

Please, Nathan, I beg you. Get tested and ask your doctor to forward the results to Danny's specialist, Dr. Gregory Parker, Head of Pediatric Oncology at the Royal Children's Hospital.

Sincerely,
Rebecca Hammerton

Still dressed in the wedding tuxedo that Antoinette Grimaldi—now Beck—had coerced him into wearing as Jason's best man, Nathan Haven sat staring at his computer. His blood had turned to ice, frozen in his veins, as he stared at the image of the boy that filled the screen. He'd been staring at that photo for what felt like an eternity, recognized those dark eyes and the cut of the boy's chin. It could have been a photo of Nathan himself at that age. It reminded him of the framed picture his mother still had sitting on her sideboard taken when he had won his first trophy for rugby league in the under sixes.

This boy was his son.

And his son was dying.

Nathan had not heard a word from Rebecca Hammerton for over seven years. Their last correspondence had been her 'Dear John' email, calling off their engagement.

He hadn't laid eyes on her since the day he'd kissed her goodbye as he'd headed off to training camp for the Green Berets Commando Unit. That was until tonight when he'd opened the email marked to his attention, sent via the Haven Security website. Nathan clicked open his inbox and read Rebecca's deceitful missive again.

The first time he'd read through the email, Nathan had known there was something important Rebecca was not saying. Like any good investigator would, Nathan had typed her name into the search engines of various social media sites, looking for answers.

He had found one, in the photos posted on her page.

A mother-fucking, mind-blowing, unbelievable omission from Rebecca's plea for his help. Her son was, without doubt, Nathan's progeny.

A son she had kept hidden from him for over seven years and one that he might never get the chance to meet if he didn't get his act together—and fast.

His contacts were far and wide, and Nathan was going to call on every one of them he thought could aid him in this battle. First on his list was Martin Shore, a medic who over the years had patched him up on many an occasion, and who was now a doctor of emergency medicine at the local hospital. Marty had once found himself trapped behind enemy lines, caught there as he'd tried to save the life of a soldier who had taken a bullet. Nathan and his team had gone in, found Marty still working valiantly on his patient and got them the hell out of there. Since then, whenever Nathan had needed medical assistance, Marty had been happy to help.

It was only four a.m. but that didn't stop Nathan from reaching for his phone. *The guy's probably up to his elbows in blood and guts this time of the morning anyway.* He punched in the numbers that would connect him to Dr. Shore. Even though Nathan knew weekend mornings in hospital emergency rooms were usually overrun with men and women suffering the effects of alcohol-related injuries, he didn't feel guilty distracting Marty from his workload.

"Shore," said the gruff voice on the other end of the line after no more than three rings.

"Marty, it's Nathan Haven. I need your help."

"Where are you? What are your injuries?" Martin Shore's no-nonsense take-charge voice exacted, without hesitation.

"No injuries. I need information and I need it yesterday." Nathan had never been known for his cordial phone manner and he wasn't going to change that now — not when every second he wasted could be the difference between his son's life and death.

"You coming to me or me to you?"

"Are you at the hospital? I can be there in ten minutes. You might need to use the hospital resources for this."

"Where else do you bloody think I'd be on a Saturday night? Scratch that, Sunday morning," Marty replied with a hint of weariness to his voice that Nathan had not heard before. "Come to the clerk's desk. I'll let her know I'm expecting you."

"See you in ten," Nathan confirmed as he disconnected the call before immediately punching in more numbers. He needed to contact Chris.

"This better be fucking important, dude. It's just gone four a.m."

Nathan didn't bother with a reply to Chris' statement. He figured Chris to be balls-deep in some woman that he'd picked up at Jason and Toni's wedding reception. He'd noticed the attention from the single ladies — and some of the married ones too — that Chris had received.

"I need you to hold down the fort here for a few days, Chris. I have some personal business that needs handling and Jason's on his honeymoon. I've left a file on my desk with the details of all our current assignments. I'll call you back in a few hours after you've had a chance to go through the file."

Nathan hung up before Chris had the chance to reply. He took time to print off a copy of Rebecca's email to show Marty and a copy of the photo of Danny, for himself, before heading to his car.

There was more soldier than man in Nathan now and it was that dominant side that took control of the situation. A battle plan was needed. Every soldier knew that. Strategy and intel were what gave you that edge over your enemy. The more you knew about your foe, the terrain you were headed into, the types of challenge that might arise, the more chance you had of returning safely with the mission completed. That was what Nathan intended to do—form a strategic battle plan to give him the best advantage in combat, to claim victory in this war. And it was a war, of that he held no doubt. His enemies, a damn disease that was killing his son and the woman who had deprived Nathan of the chance to develop a relationship with him—one he may never get the chance to experience.

* * * *

Nathan strode through the automatic opening doors of the emergency room ten minutes later. The hospital waiting room was nearly deserted. A few people were seated in the plastic chairs, no doubt waiting to be seen or to hear news on a loved one, but Nathan didn't pay any of them more than a glance as he headed for the reception desk.

"Nathan Haven for Dr. Shore, he's expecting me," he told the tired-looking brunette that sat behind it.

"He told me to page him when you arrived," the woman replied, and Nathan didn't miss the once-over she gave him, the way her eyes moved so she could take her fill of him from head to toe.

Women had a tendency to react like that around him. Usually they got the hint quickly if he wasn't interested in reciprocating their intent. When and if Nathan felt the need to fuck, he made sure the woman knew the score—no emotional attachment or promises made, just a night or two of good old-fashioned, fun-filled, orgasm-inducing action in the sack. At the moment, getting down and dirty with a willing recipient was the last thing on his mind.

"Take a seat. He should be with you soon," the clerk finally responded, her tone curt, signifying that she'd gotten the message Nathan had intended.

He didn't sit. He took a few steps away from the desk and waited for Marty to appear, his mind retreating to a memory from the past, back when Nathan's heart had still been involved in his choices, to a time when Rebecca had still meant something to him — a time when he had thought he loved her.

"You spilt some ice cream on your boob. Want me to clean that up for you, baby?"

"Well, finally you notice! I was trying to be sexy, but it's frickin' cold, so could you hurry it up, Nate?" Rebecca *giggled as she held her tits out to him, thrusting the two more-than-a-handful bounties together and in his direction.*

He'd never needed much of an invitation to lavish attention on Bec or her sexy body, and this time was no exception. She only had to look at him a certain way, enter a room and Nathan wanted her. He'd been trying to study. He was sitting his corporal exam later that month and while the physical side of the army had never been a problem, the theory and written exams always caused him concern. He put his paperwork down. Bec and her boobs were an offer not to be missed. "What flavor are we eating tonight?" *he asked, just before he licked the melting ice cream from between Bec's tits, catching some of the cold confection on his tongue and swirling it around her berry-colored nipple.* "Mmmm, vanilla and nipple, my favorite."

"Is that so? I was thinking I'd like a little cock with mine."

"Sorry. Can't help you out with that one, babe. Nothing little about my package."

The sound of Bec's chuckle let Nathan know she was about to return the favor. He let her push him onto his back as she straddled him.

"I do love the way your boobs jiggle when you climb on me, babe. Lean forward a bit and I'll show you just how much."

"What's the matter, Nate? Scared some ice cream might make the big boy shy?"

That was exactly what Nathan feared. He didn't know whether the idea of something so cold on his rock-hard cock was going to be as erotic as it sounded.

He didn't have to wait long to find out. Bec spooned a mouthful of the melting vanilla cream into her mouth and positioned herself between his legs. As her eyes locked onto his she took his cock in her hand and fed it into her mouth. The sensation was like nothing Nathan had felt before, pain and pleasure, his dick responding to the cold with a jerk before the warmth of Bec's mouth soothed over the sensitive skin.

"Fuck me..." he groaned.

"I intend to," Bec replied, her words muffled and almost inaudible as her lips remained wrapped around his dick. She massaged his balls with one hand as she stroked the other up and down his shaft, sucking him in and out of her mouth.

He was going to come any second if he didn't get her to stop. Even though the idea of shooting his load down her throat was a tempting one – and one he'd had the pleasure of experiencing many times before – tonight, for some reason, Nathan wanted to be snug in her tight little cunt when he came. He snagged a fistful of Bec's long blonde hair and gave it a gentle tug. "Up here, babe. I want to fuck you. Sit on my cock."

It turned Bec on even more when Nathan went all alpha, talked dirty to her. He knew it and was rewarded when Bec crawled up his body, straddling him again, her legs bent either side of his hips. She positioned his cock at the entrance of her cunt, his dick nudging her opening.

"Is this what you want, Nate? To be inside me, for me to ride you?" she asked, Bec's chest rising and falling in rapid succession as her pupils dilated from her state of arousal.

Nathan loved the sight of her like this. Hot and ready for him. Grabbing hold of her hips, locking her in place, Nathan bucked his hips in the air, thrusting his cock into her wet folds. Rejoicing in the feel of Bec's pussy walls as they surrounded his cock and the soft whimpering sounds, Nathan recognized her orgasm beginning to grow. Soon her body would be writhing frantically above him, against him, in an attempt to claim her release.

As he thrust inside her, in and out at a steady beat, Nathan lifted his head so he could latch onto one of Bec's nipples. He grabbed that protruding bud between his lips and sucked it into his mouth. Bec went wild.

"Please, Nathan… I need help."

With his balls tightening and that familiar tingle in his lower back warning him that he was about to come, Nathan moved his hand down between his and Bec's body, finding her swollen clit with his finger. Nathan applied a small amount of pressure – after three years together he knew just how much force was needed to push Bec over the edge – and was rewarded when he did.

"I'm coming," she cried out.

Nathan could tell this by the way her cunt contracted around his cock, pulling him over the edge with her. He continued to thrust into Bec until every last drop of his orgasm was spent and the last tremor of her pussy had subsided.

"Sorry, Nathan. I didn't mean to keep you waiting, but some kid had other ideas when he came in with a fucking hole in his face from being glassed. Fuck, I wish something could be done. I'm sick of patching up these kids—most of them just out having some fun before some fuckin' gorilla picks a fight."

Marty looked harassed, tired and angry—pretty much the same way he looked whenever Nathan caught up with him. It was the first time he'd voiced his frustrations, though. Nathan agreed with everything Marty had said but didn't have the time to discuss it with him, not right now. He didn't even know how long he'd been waiting, so lost had he been in his bittersweet memory. Nathan got straight to the point. He shoved the copy of the email he'd printed off into Marty's outstretched hand, not bothering with the intended greeting first.

"Read it. Why would a kid need bone marrow? What's he got and what are his chances?" Nathan's training was the only reason he managed to remain calm and stationary while Marty read the email. "I need some answers now, mate," he prodded after what seemed an eternity watching Marty stare at the sheet of paper.

Marty's head came up. His eyes met Nathan's.

"We need to go somewhere a bit more private. It's not that simple, mate. Follow me. I need to grab some caffeine while I think this through."

Chapter Two

It had only between thirty-six hours since Rebecca had sent the email but that still didn't stop her from checking her inbox again. She had checked the bloody thing every five or ten minutes for the last few hours and still there was no reply from Nathan. She was kicking herself for not having sent the email with a read confirmation, but knowing Nathan, he'd probably have that function turned off anyway.

Turning to him had been a last resort. Not that Rebecca hadn't written a thousand letters telling Nathan he had a son, it was just that she'd never found the courage to send any of them. This time, though, there had been no choice. It didn't matter how angry Nathan was at her deception or what the ramifications might be, Danny was more important than any of that.

Her precious little boy had suffered for so long. He needed a break, needed to find a bone marrow match that would help his poor ravaged body fight the insidious cancer that kept returning. It was a long shot Nathan even being a match but it was one that

Rebecca needed to pursue, whatever the cost. The doctors had told her that siblings made better donors—parents or a lucky hit on the bone marrow donor list did not always achieve a positive outcome. Danny had no siblings, and even if Rebecca had given birth to more children, they would only be genetically connected to Danny by her genes, not the father's.

The moment she'd found out that her bone marrow was not a good enough match for Danny had been like a knife slicing her heart in two. As a mother, to find out she couldn't take away the pain or sickness from her child was unbearable. So Rebecca had set out to find someone who could help. She'd added Danny to lists all over the world. Her brother and parents had been tested, her friends, all to no avail. Even parents at the childcare center she'd worked at before Danny had become ill had sent their blood to Pathology, all coming back without the markers needed to pair with her son.

Rebecca had sent the email to Nathan without admitting that Danny was his son. She had hoped that Nathan might reach out to her and she could tell him about Danny in person. Or that's what Rebecca kept telling herself anyway. *I should have told him in the email. If he knew Danny was his, he'd be more likely to get tested. Why do I keep doing the wrong thing? Maybe if I write again, this time being more specific…*

"Mummy, I don't want any more. I'm not hungry."

The sound of Danny's voice pulled Rebecca back from her thoughts. She looked over to her son, her beautiful baby boy who had spent the first five years of his life doing what little boys do—being mischievous, boisterous and loud—and making her heart so full of love for him that she'd spent her days with a smile on her face. Now her poor sprite was pale, quiet and always tired. His thick swatch of black hair had gone, replaced by a fuzz of regrowth over his head, but she loved him even more. Tried not to think of a life where Danny was not the center of her world.

"C'mon, Dangerous Dan, I bet you could fit one more mouthful in if you tried really hard."

Rebecca spent a great deal of time trying to think of healthy, nutritious foods to feed her ailing son, to help his body find strength in its continuing battle. Unfortunately, Danny had lost his appetite as the cancer had progressed. Gone was the little boy who would plead and beg for just one more cookie or helping of ice cream. Now she was the one imploring him to eat.

"I don't want to, Mummy. What if it makes me chuck up? I hate spewing. I hate it. Please don't make me eat any more."

"You won't spew, baby. You're not having chemo anymore. That's what made you sick. But you do need to eat more so you can grow big and strong again. One more mouthful and I will play Mario Kart with you."

"I'll just beat you again, Mummy. You're not very good at racing."

Rebecca didn't care that Danny had spoken while shoveling in another mouthful of pancakes. The fact that he had eaten was so much more important than good manners.

"Okay, but I get to be Mario this time, Danny. I think Princess Peach has let me down too many times."

Seeing Danny smile was nearly as wonderful as seeing him eat an extra mouthful. Rebecca had to fight the tears that threatened to spill at the sight of that cute grin—one that didn't appear very often lately.

"I don't think that's gonna make you win, Mummy, but okay, I'll be Luigi this time."

"You go get the game set up and I'll load the dishwasher," Rebecca said, as she collected the dirty plates from the table. "And I'm not going easy on you, Dangerous. This time I'm in it to win it, so you'd better watch your six."

"Wow, I'm scared, Mummy," Danny replied with a giggle as he took off toward his room and the game console.

Rebecca didn't say any more. She was still shocked by her choice of words. *I've been thinking about Nathan so much his words are coming out of my mouth.* It also had her remembering a time when they had been strong, a time when Rebecca had believed they had a future together that didn't involve her being in constant fear for Nathan's life.

"Well, hello, ladies, nice to see you again."

Rebecca heard the greeting coming from behind her, the sexy drawl so familiar to her. She watched the way her girlfriends' faces lit up as they noticed Nathan standing behind her. She knew why they all looked so happy to see him. Nathan Haven was one sexy hunk of man. Rebecca grinned back at her friends. Nathan was hers and they all knew it.

She swiveled her body around so she could see him. "Hiya, sexy, whatcha doin' here? This is supposed to be a girls' night out."

"Well, what can I say? I missed you, babe, and I figured you might've had a few too many colorful cocktails and might be lookin' for someone to drive you home. So here I am, ready to be that someone for you. No hurry, though. You girls keep enjoying yourselves and I'll just go sit at the bar and wait till you're ready to leave."

As Rebecca watched Nathan walk toward the bar, she took the time to appreciate the way his butt filled the blue jeans he was wearing, the way the denim strained over his muscular thighs. She also knew each one of her girlfriends was doing exactly the same thing. Rebecca was still grinning as she turned back to her friends. "Put those tongues away, ladies. That one is taken."

"What the hell you doing still sitting here, Bec? If that was my man, I'd be on my way home in a heartbeat. You're such a lucky bitch," Rebecca's best friend, Katey, said before adding a sigh at the end for dramatic effect.

"You sure Nathan doesn't have any brothers or friends you can set me up with? That man has sexy written all over him," chipped in her other friend, Sophie.

"You know what, Katey? I think you have a point. What am I doing sitting here with you desperate lot when I could be getting hot and heavy with my man?" Rebecca stood up from the table and drained her rum and Coke. "Catch you all next week," she added over her shoulder as she headed toward Nathan. His smile at her approach was enough to make her insides quiver and her panties wet.

"Hope I didn't rush you, babe," were the only words Nathan got out before she planted her lips over his and sucked his tongue into her mouth. Kissing Nathan was one of Rebecca's favorite pastimes. Making love to him was even better.

She dragged her lips from his. Her heartbeat racing and her lungs starved for air, Rebecca felt like their bodies were melding together, the heat between them so intense. It was always the same reaction for Rebecca when their bodies met in any way. "Take me home, Nate, I think all those colorful cocktails have me feeling a bit amorous and adventurous."

The moment they walked through the door, Nathan had grabbed her around the waist, turning her so they were face to face, and their lips met again. Rebecca undid the buckle of Nathan's belt, working her fingers fast to rid him of his jeans so she could hold his cock in her hands, feel the silky skin that covered his rigid shaft. Nathan was doing his best to unzip her dress at the same time and before long, they were both standing naked, bodies touching and mouths fused together, stoking a burning desire that threatened to send them both up in flames.

"Bend over the sofa, Bec. This one's gonna be fast and hard." Nathan's voice was demanding, the words growled out.

Bec loved the knowledge that she could bring this kind of sexual hunger – need – out in him and she quickly submitted to his demands.

"Fuck, woman, you get me so hot for you that I can't control myself. The sight of you bent over, waiting for me to take you… It's all I can do not to blow my load just looking at you."

He entered her then, his thick cock sliding into her wet and fully aroused pussy. She couldn't help the groan of satisfaction escaping as his cock ground past her throbbing clit.

"You're always so wet for me, Bec, so ready for me to fuck you. I love you, Bec. You're the most important thing in my life," Nathan whispered into her ear as he rocked his hips back and forth, his cock plunging in and out of her, every movement bringing her closer and closer to her orgasm. He knew exactly how to touch her, what parts of her body needed to feel his caress.

Their rhythm was close to frantic. Nathan's breathing was rapid as he took her from behind. She clung to the edge of the sofa, her butt high in the air, slapping against Nathan's groin, the oxygen in her lungs expelled in great swooshing sounds from the force of his weight as their bodies crashed together. It was unrestrained, erotic and she loved it.

"I'm so close, babe. Come with me…"

"Mummy, are you coming?"

Danny's voice was like a bucket of iced water being poured over her. Rebecca pushed the memories of Nathan away, pushed them back into that place in her mind and heart that she tried to keep locked.

Tried not to dwell on.

She'd spent too many sleepless nights wishing for Nathan's hands on her body, to hear his whispered words of love in her ear one more time, but her logical side had always won the battle over her wishful side.

Rebecca could not have remained sane and whole being the wife of a Green Beret. The not knowing where Nathan was—or if he would ever return—would have surely driven her to insanity. She'd only just managed to survive his first tours of duty and she'd known exactly where he was stationed and had been able to email or Skype him every other day.

It wouldn't have been fair to make Nathan choose between her and the military, and if she was completely honest with herself, Rebecca had not wanted to be the loser. So she had called off their engagement and moved back home to her parents. It had taken her weeks to even leave her childhood room, she'd been so distraught—her mother's coddling and understanding the only thing that helped Rebecca survive her broken heart and shattered dreams.

"Mummy, I'm still waiting. Are you *ever* going to come and play?"

Rebecca pulled herself together and affixed a smile to her face as she headed toward Danny's room. "Here I am, Danny, although I don't know why you're so impatient to lose," she said, grinning at her son as she sat on the bed next to him. Rebecca took the controller Danny held out to her, trying not to dwell on how thin and fragile Danny's arms had become since his last round of chemo. He was not much more than skin and bones. *At least he's back in remission again. I can focus on that and be thankful.*

"Okay, Mr. Luigi, time for me to show you how to race," Rebecca teased, knowing full well that Danny was going to kick her butt again. The kid was a pro when it came to computer games.

They raced three times and as predicted, Danny won each time, although Rebecca had come close the last time, but that was probably only due to Danny becoming fatigued. He was still trying to talk her into 'just one more race' when the loud knocking started at her door.

"Sweetie, why don't you take a little nap while I see who is at the door. Maybe we can play again after lunch." Rebecca eased the controller from her son's hands and climbed off his bed, ignoring his mumblings about life not being fair. She couldn't agree more with her son's sentiments but not in regard to the Mario Kart game — more the burdens he had been forced to deal with in his short life.

The knocking continued as Rebecca walked down her hallway. "I'm coming," she shouted to the closed door, curious to know which one of her small number of usual visitors was in such a hurry. She wasn't expecting it to be her father. He had his hands full. It had been just another cruel blow to endure when the doctors had told them six months ago that her mother was showing signs of Alzheimer's. Life was not fair. Rebecca had cried many times, wondering why her family had to go through so much all at once, especially when her brother Matt was unable to help, given that he was deep undercover in some Federal police operation and had been for some time.

Rebecca threw the door open. "I said I was coming. No need to break the door—" Her heart stuttered a beat, her mouth went completely dry and nausea threatened to bring back the pancakes she had eaten for breakfast.

"I've heard those words before... Hello, Rebecca," Nathan Haven greeted her in a cold, deep drawl.

The pressure in Rebecca's chest became unbearable. She'd broken out in a sweat and her head was spinning. She wasn't sure if she was having a heart attack or maybe a stroke. Nathan's tall form, his dark and ominous eyes became a blurry vision as the world began to swim before her.

"Rebecca, are you okay? I think you should sit down." His deep voice—one she'd never thought she'd hear again—sounded strange, muted, like her ears were stuffed with cotton balls. She stumbled back inside until her legs bumped the edge of her sofa and sat down. This was her biggest nightmare come true. Well, beside the one about Danny that often woke her in the middle of the night.

"It doesn't look like you're all that pleased to see me, Rebecca. I wonder why that might be. I remember a time when you couldn't wait to get me in the door before you started taking my clothes off and a few occasions when we didn't even make it inside. Looks like I've lost my appeal."

The inflection in Nathan's voice was not at all friendly. It sounded downright hostile, and Rebecca understood why. Nathan knew what she had done. He had figured it out that she had kept his son from him and judging from his words and by the way he was looking at her with such hatred in his eyes, he was going to make her pay for her mistake.

And it was a mistake. Rebecca felt the guilt weigh heavily on her every day. But as the years had passed, it had become harder to undo what she had done.

In the beginning when she'd finally realized she was carrying Nathan's child, Rebecca had truly believed that it was better for all concerned if she didn't tell him. Nathan had joined the elite fighting unit, had been on his way to passing the grueling course to become a Green Beret. It had been too late. She hadn't wanted him to leave the Army because of her or the baby. She knew he would have and that he would have regretted his choice one day. She couldn't live her life as the wife of a Green Beret the way Nathan had wanted her to, and there was no way in hell she was going to let her baby learn to love a father that more than likely they would both have been mourning before long.

Rebecca had always hoped new love would enter her life, a stable man who would treat Danny like his own. The problem had been that no man had ever lived up to her memory of Nathan. Then Danny had taken ill and there had been no time. *How am I going to tell Danny that his father is here, that I lied to him every time he asked me about his daddy, why he didn't have one like the other kids at school? Well, Bec, you made your bed and now you're going to have to sleep in it,* she told herself, using one of her father's favorite sayings. *Time to step up and deal with the mess you created. Nathan could be the answer to your prayers for Danny.*

Rebecca tried to regulate her breathing, forced herself to relax. Finally, when she thought she was more in control, she spoke. "Hi, Nate. I guess you got my email."

"I've sent a blood sample off for testing but even putting a rush on it, it's still going to take a few days to get the results." Nathan's answer to her question was delivered brusquely. "So, where is my son and what have you told him about me?"

Chapter Three

Seeing Bec sitting down, her face so pale, obviously in shock at his arrival, should have fueled the rage that had consumed Nathan on his drive to face her. But to his surprise and disappointment, the reaction he was fighting was the urge to wrap his arms around her quaking body and comfort her. He was so pissed off at his own weakness. Disgusted that his body was responding to Bec's in the same way it had all those years ago, unconcerned by the fact that she was a lying bitch who had hidden his own son from him. His dick had gone rock-hard the moment she'd opened her door.

She didn't even look the same. This Bec had short hair, was thinner than he remembered her being when they'd been together. She looked tired, worn out. She may have lost those lush curves that had once driven him wild, but still he reacted to her, just as he always had done. It may as well have been only hours or days since they'd last seen each other instead of the nearly eight years that had up until this minute felt like a lifetime. He still had it bad for Rebecca Hammerton.

But Nathan was not going to let that stop him from his mission—to claim his son and rid the boy of the disease that was threatening his life.

He did not move a muscle as he waited for an answer to his question—for Bec to tell him about his son. He stared her down, trying to intimidate her. He wanted her to fear him. She deserved it after what she had done. Not that he would ever harm her physically, Nathan was not that type of man—loathed the filthy bastards that abused women—and if Bec remembered him at all, she would know that about him. But he was angry, at her and at himself for his initial reaction to seeing her again.

"In his room, having a nap," she finally replied, her voice not much more than a whisper. "We need to talk before you meet him, meet Danny. I need to prepare you for how he looks right now. How ravaged his little body is because of the disease, the treatments, the toll that it's all taken on him. He is a beautiful little boy, Nathan. I love him more than my own life. I've done everything I could to make Danny happy and to try and make him well. I promise you that, whatever you decide to do to me. I'm so sorry."

Nathan glared at Rebecca. She was sorry, but what for exactly? Now that was the question. *Hiding my son from me, the fact that Danny is ill, that I haven't been there for him through all this or for tearing out my heart when you took off?* He was trying to give himself a chance to calm his thoughts before he spoke but there were so many questions that needed answers. He didn't know where to begin.

All through his inner turmoil, Rebecca sat on the sofa before him. She was wringing her hands together so tightly that Nathan feared she might break one of her long, slender fingers. He tried not to see Rebecca in a sexual way, tried to ignore the spark of longing that was trying to ignite in his soul. This was the woman who had shattered his dreams, ripped out his heart, leaving behind a cold, dark place that he had never bothered to fill.

Emotions Nathan had sealed away, hidden behind the ice façade that he allowed the world to see, were now starting to bubble up inside him, threatening to erupt like a volcano. His rage and torment threatened to spew forth like molten lava. He was fighting a losing battle to keep it all contained when out of the corner of his vision he saw movement.

"Mummy, I couldn't sleep…"

Seeing his son for the first time was a bitter-sweet moment. Nathan fisted his hands at his side to stop himself from reaching out to touch his own flesh and blood. The boy looked nothing like the picture Nathan had folded in his pocket. His son looked so fragile, like a small gust of wind would knock him over. He was skin and bones, and so pale. Huge dark circles ringed his eyes and his head was near bald, covered only by a tiny speck-like growth of hair.

Nathan had never felt so helpless in his life. Being caught behind enemy lines or stuck in the middle of a gun battle seemed easy in comparison. He didn't know what to say, how to react to seeing this child – *his child*. So he said nothing and waited for Rebecca to guide him.

"Come give me a cuddle then, Dangerous Dan," Rebecca said to the child.

Nathan's breath caught in his throat as he watched Danny clamber onto Rebecca's lap. Seeing them together was crushing him. It was too much and yet he could not look away. He had missed so much already that Nathan vowed to himself that he was not going to let another moment pass by without him.

"Who's that?" Danny whispered.

Nathan thought he heard a hint of fear in the little guy's voice and didn't miss Rebecca's small intake of breath at the innocent question.

Fuck, I'm scaring my own son. Crack a smile, say something funny, stop feeling sorry for yourself and acting like a hard-assed son of a bitch for a minute and reassure the kid. Bec's going to have a meltdown any minute. Tell him you're an old friend of his mum – time enough to tell the truth later. No point adding to the poor kid's problems right now.

"I'm Nathan, a friend of your mum's, and you must be Danny. Pleasure to meet you, buddy." Nathan knelt down in front of his son and held out his hand. He hoped being at the same eye level would help clear the look of fear that radiated from Danny's face.

Danny's small hand reached out to him, and Nathan gently cradled it in his own, marveling at the sensation, all the while reminding himself to be careful. *It's so small compared to my own, so soft. His fingers are long, though, like Bec's but so delicate. This is my boy, my son, my flesh and blood here in front of me, touching me.*

It was at that precise moment that Nathan realized his life would never be the same again. This small, fragile boy, as sick as he was, had given Nathan back something he'd never thought he'd regain – his heart. The battered and bruised organ was now the source of the flood of pain inside his chest, as the emotions that he'd not allowed himself to feel in years washed over him. He could not stop the lone tear from slipping down his cheek.

Nathan took a moment to glimpse up over Danny's head and see how Rebecca was coping with it all. She too had tears rolling down her face.

Letting go of Danny's hand, this first connection to his son, was harder to do than Nathan could have possibly imagined but he didn't want to frighten the boy again. He set the little hand down, rested it back in Danny's lap and sat back on his haunches.

Nathan wasn't ready to leave. He needed to make up for so much lost time. "I dropped by to see if I could take you and your mum out for some lunch. Would you like that, Danny?"

Nathan saw a flicker of interest light up Danny's eyes but the boy turned to his mother, obviously waiting for her approval before he spoke. *I'm pushing, but fuck it, I want to spend more time with my son, and if Bec doesn't like it, she can just learn to live with it. The kid looks like he could use a bloody feed. I guess he'll probably want Maccas or something.* The words were racing through Nathan's head as he waited for Rebecca to comment. *She hasn't said a bloody word, and it's not like I know what's going on in that pretty head of hers.* Nathan continued to glare at Rebecca, hoping she understood by his expression that he did not want to fight her but would if pushed.

Watching Danny and Nathan together was both a dream and a nightmare. Rebecca was struggling for words. The icy stare Nathan had been giving her before Danny had entered the room was back. While he'd been talking to Danny, his eyes had shown nothing but kindness, affection for their son—the kind of look Rebecca remembered being the recipient of back before she'd walked away from their relationship. She missed that gaze and sadly understood Nathan would never look at her that way again. Her heart was heavy with the decisions she'd made so long ago.

One thing Rebecca did know was that she couldn't keep them apart any longer. Nathan deserved to know his son, and Danny certainly could use the love of this strong man to help him through his struggles. It wasn't a great idea to take Danny out to a populated place—his immune system was so run-down that even the slightest cold could have dire consequences. *Maybe we can pick up some takeout food and go to a quieter location, have a picnic in the park maybe... At least Nathan is including me.* "I guess if Danny wants to go out, we can. What do you say, Dangerous, feel up for an outing?"

Chapter Four

Rebecca was hidden behind Danny's bedroom door, listening to the sound of Nathan's deep voice reading their son a bedtime story. It brought tears to her eyes — tears of regret and shame, that she had robbed her son of a father figure all these years and Nathan of his son. The afternoon had flown by. Rebecca was amazed at how quickly Danny had warmed to Nathan. Usually he was withdrawn around strangers and not surprisingly, considering that most of the people he met lately were medical practitioners wanting to stick a needle in his arm or run some test. Her son had smiled more in the last few hours than he had in months. Nathan had even been able to encourage Danny to eat half of his burger and fries, even though he'd eaten pancakes not too long before. It wasn't exactly the healthiest of foods, but Rebecca didn't care. Seeing Danny eat with such enthusiasm was all that mattered. Danny had even talked Nathan into reading him the bedtime story.

Not being able to stand the shame any longer, Rebecca retreated to the kitchen, deciding to boil the kettle to make coffee, just so she had something to do—something to keep her from thinking about her own selfish behavior. She had loved Nathan—she really had—but she had been hurt that he had made the decision to join the dangerous squad without even consulting her.

As Rebecca poured hot water into the two mugs she'd placed on her kitchen bench, memories of that fated night came rushing back. It had all started out fine. Nathan had passed his corporal exam and they were supposed to be celebrating that achievement with a bottle of cheap wine at a local Italian restaurant. He'd been so happy with himself that night, and Rebecca, although not crazy about Nathan being in the military, had tried to appear enthusiastic.

After the meal they had returned to their tiny apartment, seeing who could shed their clothes first as they raced toward the bedroom. Rebecca had won easily, only having a dress, panties and sandals to peel off where Nathan had been in his camos and boots. Nathan had rewarded her soundly, bringing her to orgasm three times before his cock had entered her wet and eager pussy. He'd coaxed another orgasm from her body as he'd thrust into her, his groin pressing down onto hers, the pressure on her clit just right. They had known what the other needed back then. Had made love so many times there had been no secrets between them in bed. Her body and his had been like one when they joined.

Sated, Rebecca had snuggled in Nathan's arms, her head resting on his chest, then her world had come crashing down when he'd casually informed her of his career change.

"Penny for your thoughts."

Nathan's sexy drawl startled Rebecca and she sloshed hot coffee over her hand. "Ouch, don't do that. Sneak up on me like that. You're always doing it."

Nathan took the coffee mug from her and after turning on the tap, held her injured hand under the running water. The effect of his touch was unsettling, yet comforting at the same time, the burn from the spilled coffee not even registering compared to the heat on her skin from his touch. Nathan was standing so close to her Rebecca could hear him breathing, feel the warmth of his breath against the skin on her neck.

"Are you okay? How hot was the water?" Nathan asked.

Rebecca could hear genuine concern in his voice and it made her heart break even more. The man should hate her for what she'd done.

"It's all good, Nate. The coffee had cooled. I made you a cup if you want it—there, sitting on the bench." She used her free hand to indicate the cup she'd poured for him. "Black with no sugar still the way you have it?"

He knew he should step away, let go of her hand but he couldn't. There was still such a connection between them even after all this time. Touching Rebecca's hand had sent a bolt of something up Nathan's arm. It had felt as sharp as an electric current but one full of pleasure instead of pain. He was sick of pain.

Tired of blocking emotion from his life.

Their gazes collided. Rebecca's eyes filled with unshed tears. Nathan didn't know if the impending waterworks were a result of the burn or of the situation she was now forced to face. But one thing he did know was that he needed to move before he did something stupid—like kiss her damn lips.

"I could do coffee," Nathan finally managed to reply. He gave up his hold on Rebecca's hand and walked away from her tempting closeness. "I'm surprised you still remember how I take it," he said. He picked up the mug and took a mouthful. "You could always make a great coffee, Rebecca. That hasn't changed. Shame it's been so long between drinks, though."

It was time. They needed to discuss the future. While Nathan had been reading Danny the bedtime story, enjoying an event so many parents took for granted, he'd decided that another night away from his son would be one too many.

Whether Rebecca liked it or not.

There were plans to be made, like getting the guys to take up more of the responsibility running Haven Security. Jason didn't want to spend time out in the field and away from Toni these days anyway, so Nathan didn't think he'd have a problem there. Chris might not be quite as keen—the guy liked to be hands-on in the action department—but Nathan was sure that under the current circumstances, his team would have his back. First thing tomorrow he'd start putting these strategies in motion. Tonight he needed to apprise Rebecca of his decisions.

"So, time we talked tactics. Let's both take a seat and see what we can come up with. But I'm giving you a heads-up, Rebecca. I don't plan on leaving Danny's side for a very long time. I have seven years to catch up on and I'm not about to let you get in my way."

Rebecca sat—or more accurately fell into a chair. There was fear in her eyes as she met his gaze again.

"You can't take him from me, Nathan, for his sake and mine. If you have any mercy, you won't do that to me."

Nathan had already thought of the emotional distress and confusion it would cause his son if he and Rebecca could not come up with a viable option. There was only one way this could all work out. Either Nathan moved in with them or they moved in with him. Given that Rebecca's place was closer to the hospital, it would be more practical for him to move here. The only problem was that Nathan wasn't sure he could share such close quarters with the woman and stay sane. It was truly fucked up that even after all the pain Rebecca had caused him, just being in her presence made him still want her in his arms—and in his bed. He was such a fool.

"Well then, there is only one option available. I'm moving in here until Danny recovers."

"Moving in…? But it's only a two bedroom house, and what will we tell Danny? I don't think that will work, Nathan. There must be another option. I'm sure your wife or girlfriend would have a problem with it too. You can come by and visit him every day."

"Or I can go for custody and you can come by my place and visit him. I know a lot of people in high places, Bec. Do you really want me to go down that road? Could you live with just visiting your son? As for your concern over my relationship status, don't go worrying your pretty little head over it. I'm single. I wasn't going to make that mistake again. No woman is worth it." He was being a bastard—he knew it—but there was so much at stake here. Nathan wasn't even sure he could do it to Danny—rip him from his mother's arms—but Bec didn't have to know that. "So is there any significant other in your life that might make the mistake of trying to 'come to your aid'?" — Nathan made quotation marks in the air — "'Cause I'm more than happy to show him the error of his ways. This is my son and we are doing it my way."

Rebecca was glaring at him, her eyes wide and her mouth set in a firm line. *At least she's not going to put on the tears to try to sway me.* He was a tough bastard but Nathan hated seeing a woman cry.

"No significant other. I'm not such a great catch at the moment. You know, the whole single mother with ill child doesn't hold much appeal." Rebecca tried to put up a tough front as she snapped back at him. Nathan wasn't fooled, though. She was only just holding it all together.

"I can bunk down on the sofa or the floor if I have to. I've slept rougher. Shit, if you really want, I can pitch a tent in your backyard. I'm sure the neighbors would find that interesting." Nathan paused to see how his words were affecting Rebecca. "We tell Danny I'm his father, that I've been overseas on a mission. I don't care what we say but the boy gets told I'm his dad and I didn't desert him."

Rebecca was trying to come up with alternatives or more reasons to disagree with his demands, Nathan could see that and the moment she finally gave up the fight. She placed her arms on the table and lowered her head onto them. Nathan itched to soothe her, run his hands over her hair and comfort her, but he stayed strong.

"Well? Am I going to get my gear?"

Chapter Five

Nathan woke with the knowledge that he was being watched. The little puffs of air that wisped against his cheek were another giveaway. He realized it was Danny, his son, but didn't want to let on he was awake just yet. Nathan wasn't sure when he had drifted off to sleep but guessed it had been in the early hours of the morning. He'd spent a good part of the night evaluating his conversation with Rebecca and the aftermath, which had him stretched out on her sofa. He'd also replayed every moment of the time he'd spent with Danny.

He'd gone over and over the way he had handled things with Bec. He'd been a bastard making such strong demands, but it had worked. Today they were going to tell Danny that he was his father. Nathan had tried to rehearse what he would say to his son, tried to envisage the sort of questions Danny might ask. The thing that worried Nathan the most was explaining why he had been absent from Danny's life for so long without revealing to Danny that his mother was the reason for their separation. It was no use getting the kid upset with his mum. Bec had done what she'd thought was best and that could not be changed. Nathan had decided it was better to move on from here — show Danny that he was in it for the long haul and was not going anywhere.

Nathan cracked open one eyelid just a fraction to find Danny's face was just inches away from his own. His son's eyes — big and round — were staring down at him. Nathan couldn't stop himself from grinning.

"Well, hello there," Nathan said softly, not wanting to startle Danny.

"Why are you sleeping on the sofa?"

Nathan pondered how to answer the question for a moment, deciding that the truth would work best.

"I wanted to be here when you woke up, Danny. Thought we could have breakfast together. So what do you recommend? Maybe toast and Vegemite? Or Corn flakes? What's the menu like in this restaurant?"

Danny giggled. It was the most precious sound Nathan had ever heard.

"This is a house, not a restrant, silly. Mummy makes the food. You don't get to order. She just puts it on your plate and you have to eat it all. Sometimes I just don't wanna." Danny hesitated for a moment, his face scrunched up and his head tilted to the side. Nathan could almost see the wheels turning in his son's head as he thought something over. "I think I like pancakes the best."

Danny appeared so serious as he made his choice that Nathan had a hard time keeping a straight face. He had so much to learn about what made kids tick and all he wanted to do right at this minute in time was lift Danny up and give him a big hug, make a promise to his son that he would make the sickness go away, that everything would be fine. "Pancakes, an excellent choice," he said before he lost control and dragged the boy into his arms.

"We don't have to wait for your mummy to make them, though. I'm known all over the world as the Pancake King. Maybe I could whip you up a batch, if you can show me where your mum keeps the pans and the maple syrup?" Nathan slowly moved himself into a sitting position, aware that Danny was watching every move he made. *I wonder what's going on in that head of his.*

"You have lots of hair there." Danny pointed his finger at Nathan's chest.

Okay, not something I expected. "Yes I do. Some men have lots of hair on their chests, some have only a little." Again, Nathan decided that truth was the best option for his answer.

"Come on. The kitchen is this way."

Nathan was still dealing with the sudden direction change of their conversation when he felt Danny's touch on his hand. Looking down, he saw his son's small fingers wrapped around his wrist.

"C'mon. I'm hungry." His son's little hand pulled at him.

"Okay, one humungous platter of pancakes coming up."

Nathan took his son by the hand and let him lead the way into the kitchen. The boy's small frame walking beside him might have only reached the height of Nathan's hip but his presence there overwhelmed Nathan's heart and soul.

* * * *

The sounds of activity coming from her kitchen woke Rebecca. She could hear muffled voices but wasn't able to make out what was being said. It was obvious that someone — and she assumed it was Nathan — was making breakfast. *I guess when Nathan says he's moving in, he means it, including cooking breakfast.* Rebecca wasn't sure how Nathan's plan would work out for them all, especially crammed together in such close quarters, but Danny did deserve a chance to get to know his father.

She'd spent a good part of the night thinking about Nathan and his demands. She wasn't sure if she was shocked, but what did have her wondering was if Nathan would have really followed through on them — taken her son from her. The Nathan Rebecca had known had been a dominant, take control kind of guy but she wouldn't have thought that he'd be so cruel. *A lot has happened since those days. We've all changed. If I had asked myself ten years ago would I be the type to keep a father from his child, I would've been horrified at the idea. Look how that worked out! Who knows what horrible things Nathan has seen and done and how it might have changed him. I was right not to risk it. We just have to make this work, for Danny's sake.*

Dragging herself out of bed, still weary after such a restless night, Rebecca went through the motions of getting dressed. After making a quick trip to the bathroom, she headed to the kitchen.

She stopped a moment at the door to watch the interactions between her son and his father. It was one of those fantasy perfect moments she had dreamed of — Danny standing beside Nathan, her son's head tilted up a little listening to whatever it was his father was telling him. They both had their backs to Rebecca but she could see by the easy posture of both their stances that they were enjoying the moment. Another jab of pain slashed through her heart. *I should have told Nathan about Danny sooner.*

"Are you coming in to help us or are you going to stand there all day?"

Nathan's deep, sexy voice sent shivers up her spine. Nathan hadn't even turned around but he had sensed that she was there. Rebecca shook off her pain and walked toward her son.

"Good morning, Danny," she said as she bent down and kissed her son on the cheek, before turning her attention to the man currently taking up so much space in her kitchen. "Nathan."

"Hi, Mummy. We're making pancakes with banana. Want some?"

"The kettle's just boiled if you want coffee, Bec. Breakfast will be ready in a tick."

It was too much. The whole scene so normal, yet not. Rebecca was having a hard time taking it all in. Nathan, holding her frying pan, looking so damn relaxed talking about coffee and breakfast like they had done this all before. *We have, many times, before I did the bolt and screwed up all our lives. Why does he have to look so good? Those arms, biceps bulging every time he moves the pan. Those muscled thighs filling out his jeans to perfection. Oh my, his hair is messed. In all the years I knew him, his hair was so short it didn't move and now he has bed head... And the beard, it suits him so much. Rugged and handsome with that edge of bad boy thrown in – and I gave it all up. Get it together, Rebecca. You're drooling and your son is in the room, only a few feet away, still wearing his Spider-Man pajamas. Talk about inappropriate.*

"Ahem." Rebecca cleared her throat, hoping it would stop her out-of-control libido. *What the hell is wrong with me?* "I'll make the coffee then. Danny, would you like a hot chocolate or just a glass of milk?"

"Milk please, Mummy."

Rebecca set about making the coffee, trying to keep her mind busy on the tasks at hand. She poured a glass of milk for Danny then carried the three drinks over to the kitchen table, trying her best not to make any eye contact with Nathan for fear that he would see how shaken she was. She took her seat just as Nathan placed a plate full of pancakes in front of her.

"Smells great," she managed to mumble as the sweet scent of their breakfast mixed with the pure, masculine aroma she'd long associated with Nathan wafted through the air.

"Enjoy!" was Nathan's short response as he pulled out the chair beside her.

Danny sat opposite her and he was glowing with happiness, his smile a mile wide, as he picked up his fork, ready to dig in. If this was the result of spending just a small amount of time in Nathan's company, life was only going to get better for Danny when she told him the news.

There wasn't a lot of conversation happening as they all chewed away at their food. It wasn't a tension-filled time, just three people enjoying breakfast together. Rebecca was waiting for the right moment to start up the long overdue conversation. Her palms were sweating and she fought the urge to wipe them on her pants leg again. *Just do it and get it over with.*

"Hey, Dangerous, I have something really great I need to tell you. Can you put down your fork for a minute and listen." *My God, I don't think I've ever asked my son to stop eating before. Sounds weird. Stop procrastinating, Danny looks worried.*

"I promise, Danny, this is good news. Nothing about being sick or anything." Rebecca stole a glance toward Nathan, wondering if he realized what she was about to reveal. Judging by the absolute stillness of his body, she guessed yes.

Danny was staring at her. She could tell he wasn't convinced that this wasn't going to be another hospital talk, like so many of their *talks* in the past.

"You know how you sometimes ask me about your daddy and I tell you that he isn't around. Well, things have changed now, Danny. Your daddy is around. Actually, baby, he is sitting next to you."

Danny's head swung around to look at Nathan so fast it was a wonder he didn't fall off his chair.

"My daddy? Are you really him? Not just pretending?" Danny—his eyes so round they might pop right out of his head—asked Nathan.

It seemed to take Nathan an age to answer Danny. Rebecca was trying to decide whether she should jump in and help him.

"Yes, I sure am, buddy." Nathan brushed his hand over Danny's head. "Guess that makes you the Prince of Pancakes now."

"You're not really a king. I think you are a spy and that's why you had to stay away from mummy and me, 'cause you were busy spying and stuff."

"Really, is that what you think? A spy, huh?" Nathan replied with a chuckle.

Rebecca rolled her eyes.

I think my son has spent way too much time in front of the television. A spy's not far from the truth, though, and what's the prince thing about?

"Well, why else would you not come and see us? I don't even remember you."

"Oh, baby," was all Rebecca could manage to say in reply to her son's innocent yet damning words, as she fought to hold onto the tears that were threatening to spill. *Fuck, he might only be a child but he isn't pulling any punches. He's going to hate me for what I've done.*

"It's okay, Bec. I've got this one."

"I was a soldier, Danny. Your mother didn't know where I was when she found out you were in her tummy. I've only just found out about you, too. Your mum finally tracked me down and told me. I'm so sorry that I haven't been here with you before now, but I'm here to stay, Danny."

"Were you in the war against terror? I seen it on the news." Danny's voice was so serious.

Rebecca had never heard him sound so grown up. She hadn't even considered that a seven year old would know anything about the horrible events taking place around the world. *I've been so focused on Danny's illness that I've forgotten to talk to him about other things that happen, good or bad.*

"I've been to places that are not so great, buddy, seen some sad things when I was a soldier, but I don't do that anymore. It's really nice to know I have a little boy, though."

Rebecca was pleased with how Nathan had replied. She didn't really want a discussion on war at the kitchen table.

"I'm not that little. So did you have a big gun or a tank or a plane? Did you have to wear a hat and green pants?" Danny was firing off questions faster than Nathan could answer them. "Did you know I have had to have lots of needles and sometimes they make me puke?"

"Slow down, baby. You and Nathan have plenty of time to get to know one another. Nathan is going to live here with us." Rebecca tried to distract Danny away from his current train of thought—away from the guns, the Army and his illness—and back on the issue that was hopefully good news — of Nathan being his father.

"It's all good, Bec. I don't mind answering Danny's questions. Yes to the gun, but I had to spend a long time learning how to use it. Yes, I've been in a tank and a plane. I still have my uniform packed away. I can show it to you one day, son. Your mum told me all about your trips to the hospital. You've been quite the brave soldier yourself, son. I'm really proud of you."

Danny jumped from his seat and moved to stand between his mum and Nathan.

"You just called me son. So does that mean I can call you Dad?"

"I would really, really love that, son."

"Yippee! I got a dad!" Danny shouted. He jumped around the kitchen, pumping the air with his fist.

Chapter Six

It had been a week since Nathan had moved in. Seven nights that Rebecca had spent warring with herself over inviting or even begging him into her bed. Not that she thought he would accept any such invitation, but having Nathan sleeping so close, the slightest chance to be wrapped up in his arms—so strong and comforting, holding her once again—had been a nightly fantasy she could not ignore.

During the day Nathan had been nothing short of a blessing. His help in caring for Danny was invaluable—so long she'd carried the burden on her own. Rebecca's family and friends had stepped in when they could just to give her a break but she'd always felt guilty not being with her son. Sharing the parental role with Nathan had come easier than she ever would have believed.

Some of her favorite times over the last few days were ones that she stole. Moments where she stood unseen and just observed. She watched Nathan and Danny sitting side by side on the floor, playing cars or heads down deep in concentration as they built a new

Lego masterpiece. Seeing Nathan sprawled out over Danny's bed, her son propped up between his legs, Danny's back resting against Nathan's strong chest, as they battled away on the Nintendo. They were all perfect, memorable moments. Rebecca's all-time best memory, though, was seeing Danny bowling a cricket ball to Nathan. It had been so long since her son had done or wanted to do any kind of sporting activity.

Seeing the happiness Nathan brought to her son, the way he had lifted Danny's spirits, made her feel guiltier than ever for keeping them apart. She'd thought she'd been doing the right thing, saving Danny from future heartache. She had been so wrong. God, her boy looked healthier, and had eaten more this past week than she'd managed to coax down his throat in a month.

Rebecca gave one last look in the mirror. They were going into Nathan's place of work today, meeting his friends, and she wanted to look decent. She could only imagine what Nathan's friends must think of her. *Bitch, witch* and *heartless* were the words that came to her mind first. *I deserve their wrath. His friends will hate me for what I've done and I just have to take it on the chin.*

"You ready, Mummy?" Danny asked her as he ran into the room, his excitement for the upcoming adventure clear to see by his smile.

Rebecca would never tire of seeing her son running. She'd become so used to him struggling, too weak to remain standing for any length of time, that it was almost enough for her to believe in miracles.

"Ready when you are, Dangerous. Where's Daddy?" She didn't even stumble on the word this time. She'd seen the look on Nathan's face the first time Danny had referred to him as '*Daddy*'. The hardened gruff soldier had almost fallen over, the smile on his face enough wattage to light up a room, and since that time it had been one of her son's most used words.

"He is waiting for us in the car already. C'mon, Mummy. You take forever to get ready. I wanna see where the other spies work."

Rebecca had examined her feelings long and hard about it all and had decided that she really was happy that Danny and Nathan had found so much joy in each other's company. They both deserved the love they shared with one another. To be honest, she had started to enjoy the pretense of being a happy family. *Don't start thinking about rainbows and happy-ever-afters. Nathan will get tired of sharing his son with me eventually and take him away, just as he threatened. I'll be lucky to get alternate weekends and the occasional holiday. He hasn't shown any interest in me, other than where Danny is concerned.*

Her thoughts were depressing but Rebecca did need to remember that this time would come to an end, that this friendliness was all just for Danny's benefit. *One day he will be well enough to handle the truth, and Nathan will surely tell him everything.*

Shuddering at the implication, Rebecca forced a smile to her lips and took her son by the hand. "Let's go then."

It was entirely ridiculous that the Haven Security office was not even thirty minutes from Rebecca's home. *All this time he's been right here. Why didn't I reach out to him earlier? We could have passed each other a million times and not realized. Yeah, like I wouldn't have noticed him immediately, even with that sexy new facial hair he now wears. Men with looks like Nathan don't go unnoticed. My hormones would probably have jumped up and kicked me in the face.*

* * * *

"Here we are, Danno. This is Haven Security." Nathan sounded as excited as Danny's responding squeal.

The building was an old two-story terraced house, renovated, for sure. There was a driveway entrance to the left that Nathan had pulled the car into. He punched in a series of numbers on a remote control. A thick metal door opened, allowing Nathan to drive through and enter the underground parking, then it closed quickly behind them. Lights flicked on to show a space big enough to house about six vehicles. There were some already parked, including a Hummer, two four-wheel-drive type vehicles and an old sedan.

"Can we go meet some spies now?" Danny asked, and Nathan chuckled in response at the in joke he and their son shared way too often.

The sound was one Rebecca had heard on many occasions and it still caused the same response in her—one of longing. The more time she spent around Nathan, the more she missed what they'd once had.

"I've told you, little buddy, not spies, ex-soldiers who are really looking forward to meeting you. Do you need a hand with your seatbelt, son?"

"Nup, Dad. I got it undid all by myself."

"Undone, sweetheart, not *undid*," Rebecca added lamely, feeling like she really wasn't needed on this excursion.

They all exited the car.

"This way, the lift will take us up," Nathan said as he hoisted Danny up on his hip and headed toward a wall to his right. Rebecca couldn't see any lift door in sight. Nathan held the same remote in his hand and began playing with it again. As if by magic, the cement wall opened to reveal the elevator.

"Wowee! That was so cool, Dad, it's like the Batcave, with a secret entrance and everything!"

Rebecca could not help but nod her head in agreement with Danny. It was very impressive.

The roar was deafening, nearly scaring Rebecca out of her shoes. She turned to see what was happening and a motorbike skidded to a stop beside them. The rider was dressed head to toe in black leather, his helmet just as dark as the body armor.

"Who is that?" Danny whispered to Nathan, his voice holding no fear.

"For heaven's sake, Chris, would it kill you to put a muffler on that beast? You nearly deafened us," Nathan growled to the tall rider as he approached them.

The man removed his helmet and ran his hand through his blond hair. "You know I like to make an entrance, Nate. Sorry. I didn't realize anyone was down here."

"Are you a spy, a soldier or a baddie?"

Danny was on the right track with his question as far as Rebecca was concerned. The guy reminded her of her brother Matt. Well, at least the way Matt had looked the last time she'd seen him almost four weeks ago now, dressed up in his undercover persona of a bad guy biker. This new arrival certainly fit the same image, covered in so much leather and huge in stature. Rebecca had always thought Nathan was a big guy, over six feet in height and with shoulders so wide you couldn't see around them, but this Chris was even taller and broader than Nathan and with a face that would have women lining up just for a chance to meet him. Not that Rebecca went for that type – but she knew women who did.

"Hey there, little buddy, you must be Danny. Your dad's told me all about you," Chris said as he peeled a glove from his hand so he could offer his clenched fist to Danny to bump in greeting. Rebecca was now feeling a little in awe herself at the masculinity of the moment, her little man greeting this stranger like such a big boy. *When did he learn to do that?*

"I was a soldier, once. Now I work for your dad. So I guess that makes you my boss too."

Danny giggled.

"Let's go up," Nathan said.

Rebecca nearly tripped when she felt the heat from Nathan's hand on her lower back as he ushered her into the elevator. "Chris, this is Rebecca Hammerton, Danny's mother. Bec, Chris Winters."

Chris looked her way, his eyes giving no indication of any emotion he was feeling. They just blankly took in her measure. She felt like she was being sentenced and very soon would be found guilty. Trying to exude a confidence she really didn't possess, she spoke, "Hello, Chris, it's good to meet you."

"Yes, ma'am, good to finally meet you too," he replied but his voice did not match his words.

The tension in the lift was palpable. To her shock, Nathan took her hand into his and gave it a squeeze. He was showing her support and she was the last person that deserved it. When the doors finally opened, Rebecca was relieved to step away from her close proximity to Chris. Not that she feared he would hurt her. She just didn't like the waves of condemnation that exuded from him.

Unfortunately it was straight into the line of fire of another two unfriendly pairs of eyes. *Jason and Toni, I presume.* Nathan had spoken of the couple many times. Rebecca had gotten the impression that they were his closest friends. *Great, here goes. Why do I feel like I'm about to face a firing squad?*

Nathan lifted Danny from his hip and placed him on the carpeted floor. "Jason, Toni, this is my son Danny and his mother, Rebecca Hammerton."

The couple stood still for a moment. It was the woman, Toni, who made the first move — she walked toward Rebecca, her hand outstretched in greeting.

"Nice to meet you, Rebecca," she said in a tone that was almost friendly before turning her attention to Danny and kneeling down in front of him. "My, my, what a handsome young man. You look just like your daddy."

"Hold on there, sweetheart, I hope you're not implying Nate is handsome. I'm much better looking than him," the man who had been introduced as Jason piped in. "Great to meet you, buddy. Good to have another soldier on deck," he said as he walked up to her son and did the same fist bump with Danny as Chris had done earlier.

"My daddy is hamsom... And so am I, my mummy said so," Danny told Jason as Rebecca cringed in embarrassment. Last thing she needed was for Nathan to think she spoke of him in that way. Their life was awkward enough at the moment. The sound of the men chuckling did not help.

"Thanks, little buddy. Good soldiers have each other's backs. Glad to know you've got mine." Nathan did not seem fazed by Danny's admission, thankfully.

"What does that mean, Daddy?"

"It means we look after each other, son," Nathan explained. "You want to see my office, Danny? Bec, you coming?"

"Sure, lead the way." Hell yeah she was going with Nathan—last thing Rebecca wanted was to be left with his three friends. She might not make it out alive.

"I thought Rebecca and I might go do a little shopping, have a coffee, get to know each other," the only other female in the room said, much to Rebecca's horror.

OMG, how the hell will I get out of this one? Rebecca was still trying to think of some excuse to refuse Toni's invitation as she was being dragged away in the opposite direction to the one her son and former lover walked.

"Just suck it up, Rebecca, and come with me," Toni whispered in her ear. "I think you could do with someone in your corner at the moment and I need to work out if you're worthy."

Chapter Seven

Before she knew it, Rebecca was sitting in a coffee shop with a latte and a gigantic slice of some kind of calorific cheesecake in front of her. Toni was certainly going all out to sweeten her up for the impending confrontation. At the moment, though, the woman was just sitting opposite Rebecca and had hardly said a word. It was getting pretty awkward and past time to get to the point of this charade of girly get to know each other time.

"So, what's this all about, Toni? Why did you bring me here? I'm assuming as a friend of Nathan's, you won't be all that impressed with me at the moment," Rebecca stated bluntly.

"Well, can you blame us? Why would you keep his son a secret for so long?"

Toni certainly didn't mince words but Rebecca was pleased they were getting to the point quickly. She took a sip of her latte and tried to think of how to describe the worst decision of her life.

"I'll give you the condensed version. When Nathan told me he was signing up for the Special Forces unit, I knew I couldn't make it as that kind of Army wife. It was hard enough when he was a regular soldier but at least I knew where he was and had some sort of timeframe for when he would return to me. He didn't even consult me about it—find out if I was on board with his career change. He just went ahead and joined up. I'd met some of the wives of men from that area of the Army. They were stronger than I was, able to handle the secretive and the unknown. It would have driven me insane, Toni. It was never about not loving Nathan. It was that I loved him too much to handle the idea of losing him that way. I thought, at the time, that it was better to leave him than mourn his death."

Rebecca's mouth had gone dry, so she took another mouthful of the cooling drink. Talking about that time in her life was unpleasant, especially now with the knowledge that Nathan had not only survived his time in the unit but had also left the Army, something Rebecca had only dreamed of him doing back then.

"You knew he was a soldier when you met. It wasn't fair you walked out on him for that."

"You're right I guess, Toni. I thought I could handle it all—the time spent apart, the rules and regulations. The danger." Rebecca sighed sadly before adding, "I couldn't."

"Okay, so life didn't turn out the way you wanted with Nathan. I can get that. Jason and I were in a dangerous situation not long ago. When he stood in front of me to protect me from getting shot, I realized how much I would have lost if he'd been killed. But keeping Danny a secret all this time... How could you?"

"Oh, Toni, if only I could take back that dreadful decision. How can I possibly explain my selfishness to you?" Rebecca could feel her tears forming. She tried to continue before they spilled from her eyes. "I didn't realize I was pregnant at first. I thought about contacting Nathan when I found out but he'd already gone somewhere" — Rebecca made quotation mark signs in the air — "'classified'. The more I thought about it, and the longer it went on, I convinced myself it was better for me not to tell him. I didn't want my son to go through the torment of never knowing when his daddy would be back or be going again — or die. I never told anyone who Danny's father was. I think my family probably guessed — he looks so much like Nathan — but I refused to talk about it."

"What did you tell Danny, Rebecca? Didn't he ask who his father was?"

"Sometimes I told him all he needed was me. Other times I just said his father was not around. For some reason Danny just accepted that. I think when he got so ill, everything else sort of became less important. He had to struggle to get through each day and I was there for him every step of the way. I'm so scared Nathan will take him away from me, Toni. I know I've done a horrible thing, but Danny is my life. He is everything to me — the reason I had to reach out to Nathan and ask for help. Now I have to live with the consequences."

Until Toni handed her a napkin, Rebecca hadn't realized she was crying. She did her best to try to pull herself together, wiping up her spilled tears and blowing her nose. Breaking down in front of Nathan's friends, especially his female ones, was not going to sway their opinion of her. Rebecca wasn't vying for sympathy. She was crying for what could have been if she had made other choices — the right choices.

"Have you told Nathan any of this?" Toni asked.

"We haven't really talked about anything. We just go through each day looking after Danny and making him happy. Nathan makes him happy. Once upon a time Danny fretted if he couldn't see me, if I left a room he was in. Now he doesn't care as long as Nathan is there with him."

"Does that make you jealous, Rebecca? Having to share your son with Nathan, maybe not being the center of his world anymore?"

"Not in the least. Toni, just seeing them together...seeing my son so happy, seeing how much Nathan cares for him, loves him… It's beautiful. I feel like a monster for denying Danny that love for so long and the strength Nathan has been able to bring to this horrible situation, especially at a time when Danny needed that strength."

"Has he brought you strength too, Rebecca? Being around Nathan Haven can sometimes be overwhelming. Don't get me wrong. I love him like a brother, but the man is serious personified. I can count on one hand the times I've seen him smile. To be honest, when I heard he had a son I was gobsmacked. I nearly fell over when he waltzed out of that lift with Danny on his hip. The poor little waif looks pretty beat up. I can't imagine how hard Danny's illness must have been on you—chemo, radiotherapy, all those medical procedures on your little boy." Toni paused and placed her hand over Rebecca's. "It must have been hard to stand by and see it all. I think you deserve my friendship and my help, just for what you have endured so far. You made a huge mistake, but Nathan didn't come chasing after you when you first left. Maybe if he had, things might have been different. Eat your cheesecake. I'll get us a coffee refill and then we'll head back to the office."

"It really is good cake and I never knock back a coffee. Thanks, Toni, and please, call me Bec." Rebecca was surprised at how comfortable she felt discussing her private life and her fears with Toni. The young woman certainly didn't pull any punches. She was direct and said what was on her mind. Rebecca liked that about Toni, and in different circumstances could imagine becoming close to her. It had been years since she'd had a close female friend, looking after Danny took up most of her time. But could she really befriend someone in Nathan's life? Did she have a right?

Chapter Eight

Nathan was starting to worry. He glanced at his watch again. It had been almost an hour and there was still no sign of Toni or Rebecca. He couldn't for the life of him think of what the women could possibly be talking about for so long. They'd only just met.

"You really are distracted, Nate. Did you just hear anything I said?"

"Jason, I was just wondering what was taking Toni and Bec so long. You don't think Toni will give her a hard time, do you?"

Jason laughed, and Nathan had the distinct impression that he was laughing at him.

"You really don't know women at all, mate. Cake, coffee and chat—shit it's what they do best. And talk about men, and in this case that would be you, I'd say."

Nathan groaned, "Yeah that's what worries me."

"So what's the deal with you and Rebecca? You seem comfortable around her, considering."

Nathan wasn't so sure he wanted to put into words his feelings for Rebecca, especially to Jason. He needed to figure it out for himself first.

"At the moment my priority is my son. And the best thing for Danny is Bec and me getting along." It had stirred him up a bit emotionally seeing Danny sitting at his desk earlier, even more seeing his son in front of a computer screen seated next to Chris, hearing their laughter coming from the other room as they concentrated on whatever game it was they were playing. The way his mates had just accepted Danny without hesitation made Nathan feel blessed.

Nathan was going to need these men to help him get through this. It terrified him. He couldn't stop thinking about the fact that he might only have Danny for a short time.

"I don't know what I'm gonna do if the bone marrow thing doesn't work out, or I'm not a match, mate. I can't lose him, not now — not after only just finding out about him. Fuck, why didn't she tell me, Jason? Was I that much of a prick to be around back then?" Nathan hadn't meant to voice his concerns, the thoughts had just slipped out. He wasn't the sharing type usually. But he'd felt like he'd been swimming against a raging river ever since he'd met Danny.

"I dunno, man. Have you asked her? As for Danny, let's take it one step at a time, like we did in commando training. Focus on making it through the next hour, dealing with that, before worrying about anything else. Together, as a team, we will make it work. You know we're all here for you, whatever you need. We can all get tested, just in case you're not matched. Hell, we can put the call out to every damn soldier we know if we have to."

Nathan had never been so thankful to have his team watching his back. Chris, Jason, Martin—they were all there for him and it made Nathan feel humble—and hopeful. They could do this. Danny would get well. Nathan would not accept any other outcome.

"Hey, Daddy, I'm thirsty, and Chris said I had to ask you first before he'd give me a lemonade. Can I have one, please?"

Nathan smiled at his son. "You tell Chris I said it was fine. Are you hungry, son? I think there are some cookies in the kitchen if you want one."

Danny returned his smile and headed back out of the office. Nathan could hear him telling Chris that he was allowed the lemonade and a biscuit. Nathan had learned early on that getting Danny to eat was important, so he was pleased to hear his son interested in having a snack.

"Fuck, I feel like I've slipped into some alternate universe. The kid looks like a mini you, Nate, even given how unwell he is. And you, buddy... Don't think I've ever seen you look so happy. The smile you gave when Danny came in, weird seeing it on your face. Liking it, though, mate. I really hope this all works out for you." Jason was still seated in the chair on the other side of Nathan's desk and didn't look like he had any intention of moving. Nathan had wanted to go through some paperwork, get an idea of what jobs were on the agenda but it didn't appear that plan was going to happen.

"Rebecca's the one that got away, isn't she?" Jason asked as he leaned forward, his elbows resting on the desktop. "The one you told me about that night back in Jalalabad when we were trying to stay awake and not get our asses blown off."

"Yep, she's the one."

"So you told me you regretted letting her go, not fighting for her. Seems to me that she's back in your life now. Maybe this is a chance to put things right, or at least give yourself an opportunity to put those regrets behind you."

"When the fuck did you get so philosophical? Who the hell are you, and what have you done with Jason? Toni really does have you pussy-whipped, rattling off that sort of advice." Even though Nathan reacted with sarcasm, he saw Jason's point. The idea of getting back with Rebecca was never far from his thoughts lately. He just wasn't sure that the timing was right, not with the possibility of Danny's bone marrow transplant coming up.

"I'm not sure now is the right time. Danny has a fight ahead of him, Jason. The bone marrow transplant is easy for me or whoever can donate but not for him. Martin explained it all to Bec and me, in layman terms. Those docs at the kids' hospital talk in a foreign language most of the time. Well, that's what it sounds like when they use all the medical terms for what's going to happen."

"So, tell me what is going to happen. I've already said the team is here for you, mate."

"Before they can put new marrow into him, they have to give him a massive dose of chemo and radiotherapy to kill off any cells that might try to reject the donor marrow. I feel sick thinking we are going to put him through that again. The poor tyke's been through so much already. He hates needles, doctors—anything to do with hospital. Can't blame him. He's going to be so miserable, Jason. I can hardly bear to think about it."

"But it's for the best, right? Give him a chance at survival in the long run."

That was the dilemma he and Bec faced. Bone marrow transplant wasn't always successful, especially from a parent. They'd been given the statistics. Marrow from a sibling had a far better chance of success. But even if he and Bec were prepared to conceive another child, it might all be too late for Danny.

"It's not the best option but it's the only one we have. I have to be a match. That's all there is to it. If Danny goes out of remission, the doctors don't think he'll make it. His body is too weak."

"That's just fucked up. Poor Rebecca. How the hell has she been dealing with this all by herself? She must be some strong woman. I'm struggling just hearing about it. Can't imagine seeing a child suffering, let alone my own child."

Jason had hit the nail on the head. Nathan didn't know how the hell Bec had stood up to it all and remained strong. Yet she faced each day with a smile and never let Danny see her any other way. He certainly admired her for that.

"But if she'd told me about my son earlier, I would have stood by her through it all. We could have shared the responsibility of caring for Danny."

"You're right, Nate. She should have told you from the start. There must be a reason she didn't. You need to talk to her about it. When did Danny first get ill? Were we still serving? Would you have even known straight away? We were gone most of the time back then. Would you have been able to deal with it all? A distracted soldier is a dead soldier, mate. Maybe in some twisted sense of fate, this is how it was meant to be for you and Bec and Danny?"

Nathan didn't have time to digest what Jason had said because Toni and Bec appeared at his door.

"Hey, guys, we're back. Didja miss us?"

"Nathan was just about to send a search party out to find you both, but I set him straight. Cake and coffee can't be rushed. Isn't that right, luv?"

"Oh, Jason, I have taught you well. See, Bec? Men can learn anything, given time and the right incentive," Toni said before plonking herself down in Jason's lap.

"Make yourself at home, Toni. It's only my office," Nathan grumbled before turning his attention to Rebecca who was hovering in the doorway—not really in his office or out, but somewhere in between.

"Bec, everything all right? You're welcome to come all the way in and pull up a chair. I was going to check up on a few things, but it appears the newlyweds aren't going anywhere, so it can wait."

"Thanks, Nate. I wasn't sure if I was intruding. I was going to hang with Danny, but apparently he and Chris are having boy time. I got the impression our son didn't want me cramping his style now he has a new friend to play with."

Nathan chuckled. "Well, Chris certainly is a big kid, so I can see why Danny and he have bonded. He'll be fine, Bec. I'd trust Chris with my life. Oh, and Chris gave Danny something to drink and I think he may have eaten a biscuit. We probably should get some lunch soon, though."

"Come on in, Rebecca," Jason added. "I think keeping Nathan away from working is a great idea. Life's been so much easier for Chris and me while he's been away."

"Is that right? Well, when the money stops coming in because you guys let the company go to wrack and ruin, Jason, don't complain about the lack of pay."

Rebecca had pulled up a chair next to where Toni and Jason lounged. Nathan didn't think she looked all that relaxed, though. He really hoped Toni hadn't upset her but wasn't sure what to do.

"So, what did you and Toni chat about for so long, Bec?" Direct had always worked for Nathan in the past, so he figured he might as well try it now.

But Bec didn't answer him. She just looked over to Toni and smiled.

"Women's business, Mr. Haven. If we told you, we'd have to kill you," Toni replied then gave a little giggle.

Seeing both women smiling was enough for Nathan to reassure him that Toni hadn't caused Bec any emotional distress on his behalf. How bad could it have been if they were ganging up on him already? "Well, I wouldn't want you to disclose any state secrets, so I won't push you."

"Beware, Nathan. I know that tone in my wife's voice. I think we are in trouble, buddy. These women are going to cause us some problems, I fear." Jason gave his wife a peck on the cheek.

"Ah, but they forget, Jason. Handling trouble is what we specialize in."

"Why, Nathan, I do believe you are acting playful. I never thought I'd see the day." Toni placed her hand over her heart, like she was about to have an attack or something.

Nathan rolled his eyes at her.

"I think having Bec around is going to be so much fun. It's time I had someone to watch my six—or whatever it is you guys say," Toni added playfully.

Chapter Nine

"Is Danny asleep?"

"Yes, I think Chris wore him out. But in a good way, Bec, don't panic. He is asleep with a smile on his face. I haven't seen that before."

It amazed Rebecca that Nathan could still read her like a book. Yes, she'd flinched when he'd mentioned that Danny had been tired, but it was only the slightest movement. Yet Nathan had noticed and quickly assured her everything was okay.

"Do you want something to drink — coffee, beer?"

"Why don't we share a bottle of wine, Bec? I think we need to talk. Maybe a bit of alcohol will help loosen our tongues." Nathan didn't wait for her to respond. He opened the fridge and grabbed a bottle, dispensing with the cork efficiently before filling two glasses.

Rebecca was apprehensive as she had no idea what Nathan wanted to talk to her about this time. She wondered if it had anything to do with their trip to his office. She'd thought it had gone well. After that initial introduction, when it had been a little strained, everyone had calmed down and treated her in a courteous manner. Bec really was starting to grow fond of Toni. The way she teased the big, strong men all the time, she had them wrapped around her little finger. They all loved her. That was obvious. Jason, her husband, adored her.

"Do you want to sit here or in the lounge?" she asked, nerves making her words come out a bit squeaky.

"Let's get comfortable and take our drinks in there," Nathan replied, nodding his head toward the lounge. He took the drinks and walked in that direction.

Rebecca followed behind slowly, her apprehension growing with each step.

Nathan placed the wine glasses on the coffee table and took a seat on the sofa. "Come and sit here beside me. We can talk quietly this way, no chance of disturbing Danny." Nathan patted the sofa cushion next to him.

Rebecca was frozen on the spot for a moment just watching Nathan's hand as he tapped the spot he wanted her to sit in. It was too close to him but she did as he'd requested, ignoring any thoughts she had over trying to stay a safe distance away from his oh so tempting body.

She reached over and picked up a glass of wine. "So, Nathan, what did you want to talk about?" She figured the quicker they got this conversation out of the way, the faster she could retreat to the sanctuary of her bedroom and fantasize about what wicked ways she could have pleasured him if the circumstances had been different. But for now, she needed to keep those thoughts at bay and her hands to herself.

"Us. I want to talk about us. What happened. Why you left me."

Here it was. The conversation she'd been dreading. How was she going to explain her decisions to Nathan? Would he understand her mindset at the time? Did it even matter?

"It was a long time ago, Nathan. Do we really need to go back there?"

Nathan was staring at her. His piercing gaze made her fidget. "Yes, I do, Bec. I need to understand why you ripped out my heart, why you disappeared without any reason and why you didn't feel the need to tell me I had a son. If there is any hope for us. Did you even love me at all?"

'Any hope for us' – what does that mean? Is it possible Nathan still has feelings for me or is this all about Danny? Some honorable gesture to do the right thing? Hope, a tiny little root of it, grew inside her.

"I loved you, Nathan. I really did. It was you trying out for the Green Berets that scared me enough to run. I didn't think I could handle it – you away for unspecified amounts of time, never knowing where you were, what you would be doing. You were going to be right in the thick of the danger. If I stayed and you were killed, I don't think I would have survived it. I ran before I had to face the unknown."

"I was a soldier when we met. You knew the score from the beginning, Bec. Why didn't you say something to me? We could have discussed it – how you felt. I would have done anything to make you happy, Bec."

"That's just it, Nate, I did know that but I also didn't want to be responsible for you making a decision just to please me. You were so excited about being selected to try out for the Green Berets, and I knew you would get it. You never failed at anything you put your mind to. You decided on that life. I couldn't let you give it up for me and hate me later. So, I left. You hated me, yes, but you became the soldier you wanted to be."

Rebecca took a long drink of her wine. She needed the numbing action of the alcohol more than ever. Her heart was breaking having this conversation. She'd been so young and foolish, made such a mess of everything. In hindsight she would have dealt with all the things that had scared her. They were nothing compared to what she faced with Danny on a daily basis.

Nathan was thinking about what she'd said. She could tell. She knew him as well — that tic over his right eye when he was mulling over something. The twitch of his top lip, when it was distasteful or something he didn't agree with. She'd seen them all before.

"What about Danny?" he finally asked.

"I didn't know right away. I was so upset trying to deal with not having you in my life. I ignored the early signs of pregnancy. When I finally did realize, you had been shipped out. I didn't know how to contact you. It wasn't something I believed I could tell you over the phone or by email. I didn't want you to feel like you had to do the right thing — give up the Army. Nothing had changed in that regard. The reasons why I left in the first place still remained the same. Then as the years went on, it just got harder. How did I make that confession to you? Then Danny got sick and I didn't have time to worry about me or you. I had enough on my plate and mind, just caring for our son. But I'm so sorry, Nathan. I wish I could turn back the clock and make the right decision — tell you I was pregnant, that you had a beautiful son, to stay safe so you could come home and be a father to him. I made so many mistakes, Nate, but keeping

Danny from having a father is the most reprehensible. My son deserved better from me."

Nathan had guessed most of Rebecca's reasons before she'd confessed them. Being honest with himself, he'd probably known from the start why Bec had left him. She was right. He hadn't discussed it with her before he'd signed up with the Green Berets because he'd known she wouldn't be pleased. Nathan had assumed, wrongly, that she would just accept his decision and learn to live with it. He'd been selfish. He wasn't even sure he would have been mature enough back then to take much interest in any pregnancy. Yeah, he would have been pleased, but his mindset back then—as was the same of many of his soldier buddies—had been that wives looked after the children while the soldiers fought the wars. Looking back on those years, Nathan also remembered that he'd only been able to go home a handful of times. His son would hardly have known him anyway.

Tears were rolling down Rebecca's cheeks. She looked so miserable and tired. Nathan reached for her, pulled her body against his.

"Shhh, baby, don't cry. I understand," he soothed as he stroked his fingers through Bec's soft hair. "You did what you had to do. I was wrong. I should have talked it out with you before I signed up. I was selfish, expected you to just go along with what I'd decided. I'm so sorry, Bec. I've let us all down—you, Danny, myself."

"It hurt so much to leave you—I cried for weeks, holed up at my parents place hoping you would come and find me, try to talk me into coming back to you—but you didn't."

Rebecca's voice was muffled as her face was pressed against his shoulder, but Nathan had heard every word she'd said. He'd thought about trying to find her, sweet talk her into coming back to him, but he'd been too stubborn. Pride had gotten in the way of sanity.

"It wasn't until after you left that I realized how much you meant to me, but I let my pride overrule my heart. I've never let another woman get close to me since. You were it for me, Bec. I was just too stupid to do anything about it. But I'm not that stupid, selfish boy anymore."

Nathan knew he needed to put himself and his heart on the line, show Bec how much he loved her—had always loved her. Seeing how strong she was, how much she loved Danny, how she had devoted her life to their son, only made his feelings for her that much stronger. He not only respected Bec but admired her courage in the face of such adversity, how she was dealing with the cruel disease attacking their son. It was a harder battle than anything he had faced over the years. Of that, Nathan had no doubt. But his head reigned over his heart and he kept the words to himself. *Maybe it's too soon to start making declarations like that, I might spook her. I can show her how much I want and need her, how much she means to me, though—with my hands and my body.*

Nathan gathered Bec up in his arms. He got to his feet and, carrying her, Nathan headed toward her bedroom. "Let me make love to you, Bec. Show you how much I want you. Do you want that too, Bec? To feel me inside you again? It's been so long," he whispered into her ear.

When he reached her room, Nathan gently set Bec back on her feet. He needed to hear her agree before he could continue. Had to make sure she was on the same page. Threading his fingers through her hair again, he whispered, "I like your new hairstyle."

"I shaved my head the first time Danny had chemo."

Her reply gutted him. Rebecca was stronger than any woman he'd ever met. "Oh, babe, I wish I'd been there to help you both through it."

"I know you do, Nathan. I'm so sorry."

"Shh, enough of that, babe. We need to move on. Will you let me make love to you, Bec?"

"Yes," she replied quietly, and Nathan could not help the sigh of relief that slipped from his lips.

"Thank God," was all he said before taking her back into his arms and smothering her mouth under his.

Rebecca tasted like paradise, like home. Even in his fantasies Nathan had not remembered exactly how wonderful it felt to kiss Rebecca. If he wasn't so damn hard, he would have liked to stay in this moment for a long time, but he was close to losing it.

Rebecca's little moan of displeasure when he broke from her lips proved to Nathan that she was just as into the moment as he was.

"I want to see all of you. It's been so long, Bec. I want to take my time, peel each layer of clothing off you slowly, enjoy your sexy body at my leisure."

"I don't think I can stand it slow, Nate, I want you so much," Rebecca replied breathlessly.

Nathan started on the buttons of Rebecca's shirt, releasing each fastening until he could push the material from her shoulders. Her chest was rising up and down, the curved swell of her breasts hypnotizing him. Nathan unclasped her bra and let it fall to the floor. "Your nipples are hard and just begging for my attention," he said before lowering his head and taking one of the beaded nubs between his lips.

Rebecca's back arched, pressing her body into his, and Nathan placed his arm around her hips to fasten her to him as he worshiped first one nipple before moving on to the other.

"So responsive to me, babe. I bet your pussy is wet, too."

"Nathan, please. Stop teasing me. I need you. I want to feel you, too. Take your shirt off."

He would give Rebecca that much but he had to keep his pants on, at least for the moment. Trying to keep his dick in line was becoming a problem. Nathan wanted to pleasure Bec first before he took his own, and after all this time, he was worried that once he sank into her sweet cunt, it would be over before he knew it. Nathan pulled his T-shirt over his head then dropped it to the growing pile of discarded clothing.

"Let's move this to the bed."

She giggled as he swooped her up into his arms and carried her the few steps to her bed.

As Nathan placed Rebecca on top of her flowery patterned quilt, he hooked his fingers into the waist of her skirt and pulled it down her body. She was wearing plain white underwear but on her it looked sexy as hell.

"Bec, you are still the sexiest woman I've ever seen. What it does to me, seeing you like this..." Nathan groaned before lowering his head to the junction between her thighs. He could smell her arousal. It was intoxicating. After ridding her of her panties, Nathan spread her pussy lips with his thumb and finger. Her clit was visible to him—the sight of her swollen nub made his mouth water. He needed to taste her.

"Oh, Nathan, make me come."

"Tell me what you want, Bec. Do you want me to touch you?" Nathan placed a finger knuckle-deep inside her cunt, being careful not to touch her clit.

"Yes," Bec replied, her voice a plea.

"Or do you want my tongue inside your cunt? Want me to make you come as I lick your pretty pussy dry."

Rebecca lifted her hips toward his face.

He chuckled. "Tongue it is then."

He was killing her, just as Nathan always did. Sexually teasing her into a frantic state, but Rebecca knew it would be worth it. Nathan Haven was a master at making her orgasm. It appeared that the passing of time had not changed that one bit. She was primed and ready to go just from his foreplay.

"Just do it already," she groaned.

The first lick of his tongue was like being hit with an electric shock…but in a good way. Every nerve ending stood up and took notice. Rebecca's body strained to feel the next touch. Her body buzzed with anticipation.

Then Nathan got serious. Each lave and stroke, each thrust of his finger into her eager pussy building into something immense. Pleasurable sensations were controlling her mind, sending her climbing to embrace that point of ecstasy. It was all about Nathan and what he was making her feel. At that point nothing else mattered. The past, the future, it was all about this moment.

She was so close. Her stomach muscles clenched as she reached out for that bliss. When it came, the surge of pleasure was so intense it washed over her, encasing Rebecca in a bubble of warmth.

"Oh my God, Nathan," she wept as emotion welled up inside her. This was what she had dreamed off,

Nathan touching her again. Nathan being beside her — or between her legs, as the case was — she couldn't believe it was actually a reality, had an impulse to pinch her own skin just to make sure this wasn't some dream she was about to awaken from.

No, this is real. Nathan moved from his position between her legs. Stood up, so he towered over her from the end of the bed. *So real my heart is about to be ripped in two. Please don't be leaving.* "Nate, don't go yet. I want a chance to return the pleasure you just gave me."

"Oh, honey, I'm not going anywhere. We've only just begun." Nathan's hungry gaze as he looked at her relieved Rebecca's fears. It took her breath away.

Never in a million years had Rebecca thought she would be on the receiving end of that lust-filled look again. It made her tummy go all swirly and her nipples tingle.

Nathan unzipped his fly, and Rebecca's mouth went dry in anticipation. He had the most gorgeous body, and the years had only managed to make it more sculptured. Every muscle was accentuated. Rebecca couldn't wait to explore and kiss each tempting hollow and ridge.

"Hmm, the years have been good to you, Nate. I don't think I've ever seen a man with a better body than yours. You must have had to fight the women off with a bat." The words left a sour taste in her mouth as Rebecca fought to ignore the images forming in her mind of Nathan with other women. *But it would be even more ridiculous if I tried to believe he hadn't. Like I have a right to care how many nights he's spent with other women — I left him.*

Nathan just shook his head at her comment. He had produced a condom and was rolling it onto his cock.

Rebecca hadn't seen where the rubber had come from but was glad that he'd remembered. "I hope you have a supply of those, because I've run out." Not that she'd had any at all but Rebecca wasn't about to let Nathan in on the fact that her sex life was nonexistent.

"You forget, I was a Boy Scout—always prepared." Nathan gave her a wide, toothy grin, the smile reminding her of the cheeky, playful Nathan from her past.

"You forget, I know all about your past. You were never a Boy Scout. Now get back here and let me at you."

As soon as he was in reach, Rebecca dragged Nathan down on top of her. As she knew he would, he braced at the last minute so as not to crush her. It was one of Rebecca's favorite sights. Nathan's biceps bulging as his arms, placed either side of her head, took his weight, perfectly aligned with her eyes so she could devour the view and if she turned her face to the side, she could place kisses, or bite or lick the rugged muscles.

"Decisions, decisions… I never know what to do with those tempting biceps of yours and you always fall for that move," she said and sighed as she rolled her head from side to side, getting a perfect view of Nathan's arms.

"Kiss me, Rebecca."

Chapter Ten

Rebecca was sleeping, her head resting against his chest and her leg splayed across his hips. They had made love three times, each time better than the previous. Nathan had never felt so relaxed, at ease or at peace in his life, but he couldn't sleep.

They hadn't had a chance to talk before Bec had crashed on him. He wanted her to know how much being with her again had affected him. But Nathan wasn't good at sharing his feelings, his thoughts. He'd hidden them for so long that the rush of emotions that flooded him now was hard to contain.

He needed time to digest and reflect on all of this — where it was heading, this thing with Bec. He'd already wanted forever with her because of Danny but now he knew that that was just the half of it. He wanted Bec in his life as well — wanted to share her bed, regain her love if he could. She had loved him before. He could see that now.

Nathan pondered over his part in their demise. How he wished they had spoken of her fears back then, but he probably wouldn't have listened.

This was a second chance, though, and Nathan was not going to blow it by rushing her. He would weave his way back into her heart slowly. They would join forces to rid Danny of his leukemia. Maybe in time they could get married, have another baby. He'd seen the small silver lines on her body, near her hips, whilst they'd made love, had placed kisses on them all reverently. Those beautiful reminders of how her belly had swelled as their son had grown inside her. He wanted to see Rebecca like that—experience first-hand the miracle of life developing within her.

He would be a good husband and father now that time had shown him the important things in life. He could provide well for his family. Haven Security was building a solid reputation and was receiving a steady case load through recommendations, especially from Frank Grimaldi, Jason's father-in-law. Nathan spent most of his days in the office running things. Rebecca would have nothing to fear from his job anymore.

He would make this right, no matter how long it took.

* * * *

Rebecca awoke and felt the heat from Nathan's body beside her. She had slept better in the few hours left of the night than she had in years.

Trying not to disturb Nathan, Rebecca lifted her head slightly from his arm and looked at the clock on her bedside table, the illuminated digital numbers announcing it was six-eighteen.

I need to get up before Danny wakes. I don't want him getting the wrong idea then being disappointed when he realizes Nathan and I aren't like other mummies and daddies — that we aren't going to live happily ever after. I'm disappointed enough for the both of us. What was I thinking last night? How the hell am I going to get over the memory of what happened? Hell, I didn't manage to get over Nathan the first time.

"Penny for them, Bec?" Nathan asked in his sexy drawl, his morning voice a little gruff and raspy.

A rush of heat and wetness filled her pussy. *How can just the sound of his voice turn me on? It's so unfair.* With her leg still positioned over Nathan's groin, she could feel the hardness of his cock against her skin. The thought of straddling him and letting that thick shaft sink into her pussy again was tempting. *Danny could walk in any moment.* Luckily, thinking of Danny helped quell her lust and gave her a topic to use to answer Nathan's question.

"I was thinking that we should get up before Danny discovers us in bed together—and that I need to pee."

Nathan rubbed his beard with his free hand, before reaching over and running a finger down her cheek, the act so intimate and personal that Rebecca could not help but push her cheek into his touch.

"Good morning, beautiful," he said before he leaned over and brushed his lips to hers. It was just a touch then it was over. "I don't think Danny catching us in bed would be a biggie but I can't solve your need to pee. So do I. You go first and I'll head out to the kitchen and put the kettle on to boil. Don't be too long, though, Bec. I'd hate to have to take a piss in the garden and have your neighbors complaining."

God, I love him. "I'll be quick."

Rebecca dragged herself away from Nathan, missing his touch immediately. She got out of bed without looking back. She took the gown from behind her door, shoving her arms into the sleeves before wrapping the covering around her naked form. Tying the sash closed tightly, she headed to the bathroom, hoping the time away from him would be enough to shore up her defenses — to get the lovesick puppy face she knew she was wearing off her face. They'd made no promises last night. It had all been about comforting each other and nothing else, and she would do well to remember that.

Nathan had watched the spectacular view of a naked Rebecca walking toward her door. He couldn't hide the disappointment at her covering up that lush sight with her robe. *Hey, don't forget she's got nothing on underneath.* The thought was enough to make him groan as his dick grew even harder. "Coffee — get those thoughts under control. Your son can do without seeing you sporting a boner," he told the empty room.

Nathan jumped from the bed, amazed at how fresh he felt after not much sleep. Rebecca was good for him. He grabbed his rumpled clothes from the floor and put them on. He couldn't get the zipper on his jeans to close, given the wood he was sporting, but he hoped that after he'd relieved himself, it would disappear. *Hopefully before Danny wakes.* He chuckled to himself as he headed to the kitchen.

Nathan unplugged the kettle from the wall, before carrying it over to the sink to fill it with water. After plugging it back in, he set about adding coffee to the mugs. Rebecca took sugar and milk with hers so he added them to her cup and waited for the kettle to start whistling.

"Hey, Daddy, where's Mummy?" came a little voice from the doorway.

It was so normal.

This, the morning routine, for so many families, but none appreciated it like Nathan did.

"She's in the bathroom, buddy. What do you feel like for breakfast?"

"I need to pee."

Nathan laughed. "So do I. Why do women take forever in the bathroom?"

"Maybe to make themselves pretty?" his son replied. "Do you think Mummy is pretty?"

"You know what, Danny? I surely do. In fact, I'd go as far as saying your mum is the prettiest woman I've ever seen."

Danny's smile lit up the room.

Nathan smiled back. "C'mon, son, let me show you how men have it easier than women." Nathan opened the back door and directed his son outside.

He and his boy were going to water the plants, together.

Chapter Eleven

Marty had been a frequent visitor to Rebecca's home since Nathan had moved in, so it was not a surprise to find him standing there when Nathan had gone to answer the knocking at the door.

"Marty, I know the coffee at the hospital is crap and Bec makes a mean brew, but this is becoming habitual." Nathan was finding it easier to make jokes these days. Some of that gruff exterior he'd always presented was thawing day by day.

"Glad you think it's just Bec's coffee that has me stopping by, Nate." Marty winked as he pushed past.

"Sure, come in. Make yourself at home," Nathan grumbled as Marty disappeared through the kitchen doorway. Shrugging his shoulders in resignation over Marty barging in, again, Nathan closed the door.

In the kitchen, Marty was just taking a seat, Rebecca busy pouring him a cup of coffee.

"So, what brings you around, again?" Nate asked.

Marty paused for a moment. He reached into his pocket and pulled out an envelope.

So, this is it then. Nathan stared at the rectangular object. "Results?"

Marty smiled. "You're a good match, Nathan—good enough for a marrow donation."

Nathan's head was spinning. The relief he felt from hearing the news washed over him like a warming gust of air. He'd been sure he would be. Well, at least that was what he'd been convincing himself anyway. "Thank God."

The crash of something hitting the floor echoed through the room. The mug Rebecca had been carrying to the table now lay in pieces smashed, the coffee spilled.

"Thank you, Marty. Thank you so much," Rebecca said, sounding as relieved as Nathan felt.

"Why don't you both sit down a minute, catch your breath, while I, umm, pick up my coffee?" Marty chuckled. "Maybe I shouldn't have blurted the news out like that. My colleagues at the hospital are always complaining about my bedside manner."

"Doc, that's the best news you've ever told me. Thanks, mate." Nathan clapped his hand on Marty's shoulder. "So, what happens next? When can we start?"

"Sit down, Nathan. I'll go through it all with you both. Just let me clean up this spill and grab another coffee. I've been at Emergency all night. I need some caffeine."

Rebecca took a seat next to him and Nathan grabbed hold of her hand. He wasn't sure if it was for her benefit or his own. He just felt the need to be connected with her. They just sat side by side, waiting for Marty to join them.

"Where is Danny, by the way?" Marty retook his place at the table.

"In his room watching a DVD," Rebecca answered. "He's probably fallen asleep or he would have come out to see who was here. Let's just talk among ourselves for a bit before we tell Danny what is going on."

Nathan was aware that Rebecca wasn't looking forward to telling their son he would be going back into hospital. It was a conversation that had to take place, though, and soon, as far as Nathan was concerned – the only important thing here was getting his healthy bone marrow into his son's body.

"Righto!" Marty began again, after setting his mug down on the table. "Danny will have to be admitted to the Children's Hospital, probably at least ten days before the actual transplant can be done. He will be set up in a sterile room, and a central venous line will be surgically placed in Danny's chest. Everything can be administered to him through this."

From the corner of his eye, Nathan could see Rebecca nodding her head. *She's done so much research on this, she could probably explain it to Marty.* He focused his attention back to what Marty was saying.

"We have to blast him with radiation, maybe some chemo to destroy the cells in his bone marrow before we can introduce Nathan's healthy cells. This therapy is often called ablative, or myeloablative, because of the effect on the bone marrow. The bone marrow produces most of the blood cells in our body. Ablative therapy prevents this process of cell production and the marrow becomes empty. An empty marrow is needed to make room for the new stem cells – those would be the ones we harvest from you, Nathan – to grow and establish a new blood cell production system. The marrow transplant is given through the central venous catheter into the bloodstream. It's not a surgical procedure to place the marrow into the bone, more like receiving a blood transfusion. The stem cells find their way into the bone marrow and hopefully, all going well, begin reproducing and growing new, healthy blood cells. This will not be a comfortable time for Danny, but as a doctor and a friend, I think you are making the right decision to put him through this. Yes, the odds might still be a little on the negative side for this procedure to be successful but if it does work... And I think given the team of specialist medical staff that have agreed that this should be done, we have a good chance."

"I know this will be rough but I'm prepared for it. I want my son to be given the best chance for a long, healthy life. Trust me, Marty. I've thought about this long and hard."

Rebecca may have sounded convinced but now, listening to Marty and aware that it was all going to happen, Nathan was starting to have doubts. *My son is only just starting to bounce back from the last lot of chemo, his hair growing, his eyes brighter and his energy levels have improved so much since that first day I took him out to lunch. Fuck, he's even playing cricket in the backyard with me. How can I make him go back to being sick just with a hope that my cells or marrow or whatever the fuck it is can make him well? What if they don't and we've put my son through hell for nothing?*

"Look, I know this all sounds horrendous to you, Nate. I can see by the look on your face you're starting to have doubts. We've been friends for a long time, seen and done things neither of us wants to remember. Trust me when I tell you, this is the right way to go."

"I do trust your input, Marty, and I thank you for being here. It's just..."

"Nathan, we need to do this for Danny," Rebecca cut in. "Make this hard decision. I've watched him struggle with this disease for long enough. I'm not sure he would last through too many more attacks. We are giving him this chance now before he is too weak to take it. " Rebecca hesitated. "Now all I have to do is break my son's heart and tell him."

* * * *

With the roads nearly deserted at this late hour, Nathan was feeling relaxed on the drive home. He had Rebecca in the passenger seat next to him and his son in the back. He enjoyed this new feeling of being part of a proper family unit on their way home from sharing a meal with friends. Being part of a team or unit was something Nathan was not new too but this had a totally different feel to it. A more intimate one, a connection to this woman and child that no one else could have. He and Rebecca were joined to one another through their son, they were a family but more than that he loved them both more than he thought possible.

"I think Danny had fun tonight. He's crashed out." Rebecca's voice broke the silence that filled the car. "We've never eaten in a restaurant like that one. Did you see how the waiters all fussed over Danny? He was lapping it up. I've never seen him eat so much. I'm pretty sure spaghetti Bolognese isn't normally on their menu." Rebecca sighed. "Toni must really have some pull."

Nathan glanced in the rear-view mirror. Bec was right. Danny was fast asleep in the back seat of the car. He was glad he'd installed the child booster seat in his car because his sleeping son's head rested at a comfortable angle against the padded sides. The seatbelt held Danny secured. "What about you, Bec? How did you enjoy having dinner with my team, my friends?"

The idea to get all dressed up and go out to a fancy restaurant had, of course, been Toni's. She had insisted that they should all share in celebrating the news of the bone marrow match. Nathan had been secretly pleased that she had not taken no for an answer, even taking the time to convince Rebecca that it was exactly what they all needed. Toni had been right. It had given them all a well-deserved distraction from such an emotional day.

While Danny had been clearly upset at the thought of more time in hospital, more prodding and probing of his little body, it was the idea of the surgery and more needles that had really crushed him. Nathan had shed tears right alongside his son, as the brave little boy had struggled to understand why they were making him suffer through such an ordeal.

Danny's words of hope, so full of innocence and trust, still haunted Nathan. "I know your bones can make me better, Daddy. You're so big and strong. You're going to fix me up and I will try to be very brave, just like a soldier, even if it really hurts."

With Marty's visit and the ensuing emotional fallout it had caused, Nathan had still been feeling a bit on edge when he, Bec and Danny had first arrived at the restaurant. But he'd quickly unwound surrounded by his friends. He had spent a lot of the night just watching and listening, trying to get a handle on how they really felt about Rebecca. He knew his guys and they'd all seemed relaxed and happy, understood that he and Rebecca were dealing with so much and needed support.

Rebecca was taking a long time to answer so Nathan took his eyes off the road for a moment and looked her way, to see if she was okay with his question. He wanted her to feel comfortable around his friends — his other family. It meant a lot to him that she felt like she fit in. He needed everyone to get along, especially, after today's news. So much had happened since the other night when he and Bec had talked, sorted out a few things then made love — just the memory of that brought Nathan's cock to life, eager for a repeat performance.

She turned and faced him, caught him staring at her. Rebecca smiled and Nathan's cock reacted even more.

"Get your eyes back on the road, Nathan, and stop looking at me like that. I'm fine. I had a lovely night. To be honest, I think they were too nice to me. Your friends are wonderful. I can see how much they respect you, care for you. They should be much harder on me for what I've done to you. If the circumstances were different, I'd love to have built a real friendship with Toni."

Rebecca sighed again, and Nathan took another quick glance in her direction. He was about to ask her to explain what she'd meant by her comment 'if the circumstances were different' but he was sidetracked when he noticed her lean forward, her focus on something out of the front windscreen of the car.

"That's strange…"

Nathan turned his sights back to the road ahead. They were now only a few houses from Rebecca's place, and he immediately understood what she'd meant. Her house was in complete darkness. Rebecca always left a light or two on inside when she went out. She'd told Nathan she hated coming home to a dark house, and he agreed that it was a good security measure. He'd flicked the porch light on himself before they'd left for their night out. The homes to the left and right of Bec's were illuminated, as were the street lights around them, so that ruled out a power outage in the area.

Something was off. He could feel it.

Nathan slowed the car down in front of Bec's neighbors' place and parked.

"Stay in the car with Danny while I go check it out." He wasn't happy about leaving them on their own but the thought of taking Danny and Bec with him into an unknown situation was not an option.

"We should call the police, Nathan. What if someone is in the house? I don't want you to get hurt because of me."

Nathan resisted the urge to reply to Bec that that boat had sailed long ago and that he was a little insulted that she didn't think he could handle their safety on his own. Instead, he focused on the job at hand.

"Stay in the car until I come and get you. If I'm not back in five minutes, call Chris." Nathan brought Chris' number up on the phone's display for her. "Just press this button and it will connect."

Rebecca took the phone from him "We could call him now and he could go in with you."

She really has no idea what I'm capable of. "It would be a shame to get Chris over here for the sake of a blown fuse. Let me check it out first. I've got this, Bec."

Nathan opened the car door and climbed out before she could say anything else. He pressed the lock icon on his car keys just to make sure that all the doors were secured before heading off in the direction of Bec's home.

Even though he had played down the dark state of her house, he'd known there was more to it. *It's not likely a simple break-and-enter burglar would risk being caught out smashing a street light. I should have grabbed my gun from the glove compartment. Yeah, that wouldn't have freaked Bec out much.*

Years of training and soldier's instinct kicked in as Nathan crept silently around the perimeter of the building. Reconnaissance was a much better tactic than barging into the unknown. Many missions had proven that belief beyond doubt. The more intel he had in any situation he was about to confront, the better equipped he would be to deal with it.

Nathan found the entry point easily — the back door to Bec's house was standing wide open. He couldn't hear or detect any movement coming from inside. He slipped through the door into the kitchen, his senses on high alert. The first thing he noticed, even in the darkness, was that the room had definitely been breached. The shadowed outline of the table and chairs he, Bec and Danny had sat on earlier that day were flipped over and broken on the floor, before him.

He made his way over to the cupboard under the sink, where he remembered Bec stored a flashlight, careful not to step on any of the debris around him. Finding what he was looking for, Nathan flicked the switch and shone the light source around the room. It had been trashed. Food from the fridge had been thrown against the walls, crockery and glassware in pieces on the floor.

Next he moved toward the living room. "God damn it," he muttered as he took in the sight before him. Even with just the light from the torch, he could see the destruction. *Who the hell would have done this? As if Bec and Danny haven't been through enough without some sick fuck destroying what little they have. God help whoever it was when I track them down.*

Nathan was furious—every room was just as bad as the next. Nothing had been ignored, not even his son's room. The pointless destruction was sickening. He only did a quick survey of each room, just long enough to make sure the fuckers were long gone, being careful not to touch or disturb anything.

I need to get back to Bec and Danny. What was I thinking leaving them alone and defenseless in the car. He also needed to make a few phone calls—his team first then the police. *How will I find the words to try to explain this act of abomination to Danny and Bec? I don't even want them to see it.* Nathan had seen the worst of what humanity had to offer and sadly this was just another act in a long list he'd rather not have witnessed.

At least this time he could help repair the senseless destruction, could make a difference, rather than walking away once his duty had been carried out. He had the resources to change Rebecca's and Danny's lives for the better, to never let anything like this happen to them again—unlike the civilian innocents that had been left homeless and impoverished, their only crime being caught in the middle of the war on terrorism. Nathan had never felt right about walking away from them in their hour of need, but he'd had orders to follow and they'd never included hanging around to make things right.

* * * *

I'm going to count to ten and then I'm ringing Chris. I don't care how macho Nathan wants to act. One… Two… Three… Rebecca really wanted to go and see what was happening with her house. *Danny is still asleep. I could just take a quick look and see if Nathan is okay. Seriously, why am I even hiding here in the car? I would have had to deal with this myself before Nathan came back into my life.*

Having convinced herself that leaving Danny in the car for a few moments would be okay, Rebecca quietly opened the passenger door and climbed out of the car. She took the time to look around at her surroundings. The street was quiet. There didn't seem to be any movement or people lurking around. Her heart was thudding inside her chest as she headed toward the front of her house. It was still dark. *This is silly. I just need to check on Nathan, maybe grab the car keys from him so I can move the car into the driveway and then I can get Danny into his own bed.*

Rebecca was still clutching Nathan's phone as a hand slipped over her mouth.

Chapter Twelve

As Nathan was opening the front door, he heard the screeching of tires that indicated a car had just sped away. In the dead of night, it was hard to miss. He hurried down the path toward his own car. *First I'll ring Jason and Toni, get them to come and take Danny to their place while Bec and I deal with this. The police are going to want to know if anything is missing...* Nathan stopped mid thought when he reached the car. Bec was not in it. *What the fuck? Where the hell is she? I told her to stay in the car.* It was then that Nathan noticed Danny sitting wide-eyed in his car seat. Nathan opened the back door, unhappy to find that it was unlocked. He sat down next to his son.

"Hey, big guy, did you see where Mum went?" Nathan asked, trying to keep the tone of his voice calm, even though his stress level was reaching its peak.

"Daddy, where did you go? Why did the shadow monster take Mummy? I want my mummy." Danny began to cry.

Danny's words rocked Nathan to the core. *What monster? Where was Bec? Who took her?* A million questions invaded his brain at once. He needed to comfort his son and find out what Danny had seen. He unlocked the safety harness, pulled Danny onto his lap.

"Shh! Son, stop crying and tell me what happened. Who took Mummy, Danny? Did you see him? Is he someone you know?"

"Nooo," Danny sobbed. "It was dark but I could see them. It was a shadow monster and a car started and I was all alone and scared." Danny continued to cry, his words coming out broken between sobs.

"It's going to be okay, son. I'm going to find Mummy and bring her home, but I need you to be a brave soldier for me. I have to find a phone and ring Chris."

Danny's head shot up—terror reflected in his eyes. "Please don't leave me alone, Daddy, I'll be good. Just don't leave me in the car by myself. What if the shadow monster comes back?"

"I'm not leaving you, son. I'm going to carry you inside but I want you to make me a promise. I want you to close your eyes and keep them closed until I say you can open them. Can you do that for me, big guy?"

There was no way Nathan was going to leave Danny alone, but he didn't want his son to see the damage inside, he didn't need that image added to the anxiety he was already feeling.

"I can shut my eyes, Daddy. I promise, but don't leave me."

"I won't even put you down. Wrap your legs around me and snuggle into my chest. Okay, buddy, pretend you're a baby koala and cling on?"

Danny was already clinging to him, so Nathan got out of the car, flicked on the torch and headed back to Bec's house. He went around to the rear entrance again—the phone was in the kitchen and them entering through the back door would give Danny less chance to see what had happened.

Jason stood with his back against the wall. He cradled Danny's head to his chest with one hand, his son sobbing quietly, his little body shuddering. Grabbing the phone with his free hand, he dialed the familiar number that would connect him to Jason. Nathan didn't even need to watch what he was doing, the motions were automatic. He held the handset to his ear, listened to it ring, once, twice, three times...

"Jason Beck."

"It's Nathan. I need you and Toni to get to Bec's as quickly as you can. Do you have the address?"

"Yes. On my way, Nate. We should be there in ten." There was a click as Jason cut the connection.

Nathan was thankful to have a team that didn't waste time with questions. He dialed Chris.

"Chris, it's Nathan—" he started before Chris butted in.

"Where are you?"

"I'm at Bec's. I need you here now."

"Where's your phone?"

"What the fuck does that matter? I just said I needed you to get your ass here stat. What's with the fucking twenty questions?"

"I'm on my bike. You rang me a few minutes ago. Well, someone using your phone did. I couldn't hear any voices, just some muffled noises in the background. In all the time I've known you, you've never pocket dialed me... Hold on a sec... The line is still open. I'm just going to go back and check it again."

Rebecca called Chris, clever woman. Hold on, sweetheart, I'm coming to get you. Nathan could hear the sound of Chris' bike over the line just before the sound of music replaced it. He guessed that Chris was using an earpiece to answer his phone as he drove the beast of a motorbike.

"Sorry 'bout that," Chris began again. "I should have taken the car—trying to read the GPS signal coming from your phone. By the way, I started tracking it the second I figured out something was wrong—but doing that while riding is a bitch, let alone switching between phone calls."

"I owe you, mate. Which way is she heading?"

"Rebecca has your phone? What the hell, man? What's going on?"

"We can get into that later. Jason's on his way here to look after Danny…" As Nathan mentioned his son's name, Danny stopped sobbing and lifted his head from Nathan's chest. "It's okay, Danny, stay still, buddy. I need to finish talking with Chris then I can go get Mummy."

Danny snuggled back down into him.

"Where's she heading?" Nathan asked Chris again.

"West. Just turned left onto the motorway. I'll keep following and let you know when she stops. Do you want me to engage?"

"Negative. I'm not sure who's taken her or why. Try and get eyes on her, and report back."

"Copy that, boss."

That was what was giving Nathan the most grief, wondering why Bec had been snatched, why her house had been ransacked. *My God, have I brought this down on her? Is someone getting back at me through Bec?*

Nathan tried to think of someone in his past that might go to this length to square up with him. There were plenty of things he'd done in his time that could be classed as unsavory, but most of them were when he'd been a soldier and under orders.

"Put the kid down and step away from him or I'll blow your fucking head off."

He and Danny were not alone anymore. Danny's body stiffened. Nathan patted his son's back, trying to reassure him everything was okay. *Not a chance in hell I'm putting him down, but I've got to do something to get Danny out of the line of fire. Jason will be here any minute. If I can get the fucker talking, waste a bit of time…*

"Ain't gonna happen. Not in this lifetime," Nathan growled back at the intruder, trying to put as much malicious intent in his voice as he could. "Who the hell are you? Have you got something to do with this mess?"

"I'm warning you. If you don't put Danny down, I'm going to put a bullet between your eyes."

So he knows Danny's name. What the hell is going on?

"Uncle Matt?" The sound of Danny's voice was muffled because Nathan still had his son pressed in against his chest, but he still heard him.

"Matt, is that you? It's Nathan, Nathan Haven. Why are you here? Bec said you were deep undercover, had been for over a year. So why would you be turning up here? And now, of all times?"

There was silence for a few moments.

"Well, I'll be buggered. Nathan Haven, there's a name I haven't heard in a few years, Even longer since I've seen your ugly mug. What the hell are you doing here and where is my sister?" Matt Hammerton, Rebecca's brother, asked.

"A shadow monster took her and Daddy is going to bring her back."

Danny had managed to wiggle his head out from Nathan's grasp and turn it in the direction of where his uncle stood. The thought occurred to Nathan that Matt turning up now was no coincidence. "That's right, son, I am going to go get your mother, but there are no such things as shadow monsters, Danny. It was just a man."

"Is that right, Danny? Your daddy is going to bring Mummy back. Well, what do you know! I always figured as much, Haven, but Rebecca never said a word. I think we will be having a conversation about it someday soon and you better have a good explanation for why my sister was doing the single mum gig for so long." Matt Hammerton glared at him. "I know who it is, Haven, I'll go get Bec. You stay here with your son."

The hell you will. Not without me. "We can talk about that later," Nathan answered brusquely. "In the meantime, let's go out the front. I have some friends on the way who will look after Danny."

"I'd rather not wait around. I think I need to get to Rebecca as soon as possible."

"Just chill, Matt, I've got someone tracking her. As soon as he gets eyes on her, he'll let me know. Meanwhile, we need to discuss why this has happened in the first place. Why her house and belongings have been trashed and why you seem to know something about it. If you've put her in danger..."

"Stop right there, Haven. Maybe it might be better to wait until our audience is one less before we have this, umm...discussion. How far out are your friends?"

Nathan hated to admit it, but Matt Hammerton was right. This conversation was best had after Danny was out of earshot. "Any minute now. Let's go meet them." Nathan tucked Danny's head back against his chest and walked toward the kitchen door. He didn't wait to see if Bec's brother was following.

By the time Nathan had walked down the side of the property, Jason's car was pulling up to the curb in front. Nathan continued walking until he was standing beside the passenger door. It opened and Toni stepped out.

"Hey, Danny, I thought I'd pop on over and invite you to my place for a sleepover," Toni said, her voice sounding so cheery and friendly, even though she knew something was wrong. Nathan could have kissed her for it.

"Hi, Toni," Nathan replied. "What do you say, big guy? How about you go with Toni, and your mother and I will come and get you in a bit."

"Umm, okay, Daddy." Danny hesitated for a moment—he looked at Toni then back at Nathan before adding, "As long as you promise to bring Mummy with you to pick me up."

Nathan wanted to promise his son that he would but his throat had closed up. He couldn't manage to get the words to come out. *What if I promise, and Bec is hurt or worse? How would I face him?*

"We will, Danny—me and your dad. You go with Toni and we will see you both soon," Jason jumped in where Nathan had not been able.

Had his back as usual.

And now Jason was giving Bec's brother the evil eye. Nathan needed to make introductions before everything went to hell. *I need to pull myself together, for*

Bec and for Danny. Worrying about the 'what ifs' is not going to get the job done.

"Take my car, Toni. Danny's car seat is already set up." Nathan handed his car keys over.

"Drive safe, luv, and I'll call as soon as we know something." Jason never took his eyes from Matt as he said goodbye to his wife, and to Toni's credit, she didn't move between the two men or break Jason's line of sight. She just walked toward Nathan's car and he followed her, Danny still in his arms.

Chapter Thirteen

"So, now that my son is gone, what the fuck is going on? Jason, this is Bec's brother, Matt, who just happened to turn up tonight and apparently knows who took her."

"Well, he better start talking fast," Jason grunted, "or I'm going to rip his head from his shoulders. I don't care what his relationship to Bec is. If he put her in danger..."

"Slow down, tough guy. Apart from the fact I've got at least fifteen kilos on you and a few inches so would put you on your ass quick enough, I want my sister back more than anyone."

"Huh, don't be so sure, Matt. I reckon Jason could take you, but this is not the time for a pissing contest. Tell me where you fit into all of this. The clock is ticking and we are no closer to Bec. Fuck, if even a hair on her head is damaged..." Nathan couldn't finish his sentence. Didn't want to voice the words for where his mind had been headed.

"Scrapper has her. He left me a text telling me he had my bitch and if I didn't return his, he would make her pay."

What the hell does that all mean? "Who is Scrapper and why would he think Bec is your woman?" Nathan was no clearer on what was going on.

"He's a member of the Serpents biker gang. I've been working undercover trying to infiltrate the gang. They made me a full member a few months ago and recently I've been accepted into the inner circle. At first this was all about the gang's involvement in the drugs scene, but the deeper involved I became with the gang's leadership ring, the more I discovered. The whole thing is bad. Not only are they supplying drugs to more than half the state's users, but they also have a huge firearms' racket going on."

"So, if they broke your cover, why have they taken Bec? How did they know about her and why aren't you dead already?"

Nathan couldn't have worded it better himself. Jason had asked the questions that he was about to.

"That's the thing... This has nothing to do with me being a cop. Scrapper is pissed off at me for giving his woman a safe place to stay. The sick fuck beat the crap out of her for no good reason. I couldn't just stand by and let him kill her. God only knows how or why, but he must have followed me when I came to visit Danny a few weeks ago. I've been here, like...twice in the last seven months, but I was careful each time, thought I'd made sure no one followed me. But I had to see how the little guy was doing." Matt was rubbing at his head, his chin—his erratic hand movements showing just how agitated he was.

"Guess you failed," Jason added and grunted.

"So, where would this Scrapper take her?"

Before Matt had the chance to answer, Jason's phone began to ring.

Jason took his phone out of his pocket and looked at the caller display. "It's Chris," he said. "Yeah, I'm already here... No, I didn't know. Good job... What's the location? Did you sight the prize...?"

Nathan couldn't hear what Chris was saying, so could only follow the conversation from Jason's replies. He stood, body frozen, hanging onto his sanity by a thread, waiting to hear whether or not Chris had seen Bec, if she was okay. It was as if time stood still as he waited for Jason to say something. Nathan watched Jason's facial expressions intently, looking for any hint, but there was nothing to see or hear.

Jason put his phone back in his pocket.

Nathan exploded. "What the fuck is going on? Did he see her or not? Is she okay? Where the fuck is Rebecca?"

Jason held both hands, palms up, in the air. "Whoa, calm down, Nate. You need to keep it together. Chris saw her. He said Rebecca was fighting back tooth and nail as the scumbag dragged her inside what looked to be a vacant mechanic's garage. It's on Booth Street in Granfield. Do you know the one, Biker Cop?"

"Yep, been there a time or two. Scrapper's not the brightest tool in the shed. It would have been my first stop anyway, but I hope Bec stops fighting him. He's got a nasty temper and a penchant for hitting women."

I really didn't need to hear that. "Well, should I send Chris in to get her? He can handle himself. If it's just one guy, I can't see him having a problem." Nathan aimed his question at both Jason and Matt. He wasn't used to asking advice, more comfortable being a leader, but he knew he wasn't thinking straight—not when the woman he loved was involved. *Why the hell haven't I told her I love her? Why did I wait? What if this scumbag does something to her and I don't get the chance to tell her how much she means to me?* His desperate thoughts made his legs go weak. Nathan had to lock his knees so he didn't stumble and fall.

"Given his location, Scrapper has some serious weaponry at his disposal," Matt explained. "I'm sure your guy is good, but I don't want Bec to get caught in the cross-fire. I think it would be better if we go in together, hit him from more than one front. There are a couple of offices in the rear of the building that could be breached through windows without Scrapper noticing. If we can figure out exactly where he has Bec and where he is, it would make it easier. Then one of us could rush him while the others shield Bec."

"I can help you with that, Biker Cop. I've got a handheld thermal imaging device in my go bag." Jason walked to the rear of his car and popped the boot.

The rasping sound of the zipper filled the silence as Jason unfastened his gear bag. He reappeared with the small handheld device and handed it to Matt. "We can isolate the heat signatures before we go in."

"Nice toy," Matt said as he looked at the device, clearly impressed. "Another soldier then, I presume, Tough Guy?"

"Nup, not anymore, Biker Cop, just like to always be prepared."

"Look, as much as I love this *getting to know you* phase, Tough Guy. I think we should be making ourselves scarce. I can't believe Bec's neighbors haven't called the cops by now, all this commotion we're making out here. The last thing we need is for the police to get involved, take it out of our hands.

This needs to be handled right—which means by us. It's the only way to make sure keeping Bec safe is the priority."

Matt was right. They didn't need the police getting in the way. Nathan was starting to feel redundant. Jason and Matt had a solid plan, not that he was complaining. All he wanted was Bec back safe and sound in his arms. They needed to get going ASAP. "Let's roll then. Jason, you drive. Matt, go shotgun and direct. I'm in the back."

* * * *

Yuck, the son of a bitch stinks. I need to get out of here. Rebecca looked around the garage. She knew it used to be a mechanic's because the smell of old oil and grease filled her nose. *Window looks pretty flimsy. I bet I could push it open and climb out if Stinky gave me half a chance. Of course, I'll have to figure out how to get out of these cable ties first.* Rebecca tried wiggling her hands again to see if she could loosen the restraints, but every time she tried, they just cut deeper into her wrists. The same with the ones around her bound ankles—in fact, they were really starting to hurt and her feet were going numb. She looked over to where her abductor, Stinky, was pacing back and forth. Every so often he took a phone out of his pocket, looked at it and shook his head. Then he would start talking to himself. At regular intervals between that behavior, Stinky took a healthy swig from what looked to Rebecca to be a bottle of bourbon.

If he keeps that up, he's going to drink himself into a stupor. At first Rebecca hadn't known why he'd taken her. It had all happened so fast. One second she'd been standing under the neighbors' lamp post deciding if she should go inside her home and find Nathan, the next a dirty, smelly hand had covered her mouth and she'd felt the pressure of a gun nozzle at her side. She'd gone quietly, not wanting whoever it was to discover Danny still sleeping in the car.

Once they'd arrived at this destination and Stinky had tried to drag her inside the well-lit garage, she'd seen the Serpents insignia on his dirty leather vest. This had something to do with her brother. The last time Matt had visited, unannounced, he'd been wearing the same symbol on his back.

Rebecca had fought hard to try to escape now that the threat to Danny had been eliminated. But despite Stinky's large, protruding belly, he was strong, and the fist he'd planted on her face hadn't helped. She'd seen stars for a while after. Her cheek still hurt like hell from the punch. *At least the dipshit hasn't bothered to search me.* Rebecca could feel Nathan's phone in the pocket of her jacket. She just hoped the call had connected when she'd discreetly pressed the button as Stinky had led her to his van. *Please, Chris, be listening to this. Find me and bring Nathan. I know I didn't want you to be a soldier but please, Nate, put that training to good use and find me…quickly. Meanwhile, I need to get loose of these bloody cable ties before my hands and feet fall off.*

"Excuse me." Rebecca's first attempt came out more like a squeak. She cleared her throat with a cough and tried again. "Umm… Hello, I need to use the ladies." She was taking a risk drawing Stinky's attention her way again, but if she could just convince him to let her use the toilet, maybe she could climb out of a window or something.

Unfortunately—or fortunately, Rebecca wasn't sure yet—Stinky stopped pacing and turned to her.

"Fuckin whores' more trouble than they're worth. You're just like my bitch—needs to piss every fuckin hour." Stinky did not seem impressed as he stomped toward her. "Well, I aint gonna carry ya, and I suppose you'll need to wipe your pissy cunt after, so I'm gonna have to cut all the ties. But I warn you, bitch, if you try anything stupid, I'll just put a bullet in ya and dump ya body in the river."

Stinky pulled a knife from the leather holder on his belt and knelt down in front of her. The smell of alcohol on his breath and the stench of his body odor made Rebecca gag. She had to stop herself from shrinking away from his hands as he placed the knife against her leg. He severed the cable tie and struggled to his feet, swaying a little before regaining his balance. *He's getting drunk – maybe he'll fall asleep.*

"Stand up, bitch."

Rebecca placed her wrist-bound hands on the dirty cement floor and tried to stand, but her feet were numb and not doing what she wanted them to do. She tried flexing them a couple of times to get the blood flowing.

"Hurry the fuck up, I'm not waitin' all night. Do you need to piss or don't ya?" Stinky's breath and spit rained down on her. That combined with his abusive comments gave Rebecca the momentum she needed. She stood up.

"Hold out ya arms."

Rebecca did as Stinky had asked, and the cold blade of the knife against her wrist chilled her to the bone as he split the homemade handcuffs.

"Use that door over there." Stinky pointed, and Rebecca looked to the direction he was indicating. "That one's got no window and it might have some dunny paper, if ya lucky." Stinky obviously thought he was a comedian and let out a loud, barking laugh that made his fat stomach bobble.

This man is repulsive. Wonder how funny he'd think it was if I vomited all over him.

She didn't wait for him to change his mind. Rebecca moved quickly toward the door. With her back to him—not being able to see what Stinky was up to terrified her. Was he going to grab her before she got to the door or maybe come good on his threat to shoot her? She didn't wait to find out. As soon as she was in arm's reach of the door, she flung it open then went inside, shutting the door behind her. Of course, she hadn't bothered to look for a light switch first and had to search the walls in the darkness to find it.

"Yuck, it's putrid." She gasped as the light flickered on and Rebecca got her first look at the lavatory. Any thought of using the facility was definitely out of the question. *Lucky I didn't really need to go. Please God, let someone find me before I do have to.* Rebecca tried to find something of use in the small, filthy room. *That might be handy.* The toilet paper roll was looped with a piece of wire. Rebecca put it in her pocket and as she did, the mobile phone bumped her hand. *Stupid, stupid— the phone. Check the phone.*

Taking it carefully from her pocket, Rebecca looked at the phone. She noticed two things—one, it was connected to Chris' and had been for thirty-three minutes, and two, there was not very much battery life left. She brought the phone to her lips but before she spoke, Rebecca reached over the toilet and pressed the flush button. As the noise of the water rushing around the cistern began she whispered into the phone, "I hope you are listening, Chris. I need help. I'm in an old mechanic's garage. Most of the lights are on. Someone my brother knows has me. We were on

277

the motorway for about ten minutes and then on a bumpier road for another five. Please find me. I have to go but I'll leave the phone on in my pocket. Oh and it's running out of battery."

Rebecca placed the phone against her ear. *Please let someone be on the other end.* "We know where you are, honey, and we're coming in, in about five minutes. Hang tough and try to keep out of the firing line. When you do hear us, lie down on the ground. Make yourself as small a target as you can."

At first Rebecca thought she was imagining the voice, wanting it so much she was experiencing an audible illusion, but it was real. The voice was Chris' and it was the best sound Rebecca had ever heard.

"Get out here now, bitch. What ya up to in there?"

As Stinky slammed the door open, Rebecca had only just enough time to slip her hand into her pocket and hide the phone.

"Sorry. I'm sorry. I was just taking a moment, I'm sorry. I'll go back and sit down." Rebecca tried to slide her body past Stinky's without making any contact but his hands clamped down on either side of her arms, halting her movement and putting her right in the direct path of his stinky foul breath.

"Got a bit of sub in ya, bitch? All that pleading and stuff. I didn't peg for that after the fight you put up when we first got here, but maybe you're just tryin' to hide somethin'? I'm not stupid. Whatcha get up to in the dunny?"

Yes, you are stupid, and in a few minutes you're going to be really sorry. Rebecca may have thought that but she was not going to give Stinky any heads-up that he was about to be squaring off with Nathan and his team. So, instead, she lowered her eyes and played the scared victim. "I wasn't up to anything. I went to the toilet and then I just sort of got frozen. You scare me. I was frightened to come back out. Let me go and sit back down. I won't cause you any trouble."

Stinky held onto her for a few more moments then the weight of his hand on one shoulder lifted. Rebecca thought he was going to let her go and took the risk of looking up at him. The sudden burst of pain on her already battered cheek stole her breath away as his clenched fist once again made contact with her face. She hadn't even seen it coming, had had no time to react or brace for the assault. Rebecca stumbled, and Stinky let her go.

She fell to the ground on hands and knees and tried to shake off the effects of the punch. Before her rescuers came in, she needed to put some space between them—at least get herself out of Stinky's reach. Rebecca made herself crawl away from him. Her head was ringing. She felt dizzy, nauseated, but there was no way she was going to let that bastard get his hands on her again.

"That's it, bitch. Crawl back to your place on the floor like the dirty whore you are."

Fuck you! Rebecca didn't stop. She kept moving until she was back against the wall. Then she curled up into a ball, arms wrapped around her legs, knees against her chest, and waited.

* * * *

"Over here, boss," Chris' whispered voice called to him.

Nathan, Matt and Jason followed the sound until they found Chris taking cover behind a bunch of old tires just meters away from the garage entrance. The place was lit up like a Christmas tree. Light shone over the grounds of the property like a beacon but did not reach behind Chris' makeshift blind. "Glad you could make it. Who's the big dude?" Chris asked.

"Rebecca's brother, Matt. He's the one responsible for this mess," Nathan answered.

"What are we in the middle of, some biker gang war or something?"

"Nup, buddy, this here's a real-life undercover policeman." Jason's tone was full of sarcasm. "Seems he's made a few enemies inside the big bad biker gang and it's all over a woman."

"Can we just get on with the getting Bec out of there plan." Nathan was getting tired of waiting while Chris and Jason bantered.

"Sure thing, boss. You will be happy to know I just spoke to your woman. She's a smart one. First the whole ringing me bit, then she somehow got the fuckwit to let her use the loo and while she was in there, we had a little chat. What sort of fool doesn't check for personal effects, seriously?"

"Yeah, well Scrapper's not all that bright. Nice to meet you, Chris." Matt held out his hand to Chris. "Thanks for having my sister's back."

As Chris and Matt shook hands, Nathan's patience was growing thin. It was mind-blowing that Bec and Chris had made contact. But the fact that this Scrapper guy was proving to be such an idiot only made Nathan worry more. Stupid meant he was unpredictable.

"Can we please move this along? We can all play nicely after my woman is safe," Nathan said, his frustration and concern for Rebecca growing more desperate with every second they wasted. "Have you done a scope of the area, Chris?"

"Yep."

"Okay, given you're in your leathers, you look more like a biker than Nathan or Tough Guy does, and while Bec's safety is my main objective I wouldn't mind not blowing my cover if I can help it. This way it will appear like I got one of the Serpents to give me a hand. What say you climb in through one of the windows in the back and head straight for Bec. I'll go in the front and distract Scrapper. Be warned… He's sitting on a couple of crates of semi-automatic hand guns in there. I'm not sure if he knows it or not, but better to be on guard for it. Nathan, you follow me in but try to stay in the background if you can."

Matt's plan was good. Nathan could rely on Chris to put his body on the line for Bec if he had to, and even though it riled Nathan a little that Matt was still trying to protect his cover, he did understand. Undercover work was dangerous. There was nothing more frustrating than having to pull out from a job you'd sacrificed so much for without a result. He also knew, if push came to shove, Matt could go fuck his career.

"Tough Guy, can you get that toy of yours to narrow down where Bec and Scrapper are located?"

"I'm going to use the roof next door to the garage. It's higher and will give me a better angle to scope out the area and find the heat sources. Give us a minute. I'll be right back."

Jason was gone before Nathan could blink. He might not be as ruggedly built as some operatives but what he lacked in size he certainly made up for in speed and agility.

"I gave Bec the heads-up we'd be coming in soon. Told her to get on the ground and make herself the smallest target she could."

Chris had said the right thing to Bec. Nathan was never more thankful than now to have such a well-trained, experienced team behind him, but he could have done without hearing the words target and Bec in the same sentence.

"C'mon, Jason. Hurry it up."

Chapter Fourteen

Five minutes my arse. Feels more like an hour. Where the hell are they? Rebecca stayed huddled on the floor, her ears primed for any sound that might herald the beginning of her rescue. Stinky had found another bottle of whatever he was drinking and was doing his best to guzzle it down. *I think in his drunken stupor, he's forgotten I'm even here. This would be a perfect time to come get me, Nathan.* Rebecca had only just thought his name when she heard a loud creaking sound. It was the front door. She recognized the noise from when Stinky had opened it earlier. *I figured you guys for more of the surprise attack type, but whatever... As long as it works.*

Expecting to see one of the Haven Security team, Rebecca was shocked when it was her brother that boldly strode into the light.

"Scrapper, what the hell is going on?" Her brother's booming voice echoed around the nearly empty room. "You gone insane? I get this fuckin text message saying you've got my bitch. Newsflash, dick. I don't have a woman. So I don't know who you snatched but it's got nothing to do with me."

It was obvious Stinky hadn't heard the door open. Rebecca had had to stifle her laugh when Stinky startled at the sound of Matt's voice. It took him a couple of goes to get to his feet. *I probably could have just walked out of here on my own in another few minutes. He's plastered.*

"Call bullshit, Hammer. I seen ya going into her place, followed ya a month back. You went in and didn't come back out for an hour. Seen the look on ya face. You'd got ya rocks off."

Nice, very pleasant Stinky. And gross… He's my brother. Just as Rebecca had decided to uncurl her body in preparation to make a run for it, a hand pressed down over her mouth. *Not again. Where the hell did this one come from?*

"Hush. It's Chris. Don't make a sound," someone whispered into her ear.

She nodded to acknowledge that she'd understood.

Meanwhile, Matt was still arguing with Stinky, keeping him distracted. Rebecca watched on silently as Matt inched his way closer to the repulsive excuse for a human. *Glad I recognized his voice. Wow, he looks so different. That shaggy beard really doesn't do anything for him. Geez, I must be losing it. Who cares what he looks like as long as he keeps Stinky occupied? When is Chris going to get me out of here? My face hurts, and my poor baby… Where is Danny? I just left him behind, in that car all by himself. Please let Nathan have found him quickly, not left him in the dark by himself. I need to get back to my baby. Please God, let me see my son again.* Thinking about Danny only made Rebecca even more anxious to end this.

"You decided that some bimbo I had a booty call with was going to mean something to me? Scrapper, you're a bigger fool than I thought."

"You took my missus, Hammer. I figured I needed a bargaining tool," Scrapper whined.

"Not my problem if you can't keep tabs on what's yours, Scrapper. I haven't got her. Seriously, man, if I wanted a fuck, it wouldn't be with your woman. Definitely not my type. I can do way better. No offense."

"But I seen her talking to you all the time, flirting with ya. I know she's gone off with you."

"Give us a swig of your bottle and we can talk about it some more, Scrapper," Matt said then put his arm around Stinky's shoulder, effectively locking him into place with his back to her.

"Time to go, sweetheart. Take it nice and slow and be as quiet as you can. Head toward the back office," Chris whispered.

Rebecca slowly uncurled her body and began to crawl in the direction Chris had given. She couldn't see what was happening with her brother because Chris was right by her side, blocking her view.

As soon as she reached the darkened room, Rebecca stood, Chris grabbing her arm to steady her.

"I'm going to lift you through the window. Jason is on the other side to help you down. Oh, honey, look at your pretty face." Chris drew his finger lightly over her cheek. "I should go back in there and beat the crap out of him. Nathan's going to lose it when he sees you, honey."

"Looks that bad, huh?" Rebecca replied as she tentatively touched her swollen and painful face. *How am I going to explain this to Danny? What if I frighten him?* "Oh my God, Danny!" Rebecca found she was having trouble taking a breath as she thought of her son and what might have happened to him after she'd been kidnapped. "Is he safe? Please tell me he is, Chris?

"Shh! Calm down, Rebecca. Breathe, honey. Danny is okay, and he will probably be impressed with your shiner. It's a guy thing." Chris shrugged his shoulders and grinned. "It'll be gone in a week or two, anyway," he added, as if he'd somehow read her mind and was trying to put her at ease. "Put your foot in my hand and I'll give you a boost. We need to get you out of here."

* * * *

Nathan couldn't see into the open area of the garage from his position. He could just hear Matt making small talk. He understood Matt's ploy. He was distracting the biker, keeping him away from Rebecca and giving Chris a chance to get her out of there, but it seemed to be taking a lifetime.

"Hey, boss, got someone here who'd like to see you."

Nathan thrust his elbow back instinctively at the sound of a voice, only managing to pull back at the last moment.

Chris had expected the response and deflected the worst of the elbow's force. "You're slipping, boss — never even sensed me approaching."

"Shit, Chris, I could've broken your jaw."

"Yeah, right." Chris chuckled. "Rebecca is with Jason. I gotta warn you. She's got a shiner that's not going to make you happy. I think she's worried about Danny seeing her, so if I was you, I wouldn't make a big thing of it."

Chris' suggestion made sense but it didn't stop Nathan's blood from boiling. The asshole had struck her. If he got his hands on the dirty scum biker, he'd rip the bastard apart, limb from limb.

"C'mon, man. Your woman needs you. Leave it to Matt. Don't blow his cover."

When Nathan finally set eyes on her, Bec was sitting on a tire, Jason crouched down in front of her. The weight that had been threatening to crush Nathan's chest finally lifted. Jason had wrapped a thermal space blanket around her shoulders. *The guy has everything in that go bag of his. No matter how bad it looks, how much that bastard has damaged her face, you've got to keep it together.*

The moment she saw him Bec jumped to her feet, and, shedding the silver covering, she ran at him. Nathan opened his arms and gathered her in. "I got you, babe. I got you."

"I knew you'd find me. I'm so sorry for getting out of the car. I should have listened to you, Nate. Where's Danny?"

"Shh! It's okay, Bec," Nathan soothed as he rubbed her back. He was worried she was going into shock. Her body was shivering against him. "Danny is fine. He's with Toni. He's worried about you, of course."

Rebecca began to cry, her shoulders heaving with each of her sobs. "I was so scared. I didn't want him to see Danny so I didn't fight or scream. I just went with him. He had a gun. I don't know what happened to it. I didn't see…"

A loud gunshot filled the night's silence.

Nathan picked Bec up and ran to take cover behind the tire wall. He wasn't going to risk waiting to see who was doing the shooting, not with Bec out in the open.

"What the hell was that? Anyone got eyes on what's going on?" he asked Jason.

"Dunno. I'm going in," Jason shouted over his shoulder as he raced toward the garage.

"Matt's still in there," Bec cried out and started to struggle in Nathan's arms, trying to break free of his grip.

"Jason and Chris will get him. Stay here with me, Bec."

Rebecca couldn't believe how loud it was. Like a giant clap of thunder the gunshot had rung out. *Please be okay, Matt. Please don't be hurt,* she recited over and over as she clung to Nathan. His body was warm against her, yet still not enough to stop her from shivering. *It's not even cold. Why can't I stop shaking? Why hasn't Matt come out? I just want this all to be over.*

She was crying. She couldn't stop. Try as she might, the sobs kept coming.

"Calm down, baby. Breathe through your nose. I think you're going into shock."

Nathan's voice sounded distant, like he was talking to her from a long way away. She could hear the rhythmic beat of Nathan's heart as she pressed into his chest. Rebecca tried to concentrate on the sound of it — tried to calm her rapid breathing. Match it to the steadying beat.

"They're coming, Bec. Matt's okay. Chris and Jason are with him."

Being in Nathan's arms made Rebecca feel safe, but she wanted to see for herself that Matt was uninjured. She struggled from Nathan's hold, and he put her back on her feet. She ran to Matt and threw her arms around him.

"Matt, are you okay?"

"Whoa there, sis. I'm all good."

"Who fired the gun? I heard it go off. I was terrified Stinky shot you," she said, the words flying out of her mouth.

"He shot himself. 'Stinky', that's hilarious, Bec, and so on the money. The man really needs to learn some personal hygiene." Matt laughed as he stroked her back. "Stupid fool finally noticed you'd flown the coop, got all antsy that I'd tricked him and as he was pulling the gun from his pants, the thing went off. He shot himself in the foot."

"I should go back and finish him off," Nathan growled.

"Nup, leave it, Nathan. He's actually done me a favor. I'm going to make an anonymous phone call to the cops saying I heard a gunshot. When they come, they'll find the stash of weapons. It will get this whole case rolling for me without me needing to break cover."

"Glad your sister's abduction worked out well for you, dickhead. If anything had happened to her, I would have gutted you and fed you to the sharks. What sort of rookie mistake was that, going to her home when you were undercover? You really put her and Danny in danger. What were you thinking?"

The menacing tone to Nathan's voice was clear. He was furious with her brother. As Nathan moved behind her, closer to Matt, she felt the heat from his body. She needed to calm him down before the situation got out of control and her brother and the man she loved came to blows — because of her.

Placing a hand on their chests, Rebecca tried to push them farther apart. But her attempt was in vain as neither man moved an inch. "Please, can we talk about all this some other time? I just want to get out of here and see my son. You two fighting is not going to help." She lifted her head so she could make eye contact with Nathan. "Please, Nathan, can't we just go get our son?" she pleaded.

Nathan sighed. "Sure, honey, let's get you out of here," he said before turning his attention back toward Matt. "This is not over, not by a long shot," were his parting words to her brother before he took her hand and led them away.

"Thank you," she whispered, as soon as she was out of Matt's earshot. "I'm sure he never meant to cause me any harm. He just wanted to see Danny. It was killing him that he wasn't around to help me with Danny — or Dad with Mum. You of all people should understand his career put him in a difficult position."

"But he did put you both in danger. I'm not sure I can forgive that. What if we hadn't gotten to you in time?" Nathan spun her around so that she was face to face, or at least face to chest, with him. "The thought of losing you… I couldn't bear it. Not now that I have you back in my life again. This is not the time or the place but I need to say it now. Bec, I love you — always have, always will."

Rebecca was dumbfounded. She'd never expected to hear those words from Nathan's lips again. The way he was looking at her, the warmth in his eyes as he watched her for her reaction to his words, it filled her with so much joy. *I don't deserve his love, but I'm taking it.* "I love you too, Nathan."

"That's great news, guys," Chris said, a hint of sarcasm in his tone, "like not anything we didn't already know, but kudos to you both that you finally figured it out. And while I hate to break up this romantic interlude, could we move it along a bit? I for one don't want to be here when the cops roll in."

Chapter Fifteen

"Thank you so much for keeping Danny safe," Rebecca said to Toni for what was probably the tenth or eleventh time since they'd arrived and had found Danny sleeping on the sofa.

"Maybe I shouldn't wake him until I clean myself up a bit?" she whispered.

"I think you should, Bec. He was pretty worried about you. Got himself all worked up over these things called shadow monsters. I think he needs to see you're okay."

"Why don't you wake him up and give him a cuddle? Then leave him with Jason and me for the rest of the night," Toni suggested. "I think you could do with a sleep in after what you've been through. Time to clean up. Get some ice on that eye. Are you sure you don't need a trip to the Emergency Room to get it checked out?"

"I was thinking about giving Martin Shore a call, ask his advice—maybe he can come over and have a look at it." He'd been worried about Bec's injuries but she would have no part in a visit to the hospital. All she'd wanted to do was see Danny, despite her injuries. Nathan understood Bec's need to check for herself that their son really was safe. It didn't stop him from worrying about her, though. Nathan wanted to make sure this woman that meant so much to him, who he could have lost—again—was not suffering any ill effects from the trauma she had undergone. He was pleased that Toni was giving him some backup on the issue.

"I'm okay, Toni, just seeing my little boy is making me feel so much better. You might be right, though. I do feel a little beat up and could probably use some rest. Nothing serious enough to warrant spending hours in an Emergency Room but maybe a good soak in a bath and some ice would help. As long as you are sure it's not a problem keeping Danny here with you. If he wakes up and is upset, you will call me so I can come straight over?"

"Just say hi to your son, Rebecca, and leave the rest to me and Jason. We will bring Danny home tomorrow, after you have rested. It will be better for both of you."

Rebecca knelt down next to her son. Nathan was relieved that the worst of her facial injuries were on the other side of her face.

"Hey, baby, it's Mummy. Wake up and give me a hug," she crooned in his son's ear.

Danny stirred. "Hi, Mummy," he said, sounding like he was still half asleep. "Did Daddy kill the shadow monster?"

"Shh! Baby, there's no such thing, but I'm here and I'm safe. I want you to go back to sleep and dream of Mario and Luigi. Toni will bring you home tomorrow. Okay, Danny?"

"'Kay, Mummy. Toni said she'd make me chocolate pancakes in the morning…"

Danny's eyes closed, and Nathan watched for a few moments as his son's chest rose and fell steadily, indicating he was asleep again. He pulled the blanket that Toni had placed over Danny back up and tucked it under his son's chin.

"C'mon, honey. Let's let him sleep," he whispered to Bec as he helped her back to her feet, leading her away from their sleeping child. "Time for you to get some rest, as well."

They made their way back to the kitchen where Toni, Jason and Chris had relocated to give them some privacy.

"Danny okay?" Toni enquired as she pulled out a chair and motioned for Rebecca to take a seat.

"He's gone back to sleep, I think dreaming of the pancakes you promised him."

Again Nathan was reminded just how lucky he was to be surrounded by so many good friends. People he could rely on, trust.

"Hope it's your chocolate pancakes, luv. You know how much I love them. Mmmm, better make enough for me, too." Jason chuckled before placing a kiss on his wife's temple.

"Well, if you're done with me being the hero, boss, I'm going home to hit the hay for a few hours. Call me if you need anything." Chris walked toward Rebecca, placed his hand on her shoulder. "Good job tonight, Rebecca. You kept your head and made it easier for us. I hope you know what you're taking on with that one. He's a cranky son of a bitch most days."

"I'm sure I'll manage." Rebecca gave a small laugh, and stroked Nathan's leg. "Thank you all so much for coming to help me," she said, her voice wavering a little. "I don't know how I can thank you."

Nathan placed his arm around her shoulder for support.

"Of course we came, luv. It's what we do for family."

As Jason's reply received nods of agreement from Chris and Toni, Nathan was once again moved by how quickly his friends had accepted Bec as one of their own.

"I think it's time we went home, Bec. If it's okay with you, Toni, I'll take your car and leave you mine with the car seat?" Nathan said, the lump in his throat resulting from Jason's comment about family making it hard for him to speak.

"That's fine, Nate, but I think you should take Rebecca back to your place." Toni had a grim look on her face as she made the suggestion, and Nate could have kicked himself. *Shit. Bec's house, it's a mess. What the hell was I thinking? And I haven't even told her about the break-in and the damage the asshole left behind.*

Nathan rubbed a hand through his hair as he tried to find the words to explain what he'd seen, the mess that still needed to be cleared away before Danny and Bec could go home.

"What am I missing here? Why can't I go home?" Rebecca looked like she was ready to burst into tears or stamp her foot. He wasn't quite sure which would happen first.

After everything she'd been through, Nathan couldn't blame her for becoming agitated.

"I haven't had the chance to tell you. Actually, I forgot about it," Nathan admitted, shaking his head a little at his own stupidity. "I was so focused on getting you back safely. Scrapper—well, I assume it was him—trashed your place. It's pretty bad, honey. Nothing we can't fix, but I don't think you need to see it tonight. Come back to my place and rest. We can deal with everything else tomorrow."

"He's right, Rebecca," Toni interjected. "Neither you nor Danny need to be upset any more tonight. I'll get someone over there first thing to start clearing up. I've got people for this kind of thing that will do a good job. Let Nathan take you back to his man cave for a night. I'll keep Danny here until you guys give me a call." Toni reached over and took one of Rebecca's hands in her own. "I know it all seems so much to take in at the moment, but everything will be all right, Rebecca. I promise I'll take good care of Danny. Let Nathan take care of you."

Rebecca was quiet for a few moments.

Then she let out a long sigh, the sound a barb to Nathan's heart. He hated that his woman was forced to deal with all this, to have been caught up in this mess because of her brother's stupidity in the first place. He was just so thankful that she'd managed to get out of it with just a few bruises. The house could be repaired, belongings replaced, but Nathan understood that he'd never be able to replace Rebecca. He'd tried that and failed for seven years. As for her bruises? Those he was going to make Matt Hammerton pay for, eventually.

"You know what? I am too tired to care about my house. Thanks, Toni. Take good care of my boy. When he wakes, tell him I love him and will talk to him soon. Remind Danny I came here and he was asleep, just in case he doesn't remember." Rebecca turned to him. "Take me home, Nate. I need to wash this night from my skin."

Nathan took the keys from Toni then helped Bec out to the car. She leaned her body against him, signs of her weariness apparent.

"In you get, honey," he said as he opened the car door for her.

She climbed in, and Nathan pulled the seatbelt around her and clicked it into place before racing around to the driver's side and getting in.

"We'll be home soon. Would you prefer a shower or can I run you a bath?"

"I'm not sure I could stand up long enough for a shower, my ankles are so sore. Cable ties are not that comfortable."

A wave of anger swirled up in Nathan's chest at the reminder of what Rebecca had been through. He clenched the steering wheel even harder, knuckles turning white. *Keep it together. This isn't about you. This is about making sure Bec is okay. She's got enough to deal with.* "I'll have a look at them when we get home. Maybe I should call Marty?"

"Not just yet, Nathan, please. I just want to get clean and go to bed in your arms. I need to feel you touching me, feel safe again—put this nightmare behind me for a few hours."

How could he refuse her, when that was all Nathan could think about himself? "Okay, but later we get your injuries looked at, just to make sure."

Chapter Sixteen

"I love you, Bec, I meant what I said earlier."

Nathan had helped her wash. He'd stood in his shower with her as the warm water had cleansed the filth from her body. Then he'd gently dried her and carried her naked to his very large bed. There had been nothing sexual about his touch, but Rebecca wanted him anyway.

"Show me," she said as she snuggled in closer to his naked body. "I want to feel you inside me."

"Oh, honey, there is nothing I want more than to make love to you, but after what you've been through — and your injuries — I don't want to hurt you."

"I don't care about any of that, Nathan. I want to remember the night you told me you loved me with a good memory."

Rebecca reached over and played with the hair on Nathan's chest, twirling it between her fingertips. "I bet I can convince you."

"Woman, lying here next to you is enough of a temptation."

She snaked her hand down Nathan's abdomen, tracing each groove of his six pack until she reached her intended destination. Wrapping her fingers around his cock, Bec squeezed. "Feels to me you're up for the job, big boy."

Nathan hissed. "You sure, Bec?"

She didn't bother to answer. Instead, Rebecca shifted down the bed until her mouth was in line with her hand. She could see a bead of moisture welling at the tip of Nathan's cock and she flicked her tongue over it, savoring the taste of him. Moving her hand farther down to the root of his shaft gave Rebecca the room to wrap her lips around him. "Hmmm," she murmured as she breathed in the musky scent of him. The familiar fragrance that was Nathan. Rebecca remembered it well.

"That feels so good," Nathan groaned, his hips lifting from the bed in reaction.

Rebecca stroked and sucked in tandem. Her hand and mouth working as one.

Listening to Nathan's growls of delight and the slight sting from his fingers gripping her head was spurring her on, making her wet. She loved knowing she had the power to give him pleasure, the ability to make him tremble with need for her. He was obviously trying not to push his entire length into her mouth, but she could tell it was a struggle. Rebecca wanted to make Nathan lose control.

She relaxed her throat. Breathing through her nose, she took more of him into her mouth, her hand on his cock, her fingers around his impressive girth giving her the ability to slow his progress if needed. She didn't want to spoil the moment by gagging. Rebecca wanted to bring Nathan right over the edge.

"All the way, Bec. Take my cock all the way…"

Nathan's hips bucked again as she moved him in and out of her mouth. Picking up the rhythm, her cheeks hollowing, Rebecca sucked his cock as far down her throat as she could. She thrust her pelvis against Nathan's leg as her wet pussy and throbbing clit tried to find their own release.

"Squeeze my balls."

Taking his balls in her hand, Rebecca gently rolled them.

"That's the way..." His voice was a cross between a groan and a whisper. Nathan's cock jerked in her mouth. "That feels so good. I can't hold it back. I'm going to come, honey."

Warmth hit the back of her throat and covered her tongue. Rebecca swallowed repeatedly, taking everything Nathan had to give, not willing to waste a precious drop.

I can't believe I've let her give me a blow job after what she's been through. What sort of selfish pig does that make me? I should be bringing her comfort, giving her pleasure. Struggling to shed the haze of post-sexual bliss that had reduced every bone and muscle into a lethargic, gelatinous mass, Nathan tried to drag Rebecca up his body. His brain knew what he wanted but his arms just couldn't respond.

"Honey, that was incredible. Come up here where I can get a taste of that talented mouth of yours."

Rebecca lifted her head from his groin. She crawled up the bed. Then, moving one sexy leg over his hip, she sat herself down so she was straddling him. Her tongue darted out from between her lips. She swiped it over her top lip before repeating the same movement to her lower one. "You taste as good as I remember," she purred sexily.

The sight was pure erotic temptation. Nathan's cock, only moments ago limp and sated, stirred in response. Nathan lifted his hand to Rebecca's breast. He pinched his finger and thumb over her hardened nipple, squeezing it and rolling it around. Rebecca threw back her head, pressing her breast farther into his hand.

Lifting his head from the pillow, Nathan leaned forward and kissed the valley between the swell of her cleavage. Continuing to manipulate one nipple, he moved his head so he could take the other between his lips. He sucked gently, flicking his tongue over the protruding nub.

Rebecca's soft moan rippled through her body, the voluptuous swells jiggling and vibrating against his mouth.

"That feels so good, but I need more. Make me orgasm, Nathan," she begged.

Nathan pulled his lips away from her breast. "All in good time, Bec. Be patient, sweetheart."

She groaned as he reattached himself to her, sucking until her areola was inside his mouth.

Her hips were rocking and grinding against his pelvis like she was trying to find respite. He stilled her body with his free arm, holding her stationary as he continued to suck, nip then soothe her sensitive nipple. Nathan remembered how much Rebecca enjoyed this foreplay. He'd made her come this way before, was wondering if she was still as responsive to his touch.

"If you don't touch my clit soon, Nathan, I'll never forgive you. I'm burning up inside. Please, Nathan, now." Demanding.

Nathan chuckled. With a minimum amount of movement Nathan rolled, flipping Rebecca onto her back.

"Bossy one, aren't you?" he said as he lowered his mouth to hers, before crushing her lips to his as his tongue swept inside and ravished her mouth. She tasted like heaven, like home.

Nathan had managed to keep the kissing to a minimum in his sexual trysts over the years. Had not enjoyed experiencing that act of intimacy with other women. But the taste of Rebecca on his lips, in his mouth, was one he could savor forever. He would never tire of kissing her.

But she needed more, and Nathan was not about to disappoint her.

Lifting his head and dragging his mouth from hers, Nathan moved down her body, placing kisses randomly on her skin in his wake. When he reached her pussy, he used his shoulders to spread her legs wide. Nathan positioned himself between them so that he could have full, unhindered access to her pussy. Her tight blonde curls glistened with her arousal. He swiped his tongue across those shimmering drops.

"You taste so fine, Bec. I'll never get enough of you."

Bec whimpered, her thighs quivering against his shoulders. "Just do it," she cried. She gripped his head to try to force him to move.

Nathan buried his face into her sweet cunt, swirling his tongue around her molten heat. His chin was wet with her body's response to his attention and he hadn't even started in on her clit.

Pushing two fingers into her pussy, past the slight resistance of her clenching muscles, Nathan found Rebecca's G-spot and began to tap ever so gently. He pressed his tongue down flat on her clit, making small circular motions as he kept up a slow, rhythmic beat with his fingers.

She was close. Her body was quaking beneath his touch.

He quickened the pace.

She came apart within seconds.

Hearing Rebecca shouting his name as Nathan brought her to orgasm was music to his ears. He did not stop until he'd felt the last ripple of her pussy walls.

Nathan's cock was now so hard it was almost painful. He wanted to feel Rebecca's tight cunt close around him as he thrust inside her, but he needed to know she was up for it. He hadn't forgotten what she'd been through already tonight and didn't want to push her.

He lifted his head, wiping her moisture from his lips with the back of his hand. Rebecca was wide-eyed, looking at him. The smile that had the corners of her lips turned up and the dimple in her cheek more prominent certainly gave Nathan a huge burst of masculine pride — *I know how to make my woman scream* — before he let out a little chuckle.

"Don't look so smug. Yes, that was the best orgasm I've had in years but don't let it go to your head. Well, not the big one anyway. I'm going to expect that kind of treatment regularly."

"Happy to oblige you anytime, ma'am."

"Well, stop feeling all glib and get up here, I want to feel you inside me. Let's see if you can repeat that outcome."

Nathan didn't hesitate. He jumped from the bed, his focus to get a condom from his bedside drawer and on his cock as quickly as possible. *Let there be one in there* repeated inside his head until he located his target, the small, square packet buried under some paperwork he'd shoved in there last time he was home.

Having achieved his goal and with a minimum of fuss, Nathan stretched out over Rebecca. Their eyes locked to one another.

Nathan moved his hips so the tip of his cock nudged her pussy lips. "I want us to be a couple, a family — to try again. Will you give me a chance, Bec? Give us a chance?" he asked the woman he loved more than he could ever put into words.

"Yes, Nathan, I want that too. I love you. Danny loves you. I want what you do."

Nathan buried himself to the hilt into Rebecca's wet folds. Their mouths met as their bodies joined together as one — just as their hearts and lives would again.

* * * *

Three months later…

When Nathan woke that morning the sun was shining bright through the window and the world was a beautiful place. He was in love with the woman he was meant to be with — even if they had taken the long way round to figure it out. His son was sleeping in the room next to his, his health improving day by day. Danny had only been home a few weeks and at first everything had seemed to take it out of him. He had been tired most of the time. Danny had shown little interest in his Lego or cars. Even the much-loved Mario hadn't been able to entice Danny to play his Nintendo.

Slowly the light had come back into Nathan's son's eyes. Just yesterday they had competed in a lengthy racing tournament, Danny's fingers flying over the game controller like a champ. Nathan had lost fair and square a few times. It was the best losing streak he'd ever had.

Jason would be over in just a few hours to look after Danny while Rebecca and Nathan visited the specialist's rooms once again to get the results of the latest rounds of testing. So far, it appeared that all was going well as far as the bone marrow transplant being accepted by Danny's body went. Healthy red cells were being produced. He and Rebecca were hoping and expecting the news to be good. Still going anywhere near that hospital gave Nathan the chills.

The bedroom door creaked open and a little head popped around.

"Hey, Daddy, are you awake?"

"I am now." Nathan gave a chuckle as his son ran toward the bed.

Time to go in defensive mode – how come those small feet and elbows always end up cracking me in the dick? "Wow, steady on, Dan. Careful of your mother."

"I'm awake and braced for impact. Good morning, my handsome men. What are the Prince and King of Pancakes cooking me for breakfast?"

* * * *

A few hours later he and Rebecca waited, hand in hand, in the reception area of Danny's pediatric specialist, waiting for their names to be called. Being in that room again gave Nathan pause to reflect. He had learned a great deal about himself over the last few months. He'd thought he was strong, but Rebecca had shown him up more than once.

Watching Danny suffer as doctors had destroyed his bone marrow so that they could replace it with Nathan's had been torture. Nathan had never felt so helpless in his life. Used to running head first and prepared into battle, it was hard having to take a back seat. It was as if every day another unknown complication was thrown in his path. Frustration that he was unable to help change the course of the war Danny was fighting tested his sanity. Nathan had traveled the gauntlet of emotions — love, rage, sorrow, fear, shame and joy.

Through it all Rebecca had stayed strong. She'd never left the hospital, never once shown Danny any sign of weakness. Nathan hadn't been that tough. He'd had to take regular breaks from the emotional distress of seeing his son so ill. He was forever thankful that in these times when he'd deserted both Rebecca and his son, his friends had stepped up to take his place.

Rebecca had never looked at him with disappointment on his return. Just hugged him and reassured him, as she did Danny, that it would be okay. All that training he'd gone through to become a hardened soldier and yet none of it had mattered when he was needed the most.

I should have been able to do more for them. My fear, that I wouldn't live up to Danny's image of me, overwhelmed me — the way he believed that I was some super-hero and that my bone marrow would make him better. Such faith and I was so terrified I'd let him down, that the transplant would fail.

"I know what you're doing, Nathan. Will you stop thinking?" Rebecca's plea distracted Nathan from his thoughts. "I can see by the grimace on your face you're still beating yourself up that you needed to take a step away when Danny was in hospital. Seriously, Nathan, I know how you felt. I was the same the first time Danny had chemo. I guess I'm just more used to it now. That in itself is probably all kinds of wrong." Rebecca shook her head.

"I'm sorry, Bec. I just can't help feeling like I let you both down."

"Rubbish. You're here with me now. Danny is at home probably having a wonderful time playing with Jason and looking healthier than he has in years thanks to your bone marrow. You saved our son, Nathan. Stop feeling sorry for yourself. You're my hero, no matter what you think."

"Rebecca, Nathan, the doctor is ready to see you now," the receptionist called out, cutting off anything Nathan could have said in reply to Rebecca's undeserved praise.

"C'mon, Nate, let's go get the official word our son is better," Rebecca said happily as she jumped up from her seat, her hand still in his as she tried to drag Nathan with her.

God, I hope she's right. Please, God, let the results be positive.

They followed the doctor to his office. Nathan moved aside to let Rebecca take a seat first then sat down next to her.

The doctor sat on the other side of his desk, shuffling some papers. Nathan took a deep breath. *Okay, this is it. No matter what happens, I will stay strong for Bec and Danny.*

"Nathan, Rebecca, nice to see you again," the doctor started, and Nathan couldn't help thinking he'd be happier if they never saw the man again.

"Well, the results of Danny's latest count look good. He seems to be coming along in leaps and bounds. The transfusion has certainly resulted in some positive outcomes. It's still a bit early for a definitive prognosis but I'm happy with the way it's all progressing and I think you should be, too. I would even go so far as to say that Danny is well enough to return to school — maybe give it another week or two. Obviously, I wouldn't recommend anything too strenuous for the lad just yet, but I think he can handle a few hours each day, to start off. Of course, I will recommend that the school makes you aware of any outbreaks of serious illness within the population so you can keep Danny home if the problem presents itself."

It was the best news he'd heard in a long time. Nathan turned to see Rebecca's reaction. Tears were rolling freely down her cheeks, but her smile said it all.

"Thanks, Doc. That is great news," Nathan managed to choke out. He was fighting hard to stop his tears. Just the thought of how happy Danny would be when they told him he could go back to school, see his friends again… It was something Nathan could hardly wait to see.

"Actually, Nathan," the doctor resumed speaking again but this time his tone was more serious.

Nathan's heart nearly stopped beating. *Shit, please don't be any buts in this conversation.*

"I was wondering if you could do me a favor. Actually it's more for a colleague of mine. I'm aware that you run a security company. Do you happen to take on cases that involve missing people?"

Nathan had not been expecting that. The relief that the doctor was in fact finished talking about Danny caused Nathan's shoulders to drop, relax. The breath he'd been holding, as he'd waited for the other shoe to drop — so to speak — released from his lungs with a loud whooshing sound.

"Yes, we handle that sort of thing. I'd be happy to talk to your colleague and help out any way I can. I probably won't handle the job myself. I really am focusing on Danny at the moment, but I have someone in mind that I guarantee would put every effort into the case."

"Thank you. If you leave me the office number of the man in question, I will get Dr. Stafford to give him a call direct. There's no need for him to bother you at home with this. I think he would like to handle the matter privately, though, so your discretion would be appreciated. I'm sure you understand."

Well, it wasn't like I was going to tell the folks waiting in the reception area about it. Nathan kept those thoughts to himself as he flicked through his wallet until he found Chris' number. Handing the card over he added, "Chris Winters is one of my partners. I trust him with my life, so I have no hesitation recommending him to your friend."

Rebecca's soft chuckle told Nathan that she had understood his high praise for Chris. After all, he'd also trusted Chris with her life as well.

The doctor took the Haven Security business card from him and put it in the top drawer of his desk. "Thank you. I guess that's it then. Make an appointment with my receptionist for Danny to see me again in three weeks. Until then, take care. All of you." The doctor stood and thrust his hand out to Nathan.

Nathan rose from his chair and shook hands with him. "Thank you for all you've done." It seemed so inadequate for what had been achieved under the doctor's care, but Nathan said it anyway.

"Yes, thank you, Dr. Parker. We'll see you next time," Rebecca added.

Nathan felt her hand in his, so he led them out of the office and back into the reception area. He waited as

Rebecca made the next appointment with the receptionist. Once it was all sorted they headed out to the car.

"Danny is going to be so thrilled about going back to school."

"I know, honey. I can't wait to see his face."

Rebecca stopped as she reached the passenger side door. "What do you think that was all about—Dr. Parker's colleague and the missing person?"

"My guess is it's probably a teenager that's run away from home. We've tracked down a few kids for clients in the same boat," Nathan replied.

"Not a bad day's work—a good report on Danny and a client referral in the one appointment," Rebecca added before opening the door and taking a seat.

I'd have been just as happy with only the positive report on my son. I must remember to ring and give Chris the heads-up, though. It's the least I can do after all the doc has done for Danny.

Nathan took his place behind the wheel. Putting the key in the ignition, he stopped short of bringing the motor to life.

"Bec, I've been wanting to ask you something for a while now, but wanted to wait for the right moment. I think this is it. You deserve a romantic dinner before I say this, but I can't wait."

Nathan reached over and took both of Rebecca's hands in his own. The warmth he felt resulting from her touch raced up his arm and straight to his heart. He knew they were meant to be together, forever. Yes, they'd messed it up the first go around, but Nathan wasn't going to let her slip away from him again. He needed this strong, loving woman in his life. He was only half a man without her. Seven lonely years had taught him that. It was past time that they made their family legal.

"Rebecca Hammerton, will you marry me?"

Rebecca laced her fingers through his and squeezed them tight.

"I thought you'd never ask. Of course I'll marry you, Nate. I made a mistake seven years ago and I never believed that I would be given a second chance. I'm never letting you go again."

About the Author

Sydney-born Donna Gallagher decided at an early age that life needed be tackled head on. Leaving home at fifteen, she supported herself through her teen years. In her twenties she married a professional sportsman, her love of sport—especially rugby league—probably overriding her good sense.

The seven—year marriage was an adventure. There were the emotional ups and downs of having a husband with a public profile in a sometimes glamorous but always high—pressure field. There were always interesting characters to meet and observe, and even the opportunity to live for a time in the UK.

Eventually Donna returned home a single woman, but she never lost her passion for watching sport, as well as the people in and around it.

Now happily re-married and with three sons, Donna loves coffee mornings with her female friends, sorting through problems from the personal to the international. But she's on even footing with the keenest man when it comes to watching and talking rugby league.

Donna considers herself something of a black sheep in a family of high achievers. Her brother has a doctorate in mathematics and her sister is a well-known Australian sports journalist.

An avid reader, especially of romance, Donna finally found she couldn't stop the characters residing in her imagination from spilling onto paper. Naturally, rugby league is the backdrop to her spicy tales of hunky heroes and spunky heroines overcoming adversity to eventually find true love.

A multiple ARRA awards finalist in 2013 & 2014 for her League of Love series, Donna is spreading her genre wings. In

2015 with the launch of her new romantic suspense Haven Security Series and the re-release of her contemporary erotic novella A Fruitful Intimacy.

Donna Gallagher loves to hear from readers. You can find her contact information, website details and author profile page at http://www.totallybound.com.

Totally Bound Publishing